Aroon Raman runs a research and innovation company out of Bengaluru, working in the area of materials science. He divides his spare time between trekking, advising and supporting NGOs, and travel. *The Shadow Throne* is his first novel. His second, an adventure story set in Mughal India, will soon be released by Pan Macmillan. Contact him on www.aroonraman.com.

The Shadow Throne

AROON RAMAN

PAN BOOKS

First published in the Indian subcontinent 2012 by Pan
an imprint of Pan Macmillan,
a division of Macmillan Publishers Limited
Pan Macmillan, 20 New Wharf Road, London N1 9RR
Basingstoke and Oxford
Associated companies throughout the world
www.panmacmillan.com

ISBN 978-81-923-9800-6

Typeset in Charter BT 10/13 by Jojy Philip, New Delhi 110015
Printed and bound in India by EIH Ltd., Unit: Printing Press.

For Afried, Alu and Gopu
Everything, you are everything
the sense, the substance, of everything

– 'Paripadal' 3 (63-68)
Katuvanilla Eyinanar

1

This Sunday morning was no different. I looked at the picture on the dressing table as I had done each morning of each day this past year. Yamini glancing up at me, trying to keep herself serious for the studio shot. The photographer had been mediocre, but got lucky with a rapid-fire shot. This one had caught her perfectly: the sheen of the long, lustrous tresses, eyes alight with mischief, her trademark half-smile.

My wife, taken from me not twelve months ago by cancer.

I took a sip of the coffee. It tasted like mud. I let my gaze wander round our tiny flat. Books and papers strewn everywhere, stacks of computer printouts of every article on the disease I could lay my hands on. I had feverishly read and re-read every scrap I could find as days followed nights – even as she sank and faded away in front of my eyes.

I swept the newspaper from the sofa, sat down and stared at the wall. Damp spread down from the roof terrace, peeling the cheap plaster. Splotches of green moss formed a mosaic on the wall that was once immaculate, decorated with vibrant murals that Yamini had brought from Rajasthan. The house was going to seed, taking me down with it.

The cellphone shrilled. I broke into a sudden sweat, my heart thumping. All those months waiting for the dreaded call from the hospital, and even now the body's instinctive reaction hadn't faded. The coffee had slopped onto the table when I had jerked my hand involuntarily. I placed the cup on the floor and picked up the phone.

'Hello,'

'Chandra? Chandra, it's me, Inspector Hassan. Something's turned up. You might want to come over.'

'Where? What is it?'

'A body. At the Qutub Minar. Come in by the main entrance to the complex. I'll leave word with my man at the gate.'

I got out of my night clothes into a shirt and trousers, picked up my notebook and the small point-and-shoot Olympus. The stairwell of the flat opened into a little lane that led directly onto Chandni Chowk. Old Delhi slammed into me as I stepped onto the street. I waved down a passing auto rickshaw and shouted for the driver to hurry.

Soon, we were hurtling our way past the crowds, heading south along the Red Fort. Across to my right the onion dome of the Jama Masjid loomed over a skyline pierced by multiple other minarets. Yamini used to teach history at Delhi University and had always been in love with this quarter – where the old and new danced in an ever-shifting cadence over the centuries. When we married, there was never any question that we would move into her pad just off Chandni Chowk. And so, a vegetarian South Indian journalist like me had found his true home in this seventeenth-century city of Shahjahanabad, founded by the Mughal emperor whose name it bears. And if it is a crowded, chaotic thoroughfare now, it was also once a fabled street of the East, a canalled way designed by Shah Jahan's daughter Jahanara to reflect the light of the moon.

Sunday traffic being relatively light, I made the twenty kilometres in just over forty-five minutes. I found Inspector Hassan pacing about, talking into a cellphone, his slim, elegantly uniformed figure made diminutive by the monolithic pillar that is one of Delhi's most famous landmarks – the Qutub Minar. He looked up, spotted me and waved me over. Policemen in uniform and plainclothes stood around, taking measurements and photographs. Every now and then, the air filled with the crackle of voices from walkie-talkies. A chalk circle had been marked around the body, which lay sprawled and twisted on the patchy grass. The June sun was well up; I could feel the heat building on my skin, the sweat popping through the pores. I took out my handkerchief, wiped my face and neck and moved up to the circle.

Hassan was still on the phone, but he pointed silently to the fallen figure and nodded. I went up and squatted by the chalk line. The body was that of a man. It had the boneless look that comes of a fall from a great height. I looked up at the column. The Qutub is the tallest brick tower in the world, almost 250 feet, if I remembered right. A fall from even half that height would be enough to shatter every bone in the body. I leaned in closer. It was a white man, no question about that. A very big white man. One of those foreign budget tourists, going by a first glance. He wore saffron-coloured drawstring pajamas and an off-white khadi cotton kurta. The feet were bare and I could see no sign of sandals or slippers. The head presented a remarkable sight: a high topknot of

THE SHADOW THRONE 5

hair had come partially undone and covered the back of the skull. But there was no disguising the fact that the back of the cranium was flat to the point of being practically vertical, giving the face the appearance of having been stuck to a flat piece of board. The man's face was twisted in a snarl of terror, lips drawn back over the gums. Several of the front teeth were missing, presumably from before as there was no sign of blood in the mouth. Despite the rictus, the features were almost classical in their regularity, accentuated by a curling moustache and a short French beard. I looked closer and noticed that the eyes were a shade slanted, hinting at Asiatic blood.

I leaned back on my haunches. Were it not for the rictus, it could have been one of those faces on a coin from antiquity: a throwback to another age.

'Hello, Chandra,' Hassan said, coming up behind me. 'Sorry, got caught up on one of those long outstation briefs on another case. What do you think?'

'It's so hot here, I can't think. Why don't we move to the shade,' I said, nodding at the thick shadow of the Qutub.

'Okay,' Hassan said. 'But you'd better see this before we talk.' He bent over the body and pulled back the full sleeve of the kurta on the body's left arm. The forearm had a single branded symbol about an inch high, seared into the flesh with what had clearly been a crude iron:

Hassan pulled the sleeve back into position and we walked towards the Qutub in silence. A constable dragged up a couple of chairs and we sat down. It was a relief to get into the pillar's shade. I took a quick look around. It was the quietest I had ever seen the Qutub complex; clearly, the cops had cordoned off the place.

Hassan pulled out a pack of Benson & Hedges and lit up. I used to chain-smoke before Yamini had forced me to quit but I still enjoyed the tobacco-laden aroma around those who did. He blew out the smoke through his thin, aristocratic nose.

'Well? What d'you think?' he said, regarding me intently. Inspector Syed Ali Hassan and I had met around eighteen months back in the unlikeliest of places. Yamini and I had gone one Thursday to the Nizamuddin dargah for an evening of qawwali. Under Yamini's patient tutoring, I had come to understand a little of the Sufi tradition and then to love it. The singers at the shrine were particularly inspired that night, and the sublime poetry of Khusrau had transported us into a deep inner peace. Afterwards, we decided to walk to a local eatery for dinner. As we strolled along, still bemused from the intensity of the music, neither of us noticed a shadow flit past us like a wraith, barely nudging me about the hip.

A shout from behind startled us out of our reverie, and we turned to find a man holding an urchin by the ear. Even through my surprise, I remembered noticing how elegantly turned out the stranger was: the starched, spotless churidar-kurta, neatly folded up to reveal a gold wristwatch. The pair walked towards us, and the man said firmly, 'De do vapas,' and when the boy looked at him pleadingly, said again, in Hindi, 'I mean *now*.' The youngster sullenly brought his arm into view from behind his back. And, to my astonishment, there was my wallet, looking outsized in the little fist.

To our further surprise, the man squatted down on the pavement and spoke for a while to the youngster in a low voice. Looking down at the strange duo, it seemed to me that there was a real undercurrent of tenderness in his manner. The boy listened attentively and then, with a last regretful look at me, took off at a run.

The stranger got up and said, 'Gopal keeps his eye out for marks coming out of the dargah. He says you looked particularly "juicy": ripe for the plucking.' He said this with such an odd mix of enjoyment and regret that Yamini and I burst out laughing. I held out my hand.

'I'm Chandrasekhar. Thanks for saving our

dinner for the night; it's about what I had left in my wallet. This is Yamini, my wife.'

Yamini nodded and smiled shyly, as was her wont with strangers. The man took my hand in a firm grip and said, 'And I'm Hassan.'

Of course, we then invited him to join us for dinner and that was the beginning of our acquaintance with Inspector Syed Ali Hassan. I say acquaintance because over the next many months, though we met more often, it never went beyond work. I discovered he was an inspector of police attached to the Civil Lines police station, and he that I was a freelance journalist. We both nosed around and made enquiries to get each other's measure. I found out that Hassan was regarded highly by his men for his unorthodox but effective methods. The little boy who picked my pocket was but one of his very large network of informants that spanned the length and breadth of Old Delhi. But he was viewed with suspicion by his superiors, not a little because of his blunt and outspoken ways that tended to rub the brass on the wrong side. I too was a loner in the profession: I couldn't stand the tyranny of deadlines that ruled the life of an employed reporter and instead chose the (much more precarious) existence of a freelancer. But I'd done a few scoops that had brought me some minor fame within the hard-bitten fraternity of newsmen who covered the affairs of this huge, chaotic metropolis. Whatever the reason, Hassan took to calling me on some of his more interesting cases and while that made me one of the many cogs in his network machine, it also gave me a chance to get in first on some very interesting cases of crime that periodically erupted in the city's old quarter.

I said we were acquaintances; perhaps that isn't quite the right word. We spoke little of personal matters, but he seemed to value having me around as he worked on a case; I, in turn, felt a connect to this intense man who seemed live for his work yet had unexpected depths: a love of poetry, and a wry humour that shone out occasionally like flashes of lightning in the night sky.

So here we were: standing in the shade of the Qutub Minar on this sweltering June morning, Hassan's dark, intelligent eyes fixed on me, waiting for my answer.

'Why're you here, Hassan? I thought the Qutub wasn't your beat.'

He shrugged. 'My counterpart's on leave and the ACP South is a former boss. Wanted my take before they removed the body.'

I tried to collect my thoughts, to see if I could put my observations into some sort of a meaningful pattern.

'What's our best guess about the time of death?'

'Around 6 pm last evening.'

'No witnesses, I presume?'

Hassan said, 'You presume right. The complex has of late been shutting down at midday on weekends for maintenance.'

'The guy looks spooky, like one of those Vedic sages in *Amar Chitra Katha* comics. I've never seen anyone like this. It's almost like he's been made up for the part. I suppose the cause of death is a fall from a height?'

Hassan nodded. 'Yes. The medic confirms massive trauma to the entire trunk consistent with hitting the ground at terminal velocity. His innards were literally pulverized. It's a miracle there is so little external evidence of injury. You can see the point of impact right there; the grass is flattened and sheared off in patches. The body then bounced and rolled over to where it is now.'

I looked at the tower. The base was massive: it would have to be to support the enormous column. But the top seemed almost needle-like from so far below. Hassan followed my gaze.

'We checked. The apex space inside is just about eight feet across.'

Eight feet. I looked at where the body had bounced as it hit the ground at peak velocity. The spot was around forty feet from the tower. Stunned, I looked again. No mistake. How had the body managed to land so far from the tower? There was no way the victim could have jumped off the top and landed so far out. I thought carefully about the other possibility: that he had been thrown off the top. I was no expert but even to my inexperienced eye, it seemed scarcely possible that this giant had been picked up and tossed like a shot-put from the top. The thrower had to have been some sort of a colossus, operating at the very peak of his strength to achieve anything like this distance.

Hassan had clearly been following my thoughts. He exhaled another stream of smoke and crushed the cigarette out on the back of the steel chair. 'He was chucked. There's no other explanation for the trajectory. The body follows a parabolic arc from the top. The scene forensic reckons the initial throw took the body laterally out around eight feet before it began to flip over into the descent.'

I raised an eyebrow in query. 'Do you think that's really possible? I mean, look at the size of the victim.'

'We can't think of another explanation that fits.'

A sudden thought struck me. 'Wait. You're saying the body hit the ground torso-centred. Right?'

'Right.'

'What about the injury to the back of the head, then? That doesn't square up. I can't imagine how that could have happened in the fall.'

'What injury?'

'Look at the back of the head, for God's sake. It's almost caved in.'

'Nope. It's the natural shape of his head.' Hassan then sprang his bombshell. 'We have two independent eyewitnesses outside, hawkers who swear they saw a giant – the word they used was "rakshas" – exit the main gate at around midnight, five hours or more after the killing. The guy had a flat skull. They say the shape of the head was impossible to miss in the light of the gateway lamps.'

'Rakshas …?'

'Yes. A demon. They say this guy was the biggest human being they've ever seen.'

I stared at him. Hassan's face was taut, the nostrils slightly flared. I felt a premonition of something – I could not have said what – flashing through me, sudden and fleeting, leaving me with a dry mouth and a sudden tightness in my chest. Then Hassan said:

'And the mark on his forearm. What do you make of it?'

I shook my head. 'It looks like a trident. Could be one of those fringe Hindu groups that are springing up everywhere. He wore saffron leggings and, I mean, look at him: the guy looks like he's a throwback to the ancient India of the scriptures.'

Hassan said nothing. It was almost as if he

hadn't heard me. He was looking at the sprawled body. He seemed tense and withdrawn. Then he said slowly, 'Could be.' He made a sign to his deputy hovering nearby. 'Start to clean up the scene. Remove the body to the IP Hospital morgue. We'll take a good look at it tomorrow before they start to cut him up.' He pursed his lips and squinted up at the sun, a typical Hassan habit when he was trying to make up his mind about something. In this case, I had a strong feeling he was trying to decide just how much to tell me. Then he said:

'Thanks for coming at short notice, Chandra. You were really helpful.'

'I was?' I said, surprised, then decided to press my advantage. 'This looks interesting, Hassan. I would really like to stay involved.' Seeing him hesitate, I said, 'I mean it. Not a word to anyone. It'll be just between the two of us. I want rights to break the story, but only if and when you say so.'

He shook his head, reaching a decision. 'Don't push me on this now. I'll let you know.'

'Okay. Can I at least take a couple of shots? They'll stay with me.'

He nodded shortly. I snapped off some pictures, shook hands with him and left.

2

The pad I called home sat well back from the bazaar. When I first moved in with Yamini, I remember being pleasantly surprised at how quiet it was. But I soon discovered it wasn't the silent oasis I had expected to withdraw into with my wife. Yamini, it appeared, had any number of friends and relatives who didn't seem to have much to do with their lives but to call and talk for hours with her on the phone, or drop in at any time of day or night. I, on the other hand, was a loner whom almost no one ever called – at least on a personal basis. The train-station atmosphere of our home made me quite surly for a while before I realized it was getting me nowhere. And so, I slowly got to a point where I even began to come out of my room and greet some of her friends, prompting not a little delight from Yamini – whose nickname for me was 'Karadi' or 'bear' in Tamil.

After she died, so many of her friends had called – some several times – to invite me home, to let me know they had not forgotten. But I was evasive, never responded and slowly the calls stopped. The flat that greeted me when I came home in the evening was silent as a tomb, usually the perfect foil for the numb emptiness that claimed me at the close of each day. But today, I hardly noticed it. I went straight to the fridge, pulled out some cold idlis my mother had made when she had come over the previous week and set them in the microwave. I pulled out my notebook, turned a new page, wrote 'The Qutub Case' at the top in bold letters and underlined it. I took out the idlis and set them on the small dining table.

As I ate, I thought back to the morning. Over the years, I had built up a reputation for turning in 'tricky' stories: ones my colleagues in the journalistic fraternity stayed away from – because of personal or other risks involved. Hassan had discovered that from his sources in the media: that I was a ferret that would burrow down any hole in search of the truth, no matter how dark and deep. I picked up the pen and wrote three questions in careful order:

Who was the victim?
Murder or suicide?
Why?

Most investigations start with very simple questions. Sometimes the answers emerge quickly and the cases resolve themselves with unexpected ease. But this was not one of those: something told me this was a rabbit hole that led way down. I took out my camera and replayed the shots. I looked at the ancient, violent face, feeling a faint chill in the heat of the midday afternoon. And there was at least one other just like this one: the eyewitness accounts had been definitive on that point. *Two men with misshapen skulls.* Despite the size of the second man sighted, brothers or even twins was the easiest explanation – a forceps delivery on both that caused deformation at birth. One of whom, if the time intervals were right, was a fratricidal killer. Even so, Flathead Two (as I began to call him in my mind) would find it difficult to hide for long. His size and those cranial features were a dead giveaway and Hassan would be putting out an all-stations bulletin with a picture. What was disturbing was that the man had walked out in the full glare of the gate lights – as if he cared nothing about discovery. It spoke of a sort of supreme arrogance. My imagination was clearly overheating but it seemed to me exactly the sort of behaviour one would associate with a rishi of yore, an Agastya or Durvasa, supremely confident of his prowess, answerable to no one for his deeds.

And the skin. What was to be made of the fact that the victim was a white Caucasian male? I thought about that for a bit before giving up and moving on to that last and, to my mind, more solid clue: the trident branded on the arm. Perhaps we were looking at a member of one of those tantric Shiva cults that were recently in the news for operating under the guise of holistic health ashrams. Some of them attracted even more whites than they did Indians. Surely worth running a trace. I made a note to mention it to Hassan.

I got up, washed the vessels and then my hands. A tendril of thought slowly curled up, the suggestion of a part-formed idea. I was halfway to the bedroom before I realized my desktop was down; I had bought it second hand, and a few days ago, it had clearly decided its time was up.

I pulled out my cellphone, hesitated a long moment then punched a number. She answered almost instantly.

'Hello.'

'Meenakshi? Meenu, this is Chandra.'

There was long, brittle silence. When her voice came over the phone, it was flat, carefully modulated to exclude emotion.

'Well, well … what have we here. The great Mr Chandrasekhar himself deigns to reach out to us mere mortals.'

'Meenu, I'm sorry, I really am. I know you

called, more than once. I should have called you back ... but I just couldn't ... after Yamini ... I kind of shut myself off and ...'

She broke in, her voice suddenly softer. 'I know. I'm sorry too, Chandra. That was unfair, knowing what you went ... are going through.' She sighed, a ragged inhalation of breath that spoke louder than any words. 'I miss her so much ... so much. She was like my sister, you know.'

'I know.'

A brief silence hung between us, and then I said, 'Meenu, what do you know of skull flattening?'

'A *what* flattening?'

'Skull. S-K-U-L-L. As in head. I seem to recall it existed as a practice in many societies over the centuries.'

She said instantly, 'Oh, skull flattening. Yes, of course. It's been done by several peoples from extremely ancient times. Neanderthals, many of the prehistoric Germanic tribes, ancient Egyptians ... I'm sure there were plenty others. Why do you ask?'

'Do you know of anyone who practises it today?'

'Today?' She thought for a bit and then said slowly, 'Nooo ... I can't think of any, though I seem to vaguely remember reading that some tribes in the South Pacific still do ... But what's this all about?'

'Do you have your laptop and an Internet connection?'

'Yes, of course.' Then more insistently, 'Chandra, what's with the twenty questions?'

'I'll tell you when I see you. Bring your computer.'

There was another silence, then she said, 'So you want me to come over?'

'Can you?'

'Sure. It's Sunday. See you in an hour.' She hung up.

Meenakshi Pirzada, to explain her rather unusual name, was born of a Kashmiri Muslim father and a Hindu Maharashtrian mother. Her family had moved to Delhi when she was young, but beyond this, I knew little of her family. She was an associate professor of history at St Stephen's College and Yamini's closest friend and colleague.

I reflected over what she had just said. When Yamini died, she was clearly as much reaching out to me in her grief as to give me comfort – and I had rejected her, intent only on wallowing in my own private sorrow. I sat on the sofa, feeling suddenly small and rotten.

The landline shrilled. It startled me, and it was a while before I located the ringer beneath a pile of old files. The landline was an old, practically defunct connection ever since mobiles had taken over. I snatched it up.

'Chandrasekhar.'

The voice came low and urgent. 'Hassan here.'

'Oh, hello Hassan. I was going to call you. Listen, about the body ... There are a couple of things I wanted to ...'

He cut me off. 'Chandra, have you used your cell to talk about the morning's case with anyone?'

'Only indirectly.'

'But enough for anyone in the know to make a connection?'

'I guess so. What's this all about?'

But Hassan was already swearing. 'Shit. Listen Chandra, I've been pulled off the case.'

'What?'

'The file's been transferred, so has custody of the corpse.'

'To whom?'

'A bunch of muftis came over and took my notes, files, photographs, forensics – everything. It's a complete clean-out.'

Muftis. Plainclothesmen.

'COD – Corps of Detectives?' I said.

'No.' Hassan's voice was definite. 'RAW, most likely. And then I got a call from the DGP. He was polite, but I got the message: *This is a national security matter. Forget you were ever there at the Qutub.*'

I drew in a deep breath. 'So that's it, then?'

Hassan was quiet for such a long time that I thought he had gone off the line. Then he said:

'Not quite. Chandra, can I come and see you this evening?'

In the few cases where I had seen Hassan in action, he was the quintessential cop: decisive and tough as nails, a bloodhound who gave no quarter as he went after his quarry, using me ruthlessly as he used everyone who could help him break his cases. Now there was something in his voice ... I swallowed my own unease and said:

'Okay. When?'

'Seven o'clock. One last thing: they asked me who else was on the scene and I had to tell them. Don't use your cell for anything to do with this case. I'm talking to you from a booth near the station. Both our cellphones may be tapped.'

My stomach was suddenly churning, taut with tension. I felt a sudden need to break out a cigarette, a fix I thought I had gotten over; but the nicotine craving was right back.

I knew cops retained extensive links with the COD and the IB – the intelligence bureau that handed domestic security issues. Personnel were freely traded between them, and there were large areas of overlap. Hassan would know enough to eliminate those two, which left only one organization with the clout to pull off what I had just heard – RAW. The Research & Analysis Wing, attached nominally to the Cabinet Secretariat but reporting to the national security advisor and, on occasion, direct to the prime minister. I tried to recollect what I knew or had heard about it, which wasn't much. It was the most shadowy of our intelligence agencies, tasked with protecting the external security of the country. Rising from the ashes of the 1962 China debacle, RAW had been led in its formative years by the legendary China hand then attached to military intelligence, R. N. Kao. Over the years, it had steadily gathered into itself the whole gamut of stealth operations, external intelligence and counter-terrorism. It ran extensive cross-border HUMINT or human intelligence networks backed by an array of aerial and ground recon technologies, satellite imaging, advanced communication and interceptors. I now remembered a news report I had read a couple of years ago on the morphing of RAW into *the* uber agency of Indian intelligence. Post 9/11, given India's own vulnerability to global terror networks, it had intensified its focus on Pakistan and acquired carte blanche power of surveillance and even rendition of *domestic* terror suspects. Its other main obsession was said to be China. No wonder, the article said, practically all its directors were Pakistan or China experts.

If Hassan was right, this was the agency that was likely tapping my phone. On an impulse, I walked to the other end of the living room and, standing to one side, took a careful look at the street below. Nothing I could see. Feeling slightly foolish, I came back, pulled the notebook open and wrote:

RAW?

The three letters stared out malevolently from the page. The flat was quiet, but I had a distinct feeling that something or someone else was in the room with me, watching. I tried to think but soon gave up. I was wound up tight as a spring. Then it suddenly struck me that I had called Meenakshi from my cellphone. Had I inadvertently brought her into a possible surveillance loop? The thought spooked me and I was reaching for the landline when the doorbell chimed.

3

The fence was a snake that dipped and coiled its way into the mountains as far as the eye could see. 'Fence' was really a euphemism for its military name: 'anti-infiltration barrier' or AIB for short. It was a double fence: two lines of twelve-foot posts topped with loops of tightly packed, barbed concertina wire facing each other across a narrow strip of land. The strip itself was strewn with mines, among them anti-personnel M-18 Claymores designed to fragment on detonation, literally eviscerating anyone within range. The entire barrier was electrified, equipped with thermal and motion sensors and, recently, with high-resolution night-vision video cameras. The AIB stretched unbroken for close to 600 kilometres from Jammu along the border with PoK and up until a little beyond Kargil, where the terrain became too wild and forested for even the AIB. The fence, completed by the Indian army in late 2004 after the shock of the Kargil attack, ran inside Indian territory parallel to the Line of Control – the operational boundary between India and Pakistan and geopolitically one of the most sensitive borders on the planet.

At two o'clock in the morning, the high peaks surrounding the valley stood etched against the night sky like silent sentinels of the border. Six men crouched beside the wire on the Indian side. All were identically dressed in black jerseys and combat boots, their faces covered by ski masks. Sophisticated electronic gear lay in neat rows on a rubber sheet on the ground and a small satellite dish powered by a field battery scanned the heavens in a parabolic arc. One man intently scanned a hand-held monitor. The satellite image showed up the terrain in remarkable detail: the barrier posts, the wires, even the men – etched in sharp detail against the screen. He pressed a button and the shot panned out into a larger area beyond the fence – into Pakistan. He kept an eye on it, and then raised his arm in a thumbs up.

One of the others immediately pointed a walkie-talkie-like device at the fence. There was a short, high whine and then all the small blinking lights along the posts went out. He turned to the four others just behind and made a slashing movement across his throat. They nodded and, pulling out giant wire cutters from their bags, started to cut through the wires close to the ground. Soon a two-foot hole opened up and the men began to assemble a cantilevered collapsible step, which they placed across the mined strip. A cut through the second fence, and all four wiggled through. Bulky rucksacks were quickly relayed through the gap. The men grabbed them, slung them over their shoulders and took off at a shuffling run towards the rim of the forest forty yards away. They had not even disappeared from sight before the remaining duo set to work with small soldering irons, welding the cut parts of the fence back into place. The collapsible bench was quickly drawn back in, telescoped back into the bag and the wire on this side re-fixed. The leader hit the sat switch. The screen went blank. They dropped everything on the mat, rolled it up and jogged out twenty yards. The walkie-talkie man pointed his device again at the fence. The whine went up and the sensors started to blink once more, the cameras resuming their ceaseless scan of the night.

Next morning, the overnight electronic AIB log showed up a glitch at a specific spot along the LOC. The duty officer stationed at the Kargil SIGINT (Signals Intelligence) station took it to his commanding officer. They scanned the video footage, which showed up blank for exactly eight minutes from 0200. The thermal sensors had also malfunctioned; all facts pointed to a power trip caused by a temporary overload to the batteries, a fact confirmed by the videos showing up an electrocuted fur-tailed fox lying on the Pak side of the fence. This was not uncommon; the whole area had seen a big resurgence of wildlife post the Kargil conflict – what with the Pakistanis staying away from the area they seemed to view as somehow ill-fated. At the station, they filed a report under 'malfunction due to animal intrusion', a blip that called for no further review.

A little over 900 kilometres south of Kargil as the crow flies, a man sat in a cubbyhole of a nondescript government office in a lane off New Delhi's Lodhi Road – not ten minutes away from Parliament House. His desk was completely bare save for two phones: one black and the other red. He sat still, unmoving, staring at the lime-washed wall opposite, traced with cobwebs and hung with a dusty portrait of Gandhi. The light on the red phone blinked. He waited for three flashes, picked it up, listened and hung up again without a word. He went back to waiting, but now small droplets of sweat beaded his forehead. After a minute, he wiped his face with a dirty towel draped over the backrest of his chair and then picked up the receiver from the black cradle.

This time there was no pause. Whoever was on the side was clearly waiting. He said: 'Kaam ho

gaya, sir. It is done. Shadow Throne proceeding
as scheduled.'

Meenakshi Pirzada zipped past Gauri Shankar
Mandir, flicking the steering wheel of her Maruti
800 to expertly weave through a pair of cows
with red tilaks that sat with bovine indifference
in the middle of the lane. The Lal Qila – that
magnificent legacy of Shah Jahan – loomed up
ahead, its crenellations etched like giant teeth
against the sky. She hooked a left onto Chandni
Chowk, checked her watch and looked at herself
in the rearview mirror.

She told herself she was being silly but try as
she might, she couldn't rid herself of a frisson of
anticipation at the thought of seeing him again. It
had been over a year now since they'd last met.
Time had blunted the sharper edges of her grief
but the ache still lingered – as did the memory
of that day: the huge crowds at the crematorium;
the shattering sense of loss as Yamini's body was
pushed into the furnace; Chandra swaying by her
side as if buffeted by a sudden squall.

Yamini had first introduced Chandra to her
around four years ago. She still remembered her
first impression of him: a big-boned man with a
stoop to his shoulders, shaggy hair framing a baby
face that reminded her of Rishi Kapoor's in the

film *Bobby*. Rightaway she knew: this was serious. Yamini and she had been inseparable since their days in high school and in the months that followed she'd struggled to come to terms with her friend dating and then marrying this stranger.

She kept away from them for a while, till she realized how childish it all was: the resentment and imagined sense of loss. It was when she got to know Chandra better that she understood a little of what Yamini saw in this taciturn man with his stooped shoulders and melancholic dark eyes. From bits and pieces gleaned from Yamini and from those rare conversations when Chandra relaxed and let go, she came to realize that behind that reticence was a widely read, sensitive person. The Internet also had enough on Chandra for her to learn that he was an ace journalist with an uncanny nose for a story. A piece he had done titled 'Politics and Osmosis on the Indo-Nepal Border' was a brilliant exposé on how India's borders were a world within a world: complex negotiated realities of corruption and power that were a far cry from the geographical lines on maps.

He appeared to have quite a reputation within the hard-bitten journalist fraternity. A friend of hers from the media had said as much: that he was regarded as someone who could go extremely far in his profession if he was not such a maverick, a fiercely independent loner, refusing to compromise on what to others might seem a minor matter of principle.

Yamini called him her karadi – bear – and it described him perfectly: a shambling hulk of a man without social graces, who doggedly went burrowing in thickets that others left well alone.

He'd stood there in the crematorium ante-chamber, receiving the murmured condolences of the queue like an automaton. And then – after what seemed interminable hours – it was all over. The two of them alone in the crematorium -- with the yawning hole left by Yamini.

He was staring into the distance, his eyes unseeing and haunted, already withdrawing into his private torment. Then he'd muttered his thanks and turned away.

That was the last she had seen him. Her string of calls went unanswered; she had even gone to his place a couple of times only to find it shuttered. Over the months, Chandra acquired the texture of an old photograph in her mind: a fading, sepia-tinted backdrop to the sharp, vibrant image of Yamini. Till today's call.

She pulled into a cul-de-sac off Chandni Chowk and screeched to a halt. Grabbing her laptop case, she set off up the stairs to her right.

I opened the door and there she was, pretty much as she had been when I last saw her – which was at the funeral: short and extremely fair, inclined to plumpness, windblown hair framing an oval face with its cleft chin and a sharp, inquisitive gaze. We stood looking at each other for a long moment. Then she smiled awkwardly.

'Aren't I coming in?'

'Sorry.' I stepped back. She walked past and stopped, looking around. When she turned, there was a tiny frown creasing her brow and her lips were compressed into a thin line. I pointed to the sofa and she sat on it primly, her back erect with disapproval.

I set myself down in a chair opposite. There was another silence, then I said, 'Go on, you can say it. I know it's a mess.'

She shook her head. 'It's your home, Chandra. I'm just visiting.'

'But ...?'

Her face wore a melancholic expression. 'Why remove everything? The pictures are gone and really ... this mess. You know how house-proud she was.' She said abruptly, 'Are you okay?'

'Sure. Going to work, filing stories, all that. Yeah, I'm perfectly fine.'

'Really? What's the score in today's match?'

Before I could stop myself the words were out: 'What match?'

She said nothing; my reaction had said it all. I *really* was not okay. If there was one thing I had inherited from my father it was an absolute passion for cricket. In fact, he had named me after B. S. Chandrasekhar, the legendary leg-spinner of the 1970s. I went on to captain my school and then Madras University and was even selected to play the Ranji Trophy for Tamil Nadu before a debilitating knee injury took me permanently from the game. But it didn't stop me from catching what I could on TV, or spending the odd blissful day in the stands at Feroz Shah Kotla when the matches came home to Delhi.

'England's playing us in an ODI at Mohali today.' Then, probably wanting to save me more embarrassment, she flipped open the flap of her leather case, pulled out her laptop and said, 'Let's get started.'

I moved over to her side, this time carefully stacking the papers and placing them on the centre table. She raised an eyebrow at that but didn't comment. She punched the start button, plugged in her Internet stick and soon the Google homepage popped up on the screen.

'So, where to?' she said in Hindi, 'Kahan jayein?' In the manner of a Delhi taxi driver.

I smiled and said, 'Take me to skull flattening, if you don't mind.'

'Okay – skull flattening it is.'

It appeared that Meenakshi was one of those speed readers who also play the Internet like a

violin, so I was content to sit back as she started a
high-speed scan of that immense electronic ether
that is the World Wide Web.

It soon became clear that she was right; artificial
cranial deformation had been practised widely since
ancient times by many peoples. There seemed no
geographical or ethnological connection between
societies that did it: the custom seemed common
to some Pacific Islander groups, American Indian
tribes, ancient Egyptians, the Incas and marauders
from Asia like the Huns. Reasons for it varied:
beautification, social advancement and religious
sanction. There were a whole set of reports on a
recent increase in flat skulls in infants in the USA,
a condition called positional plagiocephaly that
arose from poor sleeping positions of newborns.
There was nothing I could see that threw any sort
of light on the body at the Qutub – except the
possibility that both Flathead One and Two were
plagiocephalic twins.

Meenakshi must have seen my expression for
she said firmly, 'Look, if I know what you're after,
it might be a whole lot easier for me to help.'

I thought about it. I had told Hassan that I
would keep everything under wraps. But events
since had moved with the speed of an express
train. He had been summarily taken off the case
and now suspected that both of us were being
bugged by Indian intelligence. There was a big

story here, the biggest I had come across and the gloves were off as far as I was concerned. But what about Meenakshi? I told myself I was being paranoid; she was just a friend on a social visit and there could be no danger to her whatsoever. What possible connection could ever be established between her and the case? Yes, I had called her for some information on skull flattening, but there was nothing in the conversation to indicate it went beyond what a journalist might ask a professor friend – on a storyline he might be working on.

I said, 'I'm going to trust you, Meenu. Not a word to anyone else. Okay?'

She nodded. Her face was alight with anticipation. 'Sure. Word of honour.'

I made up my mind. I took out my camera and, in the most fateful decision I would ever make, clicked it on. I say 'decision' but well into the future, I would look back at this moment as one of those instants when we appear as but actors on a stage, performing to a script already written for us by a higher fate, a script which would soon plunge us into a terrifying vortex of danger and death.

I showed her the pictures and explained Hassan's call. Like me, she stared at the shots and, like me, she shivered. She handed the camera back to me as though it were contaminated and sat silent for a long time. I thought the photos had shaken her even more than I had imagined, but she was actually thinking. She got me to scroll down to the shot of the trident mark on the arm and looked hard at it, chewing on her bottom lip. Suddenly she said:

'If you had to put a nationality to the dead man, what would you guess?'

I didn't hesitate. 'Greek. If I didn't know it was impossible, I would say ancient Greek.'

'How about ancient Asiatic Greek?'

Our eyes met. I nodded and said quietly, 'That's *exactly* what I would say.'

She clicked on the mouse, scrolled down, turned the screen to me and there he was: the dead victim.

I took the laptop from her. I could scarcely believe my eyes. If the corpse itself had walked in at that moment, I could not have been more astounded. Meenakshi had located him in under fifteen minutes. Before I could scroll down further, Meenakshi relieved me of the laptop.

'Wait, there's more.' Her fingers practically flew over the keyboard, purposeful and assured, as if she knew exactly what she was after. There was a moment when the connection flagged and she waited impatiently, fingers drumming the laptop lid as the small light blinked on the stick, extracting the billions of bytes of data she wanted from the vast reaches of time and space. The screen started to come alive. A picture was forming slowly. Even as it started I knew what it was; in less than twenty seconds it stood clear and stark against the screen. It was the trident, exact in every detail to the one on the body.

She handed me the laptop, bowed briefly and said, 'Elementary, my dear Watson.'

I sat absolutely dumbstruck. She broke into a shy yet triumphant smile at my flabbergasted expression. I tried to say something, but ended up putting my hands on both her shoulders and giving her a squeeze.

'Meenu, you're Holmes and Poirot rolled into one, an absolute genius. Now tell me what it's all about.'

Her countenance changed. I saw a shadow flit across her face, leaving it pale. 'I don't know, Chandra. What we've come up with is impossible. Your man's a Kushan.'

'A what?'

'A Kushan. Someone who went extinct over 1500 years ago.'

4

The Khayaban-e-Suhrawardy Avenue is a mid-sized thoroughfare in the heart of the Pakistani capital of Islamabad. A mix of government offices, aid agencies and some residences line both sides of the street except at the western end, where a high wall stretches for some hundred metres along the road and then veers off a right angle to the south. It has the appearance of a fortress, which it is: the general staff and planning headquarters of the Directorate of Inter-Services Intelligence, more commonly known to the world as Inter-Services Intelligence or ISI – one of the most feared secret services in the world.

Since its creation after the abortive India-Pakistan war of 1947, ISI's power waxed and waned until a fateful day in December 1979, when Soviet tanks rolled into Afghanistan. In the decade that followed, ISI grew enormously in money, power and influence. It was now America's main striking

weapon of organizing Afghan resistance to the
Soviets. Throughout this decade, its covert action
division worked in close tandem with the CIA
as a conduit for gunrunning, training of Afghan
resistance fighters (many of whom would later
morph into the modern Taliban), extortion and
bribery: in short, the whole gamut of clandestine
operations designed to defeat and then drive
the Soviets from Afghanistan. There was a brief
cooling-off period with the United States after
the Russians withdrew – when ISI turned the
full spectrum of its newly acquired capabilities
to support Kashmiri independence. The heavily
militarized Indo-Pak border quickly became one
of the most dangerous flashpoints in the world, as
no less than six divisions faced each other across
the LOC: overt manifestations of a deadly covert
struggle between ISI and RAW in the shadow
world of Kashmiri politics and insurgency.

With close links to the army, and given
the army's almost overwhelming influence on
domestic politics, ISI also spied on Pakistani
politicians to keep them under control – largely
subservient to the military's interests. By the mid-
1990s ISI was effectively a state within a state
with practically untrammelled power and beyond
all civilian oversight. It was a characterization
widely accepted by most observers of Pakistan. Its
public persona, moreover, derived from its image

as the country's greatest bulwark against external security threats, especially from arch enemy India. Its moment of crowning glory came on 28 May 1998 when Pakistan exploded five nuclear devices in the Chagai Hills of Balochistan, taking it into the rarefied nuclear club and changing the geopolitics of Asia forever.

9/11 and the American War on Terror provided a new trajectory to ISI as Pakistan now became the frontline state for the capture or killing of Osama bin Laden in the largest manhunt ever mounted in history, and for the NATO's struggle against the Taliban. Not only did ISI grow exponentially in size and reach during this time but it also began to acquire a distinctly Islamist character in its middle ranks, a development that would have far-reaching implications for the agency.

On that sweltering June afternoon, four men gathered in the briefing room of the ISI basement floor. Together they comprised the operating apex of Pakistani counter-intelligence, men with decades of experience in the brutal world of espionage. Shaji Mir headed the JID – Joint Intelligence Directorate – tasked exclusively with India-centric operations. On his right was Iftikar Ahmed, chief of the SSD or Special Services Directorate that handled covert action. The man opposite them was Gul Mohammed, head of JD Technical that was responsible for all SIGINT and electronic espionage. At the head of the table, dominating the room, was a short man of swarthy complexion, with deep-set eyes of coal. He was Salman Qazi, Director General, ISI, and with the possible exception of the chief of army staff, the most powerful man in Pakistan.

The room had been swept no less than six times for bugs, a paranoid number by even the standards of the secrecy-obsessed ISI. However, this was no ordinary meeting, and it came at a fraught moment in ISI's history. For the first time in over three decades, Pakistan's all-powerful intelligence agency was deep in the throes of a crisis. The stealth raid and subsequent assassination of Osama bin Laden by American Navy Seals in the previous month had done irreparable damage to ISI. International suspicion now coalesced into certainty, exposing ISI as a double-headed hydra in the war on terror. Relations with the West – the US and the NATO – plunged to the lowest ebb ever, amidst intense pressure on Pakistan to turn on its Afghan support groups.

However, what alarmed the military leadership most was the loss of national faith, a shattering of ISI's carefully cultivated image as a frontline guardian of Pakistan's national security. In the midst of an outpouring of national shame at the impunity with which the Americans took out bin Laden – not 500 metres from the military HQ at Abbotabad – ISI found itself with its back to the wall.

To cap it all, the Indians had just concluded a wide-ranging security pact with the Karzai government in Afghanistan. Far from the 'strategic depth' long sought by Islamabad with its western neighbour, Pakistan now faced the ultimate nightmare scenario from the perspective of its security planners: a strategic encirclement of the country on both sides by India.

Hard as it was to comprehend, what had today brought the top echelon of ISI together was none of these things. It was a development so extraordinary that even the hard-bitten and ruthless men in the room could scarcely credit it.

'Show them the reports, Gul,' Qazi said in his hoarse voice. As usual he spoke Urdu, the language they were all most comfortable with.

Gul Mohammed passed around the electronic printouts. They showed blips on a running line, rather like an ECG report. As the men scanned them, the director of SIGINT started to speak softly.

It had all started about ten months before, with reports by army intelligence of mobilization by the Indians near the Siachen Glacier, 200 kilometres northwest of the AIB at Kargil. The Pakistanis had moved to high alert in response, but the activity soon subsided. A similar incident was again reported two weeks later, and again the Pakistani Siachen Brigade was moved to a heightened defensive posture. Again, the Indians seemed to subside within a few hours. This was repeated twice over the next two months, but thereafter all had gone quiet for several months – till another occurrence the previous week. In normal course all this would have been put down to the usual sabre-rattling. Both armies played hide-and-seek along the border and provocation was sometimes a way of relieving plain boredom and the bitter cold at lonely outposts. These minor excitements would not have merited a second thought had it not been for one very alert SIGINT officer who had connected the dots.

'Our border stations only monitor electronic activity on the AIB; we don't have visuals along the whole length, but our sensors keep a tab on the electronic signature of the fence. The dates of the Siachen activity are set down against the surveillance SIGINT over the AIB. Gaps in the line are when it went down,' Gul Mohammed said, pointing to the sheets.

The men stared. The fence malfunctions coincided exactly with the dates of the Siachen incidents.

'A goddamn feint,' Shaji Mir said softly. 'The bastards are breaking in through their own bloody fence.'

Gul Mohammed nodded shortly and sat back. 'Given the short time windows we're seeing, only a few could have gone through.'

'How few totally?' Mir asked.

Mohammed shrugged and replied, 'Twenty people at most, but that's just my guess.'

There was a short silence, then Qazi said, 'The numbers don't matter. What matters is what has been coming in from Qakshal.'

Qakshal was the code name for Agent 24, the highest-ranking ISI mole within the Indian government, an officer working for RAW at the level of deputy director in JD (Joint Directorate) III and handling countries other than Pakistan and China. Over the years, 24 had proved to be a spy of genius, time and again providing intelligence of extraordinary quality. Qazi leaned forward, holding their undivided attention.

'Brothers, we have all been in the intelligence business long enough to understand that the Indian view of Pakistan has changed decisively over the last decade. We now recognize three tipping points, each occurring in rapid succession in just three years: our nuclear explosions of 1998, the Kargil jung of 1999 and the attack on the Indian parliament in 2001. Each shook the Indians – which was intended – but also set into motion consequences which we could not foresee.'

'As tends to happen when trigger-happy morons sit in positions of power,' Gul Mohammed said sharply. It still rankled at him that the military brass could have been so stupid. The 1998 explosions had placed Pakistan firmly in the nuclear club. It was a time for extreme circumspection, a time to present the country to the world as a mature, reasonable power that could act with restraint. Instead, they had plunged headlong into a disastrously miscalculated war with India. American intelligence had caught nuclear launchers moving into the theatre of conflict. So much for Pakistani restraint.

The others in the room said nothing. After a pause, Qazi continued, 'One was that hardliners within the Indian establishment came into their own. We have known for some time that their influence has been growing, but we had no idea of the extent of their penetration into the security apparatus – till now.'

Qazi paused again and took a sip of water. He let his gaze travel over the table, taking in each of their faces. Then he said, 'RAW has been taken over by anti-Pakistan elements so extreme that even our Talib look tame by comparison. There is no doubt about their agenda: the unleashing of a nuclear barrage from Pakistani soil aimed at key Indian cities. The missiles are very likely being assembled somewhere in Afghanistan even as we speak.'

The words were spoken softly, without emphasis, but a chill permeated the room. He could see the naked shock on their faces. Nuclear war. Between two countries whose landmass was home to over *1.6 billion* people, close to one-fourth of population of the planet.

Qazi paused once more for them to absorb the enormity of it. '24 is not clear on how many of these maniacs exist, but it appears that at least some of them sit at the top or very near the top in JD I and II. It is unclear if AD-RAW is in with them, but Qakshal is certain they have extremely powerful connections in the prime minister's office and the office of the NSA, the national security advisor to the Indian government. We *do not know how much higher this goes.*'

'How did Qakshal get access to this information?' Mir asked.

'As DD in JD III, he's been taking a distinctly hawkish position on Pakistan gradually over the last year. He's been hearing a few things; some people are opening up. Nothing overt, just a few hints. It's an incredibly shadowy group and keeps a tight lid on everything. Qakshal thinks he's been very lucky to get even this far. He's bedding two women at the same time, both working in different sections of the NSA's office. They're low on the totem pole but there's enough classified material passing through them that he's pieced together with reports from his own desk. Qakshal has no doubt about what is brewing – right under the nose of the unsuspecting Indian government. The bastards have chosen the perfect moment; the Indian leadership is practically rudderless.'

Iftikhar Ahmed spoke for the first time. 'So who can we go to on the Indian side?'

Qazi turned to Mir in query. 'Well?'

Mir grimaced. 'You're right. The politicos have screwed up big time. There's a huge power vacuum. This is the weakest Indian civilian government since 1947. The corruption scandals have all but paralysed the administration. No one wants to take a piss without posting it on a file first. Even if you get someone to hear you out, it will take months to get a reaction. They don't trust us one inch. This is *us*, for God's sake, the goddamn ISI – their worst enemy. And then what? They'll pass on our concerns to RAW. No, we're fucked either way.'

Gul Mohammed nodded. 'I agree with Shaji. We just don't know how high this goes, within either the elected government or the armed services. I've considered third countries, but they'd have to process our information through the same channels and,' he cleared his throat, 'we have a very specific problem of credibility with them as well.'

Qazi tried to think. He passed his hand over

his forehead and found it came away wet. 'We've tried everything we can to figure the likely point of launch, but the border is too big and porous. They can cross us practically anywhere and fire the missiles from within Pakistan. Make no mistake, if those missiles get away we have *zero* deniability. It's exactly what the world thinks can happen in Pakistan. There will be no second- or third-strike options: the Americans will be on us like a ton of bricks, clamping down on all our nukes.'

Ahmed said in a strangled voice, 'And if the Indians counter-launch when we have both hands tied behind our backs? It'll be the end of Pakistan!'

Qazi said heavily, 'Either way it'll be the end of Pakistan as we know it. We'll be finished forever.'

Gul Mohammed interjected angrily, 'What are you both blathering on about? Forget Pakistan. Frankly, I could give a shit about what happens to the country politically, whether we even survive as an independent country. Think of it in human terms, for God's sake: the millions that are going to die if those madmen succeed.' He said to Qazi, 'How much time do we have?'

Qazi had not reacted to Gul Mohammed's words. If there was an officer who was universally respected for his contributions to Pakistani intelligence, it was Gul Mohammed. Incorruptible in a country besieged by graft, a patriot and, above all, a supremely competent professional, Gul Mohammed was a legend in his lifetime within the espionage community. He could say what he wanted and no DG of ISI was going to stop him.

Qazi gave the question his full attention and then replied, 'I think the trigger mechanisms are what have been taken through the fence. We have to assume that the main missile parts have probably been shipped into Afghanistan with the Indian aid and reconstruction convoys. So even as we speak the full projectile and launch systems could be getting assembled.'

Mir said, 'Missile and warhead assembly need space; they'll need minimum rigs, infrastructure. Can we find out where it's being done – put our networks on it? We can reach into most parts of Afghanistan.'

Qazi said nothing for a minute. When he spoke, it was as if he was weighing his words carefully. 'We're almost sure they're working with Xiphos Soter.'

The others said nothing. Qazi had said it all: no other explanation was needed. They just sat there, white-faced. Shaji Mir took out a cigarette and lit it with shaking hands. All the others followed and soon the room was fogged with smoke as they dragged furiously at their cigarettes.

Gul Mohammed finally said, 'There is one to whom I can reach out. He is a cop, an inspector of police in Delhi.' He saw the open disbelief on their faces but continued doggedly, 'He has an exceptional record and, what is more, he never gives up.'

Qazi said, 'Gul, you can't be serious. What can this man do? What is he to you?'

'We have no other option. Time is running out on us. His name is Syed Ali Hassan and he is my cousin.'

5

Meenakshi's miraculous Internet act turned out to be a case of luck favouring the prepared mind. When she had clapped eyes on the dead man's head in my photograph and we had both agreed on 'ancient Asiatic Greek' as best describing him, she remembered a cross-reference at the bottom of the Wikipedia article on skull flattening. Some link to the Kushans and their coins. To a historian like Meenakshi, the connect was immediate.

I had but the vaguest notions about the Kushans: just scattered fragments of memory from long-forgotten history drones at school. However, Meenakshi was a born teacher making up for lost time and I listened, suddenly fascinated. It was Alexander the Great who first brought the Greeks to Asia and almost into India. When he died in 323 BC, the easternmost parts of his empire fell to his general Seleucus, whose successors ruled over the area – now eastern Iran and a large part of northern Afghanistan – for the next two-and-a-half centuries. The result was the Greco-Bactrian kingdom, a vast area to the west of India that acquired a decidedly Greek character but melded over time with the social geography and customs of Asia.

The Seleucids declined over time and the Kushan Empire came into being when a tribe from northwest China pushed westwards and gradually took over the region from around the middle of the first century AD. Within the next century, the Kushans had pushed the boundaries of their rule further east and south, taking over large swathes of Pakistan. The crowning glory of the Kushan era was the rule of Kanishka – the greatest Kushan emperor ever – who extended Kushan rule to almost the whole of northern India.

'Imagine it,' Meenakshi said. 'Kanishka's summer capital was Bagram in Afghanistan; to the west it was Mathura. He maintained political contacts with Rome. At his zenith, Kanishka would have been a sort of Greek Akbar.'

For the Kushans were by now an extraordinary amalgam: they had adopted many remnants of the Hellenistic culture of the old Bactrian kingdom, but overlaid them with the new. They worshipped gods from Greek, Zoroastrian and Hindu pantheons. As time went on, they came to be predominantly Buddhists but maintained

Greek as the lingua franca. As was to be expected from such a potent cultural fusion, the Kushans were supreme aesthetes. Meenakshi had pulled up images of their coins, stone sculptures and reliefs on the computer, and even to a poor judge like me, they were breathtaking.

And they flattened their skulls. Many coins and Kushan stone figures showed the deformed cranium starkly; the bust Meenakshi had pulled up was that of a soldier, discovered at the Khalchayan Palace in Uzbekistan.

'And the trident?' I asked. 'Anything on that?'

'Yes. It's a tamga, a royal seal of Kanishka.'

There was silence. I was trying to digest all this stuff, but none of it made any sort of sense and my own thoughts were whizzing around in clueless circles.

'You mean this guy could be a member of a sort of Kanishka cult?'

'I mean nothing,' said Meenakshi a trifle tartly. 'I'm telling you what we're seeing.'

'But …?' I let the question hang.

'Anything's possible, of course,' she said slowly, reflecting on it as she spoke. 'But think of it, Chandra. The Kushans went into terminal decline in the middle of the third century AD. First, it was the Persian Sassanids, and then the Guptas, who overran them. All that was left of the Indo-Greeks culturally and politically was wiped clean by the wave of Islam that spread throughout Central Asia from the seventh century.'

'You mean nothing's left of the Kushans of old?'

'No, nothing. At least nothing that we would recognize as Kushan. The Tajiks and Hazaras of Afghanistan are said to have descended from the Asiatic Greeks, but they are pretty completely Islamized.'

'So we're looking at a ghost?'

Meenakshi was looking down at the ancient bust on her laptop. 'Yes, we are. The man we saw cannot exist.'

So there we were: ground zero. We decided to break for tea. I offered to make it, but she said she knew where everything was in the kitchen and made for it before I could stop her. Which was a mistake. She took one look at the ready-mix packets, the vessels carelessly piled up on the counter, and the disapproval was back – with gale force this time. Nothing was where she remembered, so I brewed us a pot in cold silence. I guess I should have had my own reaction: irritation perhaps or even resentment; what I felt instead was a strange comfort. The place had not seen a real visitor in over six months. It was my fault, of course. I had withdrawn from everything that reminded me of my wife, sealed myself off in a tomb. Now here she was, a woman whose anger spoke louder than any words and I was glad.

I said, 'Thanks for coming, Meenu. Really.'

She looked at me over the rim of her cup, not sure if I was serious. When she saw I was, she smiled sadly, put the cup down and said,

'Yeh dil na umeed to nahin, nakam hi to hai
Lambi hai gham ki sham, magar sham hi to hai.'

The couplet was an old favourite of Yamini's, by the great Pakistani poet Faiz Ahmed Faiz.

The heart has not lost its hope, it is but sad
Long is the evening of our sorrow, but it is still
*   an evening.*

Her eyes filled with tears. There was nothing to say and we just sat there, in the silence of the kitchen, in the void left by Yamini. Then the shrill of the doorbell shattered our reverie.

—⚊

I made the introductions. 'Meenu, this is Inspector Hassan. Hassan, Meenakshi Pirzada, an old friend of Yamini's.'

Hassan sat on the couch. I poured him some tea, trying to hide my disquiet. The man was usually so dapper; not quite a dandy, but I knew he took his appearance seriously. And right now, he looked terrible. He had changed out of uniform, but his shirt was crumpled and a semi-circle of sweat had pooled out from the armpits. He kept mopping his face with a kerchief.

I sat facing him. He sipped perfunctorily at the tea. I could see he was having serious difficulty in starting, and he kept looking at Meenakshi.

As usual, she got right to the point. 'Inspector, do you want me to leave?'

Before he could reply, I said, 'She's the one who brought this up.' I turned and showed him the bust on the laptop screen. He jerked back as if struck. I clicked on the other tab and showed him the trident. He took it from my hands and then breathed a long, 'My God.'

'Will you go first or should we?'

'You first.'

I asked Meenakshi to take over. For the next twenty minutes, except for wiping himself with his kerchief, Hassan sat immobile as she led him through what we had discovered. Like me, he had also heard vaguely of the Kushans but, unlike me, he didn't seem to want to look at all the other stuff on them on the Internet. No question he was shaken and excited by our account, but something else was consuming him and it was clear that he did not want Meenakshi around.

She took the hint smoothly and got up to leave. Hassan also rose and said with an old-world courtesy, 'Ms Pirzada, that was a superb piece of detection on the Internet. I mean it. I would very much like to talk more with you about it. Till then please don't mention it to anyone. *Anyone*.' The emphasis was unmistakable and Meenu's eyes widened just a bit. She nodded shortly.

I walked her to the door. At the head of the steps I said softly, 'Meenu, Hassan's deadly serious. Please keep all this stuff under wraps.'

Meenu said, 'The man's under severe stress, in case you haven't noticed.'

'I noticed.'

'Is it about the case?'

'Could be. I think it is. He's been like this since the morning. Frankly, it's not like Hassan. I think the phone tapping was …'

I stopped, but it was too late. Meenakshi had gone still. Then she nodded to herself as if something had just been confirmed and said, 'You've been tense too – all morning. There's more you're not telling me, isn't there?'

When I did not reply, she continued, 'Chandra, I can't leave like this. I think I've earned the right to know what is happening, don't you think?'

'Please, Meenu. Just leave.'

'Why?'

'Because I don't know what we're starting to get into here and the less you are involved the better.'

'You mean there's some danger?'

'No, I meant just what I said. Now, Meenu, please just …'

She cut me off. 'Okay, I'll go on one condition.

You'll keep in touch and let me in on what happens.'

'I will. I promise.'

She capitulated. 'Well, I'm full up with classes the whole week. My mobile will be on silent mode, so I'll return calls during breaks. You will call, right?'

I assured her I would and went back in. Hassan was sitting right on the edge of the sofa and he got to his feet. He was looking even worse than when he came in, his face pasty in the neon wash of the tube light.

'Hassan, are you okay?' I said, concerned. 'Frankly, you're not looking good, man.' He flapped my question away with a curt wave of his arm and then dropped his second bombshell of the day – one that exploded in my living room with the force of a grenade.

'Chandra, I've been contacted by ISI.'

'The … what?'

'The Inter-Services Intelligence Directorate of Pakistan. ISI.'

My first reaction was this was some sort of obscure joke. 'ISI?'

'Yes.'

He was deadly serious. I felt a huge spurt of adrenaline and my pulse rocketed, going now like a trip hammer. I held myself as tightly as I could and said, 'Earlier it was RAW and now it's … ISI?'

He began to shake his head. 'No, it's both. They are both ...' He began to walk about agitatedly. 'I got the first call at 7 am today, just before the report of the Qutub killing came in to the station. It was from my cousin Gul Mohammed who lives in Karachi. I couldn't talk to him as I was in the middle of my morning debrief and then was rushing to the spot, so he called me again around lunchtime. He wants to meet: said it was a matter of national emergency.'

'Cousin? Who ... what did he ...?'

'Gul's grandmother and my grandmother are sisters. Our families have lived on opposite sides of the border since Partition. I was told that Gul had taken over his father's construction business in Karachi, but it didn't work out and so for the last ten years or so he has been in some minor government department.'

'Okay, so ...?'

Hassan took in a deep breath and let it out with a whoosh. 'That was obviously a cover-up. Gul is a deputy director general with ISI.'

One could have cut the air with a knife. My jaw was clenched, my whole body painfully rigid. 'He called you on your cellphone to say this?'

'No. On this.' Hassan held up a black instrument. It was one of those cheap Nokias available in any store. 'It was delivered to my house by an anonymous courier this morning.'

I stared at the phone. 'He wants to meet you where?'

'There is a small sit-down place near Ghantewala's. He'll meet us there at nine o'clock.'

I sat tight, trying to get a hold of myself. 'Hassan, let me get this straight. What you're saying is that the big boss of ISI is here *in Delhi*, in fact right round in the corner in Chandni Chowk. Waiting to meet you. And all the while RAW is likely tapping your phone, maybe even tailing you here.'

He shook his head at that. 'No. No tail. I would know, believe me, especially here on my home turf.'

A burst of raw anger propelled me to my feet.

'Get the hell out of here! Now. I don't know why you came here, and I don't want to know. This is not what I signed up for. Get out.'

Hassan did not move. Instead, he said, 'What are you going to do?'

'I am going to report it to the government. The man you're going to meet is a sworn enemy of the Indian state.'

'Who will you speak to?'

'None of your damn business. You had no right, *no right*, to get me involved in something like this. The guy's bloody ISI, for God's sake.' Despite myself, my voice began to rise. 'Is this some spy ring? Is that what it is? Working for Pakistan? *What the hell is going on, Hassan?*'

Hassan's face turned ugly. His smoker's voice, when it came out, rasped like metal cutting at stone. 'Hey, hold it. *Hold it just a minute.*' He pointed a finger at me. 'You think I'm plotting all this? That I'm a fucking terrorist. Or better still, a Pakistani. *Is that it? Is it?*'

I said nothing. The wall clock ticked loudly in the dead silence.

Hassan's shoulders slumped. Then he said in a low voice, 'It's a bloody big shock for me too – even bigger. Gul is my relative, for God's sake. That *exactly* why I have come to you. Just listen to me for a few minutes. Then I swear I will leave – and you can call whoever you want.'

I started to shake my head when he said again, 'Chandra, please.' There was in his voice a plea that I never expected to hear from this tough cop: one with a desperate edge to it. And a core of truth. I hesitated a long moment, then sat down. 'Okay, you've got five minutes. And you'd better believe I will make that call.'

Hassan also set himself down on the couch. 'Chandra, believe me when I say Gul Mohammed's occupation was a nasty surprise. We have met over the years as families: sometimes in Karachi and sometimes in Delhi. There has been absolutely nothing between us; we have never really spoken of our work to each other. He always said he was in government accounts and I never thought to ask him about it. Whatever it was, it seemed deadly dull to me. And he's never made any sort of a … approach. Never. I think he read me as well as any intelligence officer would.'

'You're saying you were … are just cousins – is that it?'

'Yes, that's exactly it.' Hassan paused here. He seemed to be collecting his thoughts as if what he would say next would make – or break – the moment. 'But I've been enough with him, seen him at close quarters over the years. I think I am a good judge of character. It's a cop thing, a gut feel for people. I usually know when the other guy is shitting me. Sure I've made wrong calls, but I have been right far, far more often. When Gul Mohammed spoke to me, my reaction was the same as yours. I almost got on to the phone with the DG direct. But he was begging me to hear him out before I did anything. He said just one thing: it's a matter of millions of lives – Indian lives.'

'And you believe him?'

'I don't know what to believe; my logic rejects the whole thing, but my gut says otherwise.'

I pointed a finger at him. 'Hassan, your gut means shit. This guy is a spymaster, for God's sake. He's trained to deceive. He can pull wool over you so thick you'll be buried forever. This is a crazy conversation.'

We stared at each other through a fog of

tension. I said, 'Hassan, please report this to your superiors, or to the IB or whoever. But do it. Don't take the meeting. Please.'

Hassan's head drooped. He gazed down at the carpet and was quiet for a while. When he looked up, his thin face was drawn but determined. He shook his head. 'No.'

'Hassan …'

'No, Chandra. Think what you like, but I am Indian, and a cop. I'm going to meet Gul Mohammed. Make your call.' He stood up. 'I'll see my way out.'

And suddenly there it was, rearing up stark and deadly before us: my own moment of truth. Hassan had said he was Indian, and a cop. That was very likely true. But India was changing: identities were becoming more visibly assertive on all sides of the religious divide. Several of the influential Hindu orders were now overtly political, more nakedly right wing than before. Madrassas and mosques were also proliferating, many of them preaching a heady radical theology to the young. The signs were all there – and frightening.

I felt very strongly that religion was dividing us, that the way forward for this country *had* to be to open our hearts and minds, to trust in each other – Muslim, Christian, Sikh and Hindu – no matter what. But that was in the comfort of the collective. Here, now, it all came down to

one man: Inspector of Police Syed Ali Hassan – a
Muslim. Going for a clandestine meeting with a
Pakistani intelligence officer.

I thought of our cases: the long hours poring
over the evidence, the forensic and witness reports.
We had even done a couple of stakeouts together.
We'd fenced with each other using our wits, each
trying his solution on the other. One does not spend
that kind of time with another without building a
feeling – a bond even – to some degree. I felt that
bond now, and it was telling me something.

Hassan had his hand on the door latch. He
turned around as if to say goodbye. I saw his
lined, tired face: bitter, but touched with a kind
of understanding.

'Wait,' I said.

Ghantewala fronted Kinari Bazar on Chandni
Chowk. The sweetmeat shop had been around
since the late eighteenth century and had its niche
in Delhi's history; it was said that the sepoys of
the 1857 mutiny lost their urge to fight on after
gorging themselves there. The Sunday crowds
were out in full crush. Music blared out from
shops and the smells of chaat and samosa filled
the air. Bright coloured lights lit up the whole
place like it was a festival. I never tired of my
neighbourhood and would normally have soaked

it all in but as Hassan and I pushed and shoved our way forward, I cursed myself for my weakness. For all my misgivings, when it came down to the wire I was a journalist, a goddamn newshound. I was very afraid, but the story was so implausible it had the smell of truth. And I was hooked.

Hassan spoke briefly into his black Nokia and led me into the sweet shop. A figure sitting at a table at the rear raised his hand and then we were facing him: Hassan's cousin and one of Pakistan's top spymasters.

Despite my nervous tension, I found myself studying him with open interest. I had half-expected a James Bond-like figure, but the man before me was anything but. Gul Mohammed was of medium height and average bulk. His clean-shaven face was bland to be point of being completely undistinguished. Even later, after seeing him many times, I would still have some trouble recalling him exactly. The only memorable feature about him was that he was bald. A completely forgettable man, with a completely forgettable face. I could certainly see him as a minor accountant in the government. Perhaps all spies outside of thrillers were like this.

We pulled up our chairs and sat down. Gul Mohammed took out a packet of unfiltered cigarettes and offered it to Hassan and then to me. I declined and the two of them lit up. He then ordered some tea for us. While we waited for it, he looked at me in frank appraisal. Then he picked a small fleck of tobacco off his lips and said:

'You know, Mr Chandrasekhar, I almost called this meeting off. I did not think having you here was a good idea, but Hassan refused to come without you. He seems to think of you as his ... insurance. I told him I didn't think you would come, that you would report him to your authorities. But he said no. Was he right?'

A cop thing, a gut feel for people. Hassan the cop had read me like a book and thrown me the bait. I felt suddenly trapped, the walls closing in on me.

Hassan saw my face and said uncomfortably, 'Enough of the bullshit, Gul. He didn't want to come. Now get to the point.'

I leaned away from both of them and said tightly, 'Mr Mohammed, Hassan may have hooked me enough to be here, but let's be clear on this: I am an Indian – first and last. If I hear anything that even remotely puts my country at risk, I am out of here and straight to my contacts with the authorities. So please be warned before you start.'

The Pakistani smiled gently at my open hostility. 'A straight shooter: that's what Hassan said. But you make a very poor spy, Mr Chandrasekhar. You should have heard me out and *then* got to your government. Not warned me beforehand.' He crossed his hands and leaned forward, suddenly businesslike. 'Let me speak equally frankly. We need someone exactly like you, someone incorruptibly Indian. Your country is at risk – at the edge of catastrophe – and so is mine. Please hear me out. Then it is entirely up to you: whether you will act with us or go to your government.'

In a *Star Wars* movie – I forget which – one of the Jedi knights tells the young Anakin Skywalker, 'Always remember, your focus determines your reality.' All three of us had unconsciously moved close to one another, hunched over the table. For the next half hour Gul Mohammed spoke without pause. He kept his voice low: just audible through the Bollywood song on the wall TV and the chatter of customers. Within moments, I was transfixed. Everything around me faded away, replaced by a total intensity of focus. The Pakistani spoke, then ended as simply: no verbal flourishes, no dramatic turns of phrase but if anything, the impact was even more chilling. My stomach began its familiar churn. I held on to the thick tea glass tightly, disoriented, almost concussed, as I struggled to absorb what I had just heard. Hassan's face was pinched, every line rigid with tension. Only Gul Mohammed seemed exactly as before: calm and expressionless as a stone Buddha.

I tried to rein in the chaotic swirl of thoughts, to make some sense of it all. If the ISI man was to be believed, the genie of thermonuclear war was about to be uncorked from its bottle. In the most populated part of the planet. The mother of all nightmares for every government in the world.

I looked over at Hassan. He was holding his head in his hands. He turned towards me. His eyes were wide open with the same shock, the same disbelief. He shook his head in a way that was clearer than any words: *What the hell do you make of it?*

It was impossible. It just could not be. The whole thing had an unreal feel to it: one of those plots right out of a Tom Clancy novel complete with rogue elements and over-the-top conspiracies backed by techno-wizardry working to unleash a world war. Supposedly, the crazies behind this were ours. How could they have spread right through our command and control structure? The notion was bizarre. I remembered a press briefing I had attended to announce the setting up of a nuclear hot line between India and Pakistan with American help in 2004. I had researched a small piece then for the *Hindustan Times* on nuclear power and equations in the subcontinent. India had a nuclear command authority reporting to the Cabinet Committee on Security and a Strategic Forces Command. They mirrored the structure of the US's own command and control and were reputedly rock-solid.

Then Gul Mohammed said something that I

could not dismiss: that power abhors a vacuum. The Indian political dispensation in scandal-ridden paralysis, wheelchair-bound for the last several years had left a huge vacuum. Power equations were shifting, some of them widely reported. The jostling between the civilian and military bureaucracies, and their shenanigans with their political masters regularly provided cannon fodder for a gleeful press. The recent fracas between the army chief and the defence minister was a case in point: it had filled reams of newsprint and exposed a severely dysfunctional civil-military relationship. Beneath this chaos, perhaps other power shifts were happening: quiet, unreported for the most part – but tectonic.

I looked around, and the noise and bustle surged back into my consciousness. Just across, a bunch of youngsters – from college or perhaps some software company – was buried up to their chins in kulfis. To our left, a couple of foreign tourists were reading intently from their *Lonely Planets*. I tried to imagine it: this place, the tourists across, the students … the throngs everywhere … the whole of Shahjahanabad, old Delhi … the capital itself – all vaporized.

I felt nauseous, giddy as it all hit me together. I knew I could not walk away now. Not after what I had just heard. Perhaps the ISI man was playing some bigger game. Maybe there was an altogether deeper motive to this meeting, to use me as a pawn for some Pakistani mischief on Indian soil. However, that was beyond me. I would keep my eyes and ears open, but I had no illusions that I could match ISI in a double or triple game of deception. But right now – at this moment – I would have to assume he spoke the truth.

Hassan said, 'Do you know where into India they are aiming these ... the warheads?'

Gul shook his head. 'No. That decision will be made at the very apex of the group and we don't have penetration at that level. We cannot even hazard a guess.'

Hassan said, 'Gul, you surely have *someone* on our side you can turn to.'

The Pakistani said regretfully, 'After Kargil, inter-agency communications between the countries took a massive hit. The attack on your parliament ... and then the recent Bombay terror outrage. We've stopped talking. No, Hassan. There's no one we can turn to.'

We sat in silence for a bit, and then Gul said, 'We don't have time. These people are turning nukes on their own country to destroy Pakistan. I repeat: we don't know who to get to in the Indian government that we can safely say is a 100 percent in the clear and who can act decisively within the power structure *without referring it to Indian intelligence.*'

'Someone who won't dismiss it as one of your usual ISI ploys,' Hassan said acidly.

Gul nodded. 'Exactly. For what it is worth, let me say that we – the army and ISI – have screwed up big time. We played our stupid games too long and now no one will believe us. For years I argued with my people in the military and intelligence communities that we were cutting our nose to spite our face, that we were losing our biggest weapon: credibility. I failed to carry the argument, but that is neither here nor there.

'We're trying like hell to find the missile assembly site. We're using everyone we can – the ISI network, the Talib, the tribes on our side. But the country is huge and so far we've got nowhere.'

I tried one last time. 'Look, if you with all your resources don't know what to do, what chance do the two of us have? I mean, we're not the government or the military; we … I'm not even that well connected. What do you think we can possibly achieve?'

Gul crushed out his cigarette. 'I'm not sure. Let's just say I'm grasping at straws.' He paused. 'But I've seen enough of your records to be … impressed. You've both pulled off complex investigations, stuff that would have challenged anyone. And – crazy as it may seem – you're the only people on the Indian side I can trust right now.'

Hassan said, 'What do you want us to do?'

'We want you to track down and discover the site where the missiles are being assembled. We need you to take photographs and any other evidence that will convince your government that the threat is real.'

I looked down at the tea glass, trying to hide my shock.

Hassan said, 'And you think the two of us can do it. ISI must be even more fucking stupid than I thought, or else you guys know something we don't.'

Gul Mohammed said tonelessly, 'We know damn-all; we don't even know what we don't know.' He paused. 'But we know something about you – both of you.' He shifted and looked around. 'Look, we've run out of time. You need to make a decision here.'

I said nothing. In a space of less than twelve hours I had been called to a weird murder case involving an extinct cult, was apparently being bugged by Indian intelligence and was now being asked to save the subcontinent from nuclear war by a Pakistani intelligence operative. There is only so much the mind can absorb, and mine was setting up a reaction by going blank.

Hassan said, 'I'll go. But I have some conditions.'

'Name them.'

'We will communicate with you, not the other way around. You don't control us. We'll operate strictly freelance. We'll call as and when we have something to report. Whatever we need you will provide – without questions.'

Gul Mohammed sat thinking. Then he nodded slowly. 'Okay. I agree. You say "we". Do I take it that you speak for Chandra here?'

Hassan said, 'No. It was a figure of speech. Chandra needs to make his own decision.'

They went quiet, waiting. Another moment of truth. I drained the remains of my cold tea, set the glass down and nodded weakly.

Hassan smiled. He straightened up: a man who has suddenly had a big weight lifted from his shoulders, 'One final point, Gul. No tailing us. If we even so much as spot a tail, we will stop looking. And we will go to RAW.'

This time Gul didn't hesitate. 'Agreed. Now: have either of you ever heard of a secret sect called the Sword of the Saviour?'

We shook our heads.

'Gentlemen, with your permission, Pakistani intelligence will place you deep inside Afghanistan within the next two days.'

In the nondescript office off Lodhi Road, a light started to blink on the red phone. The man at the desk reached out and held the receiver to his ear. He waited until the hiss of the scrambler kicked in, then said, 'Yes?'

The voice on the other side had a hollow ring as if coming from a great distance. 'Numbers 1 and 2 are ready. System testing of all circuits to commence 0400 tomorrow.'

'Time track for all systems go?'

'T minus twelve days and counting.'

'Good. Report back at 2100 tomorrow.'

He disconnected but kept the receiver to his ear, then punched a single number on the button array. There was a click as the call was answered. He waited a beat and said, 'What is the status of targets?' He listened intently and said, 'They are both not at home? Co-incidence bhi ho sakta hai. Mount both audio and video surveillance inside the houses and a twenty-four-hour watch as soon as they get back. Control pucca hona chahiye.'

The voice at the other end squawked something. The man's lips tightened. He paused, keeping his eyes on the Gandhi portrait on the wall. 'Yes, keep them on stand-by alert. I've read the report: the cop is a loose cannon; he's pissed off that the case has been taken from him and the journo's a nosy bastard. If necessary we'll have to take them out.'

6

The hall was vast, a cavernous immensity of rock gouged out of the heart of the mountain. A colonnade of gargantuan ionic pillars on either side soared away to the roof so far above they seemed to vanish from sight into a distant emptiness; from there cleverly placed recessed arc lights shed a ghostly light over the entire hall – like starlight from a luminescent sky. Four wide steps led up to a stage at the head of the central atrium between the columns. A single high-backed stone seat of mammoth proportions dominated the podium, against a backdrop of rough-cut pink granite with a trident carved into it. The throne was empty, but flaming torches mounted on stands on either side bathed it in a red glow, magnifying its size and investing its emptiness with a strange power.

The sound of a gong reverberated from deep within the mountain. As if they were waiting for the signal, a line of white-clad figures emerged from an entrance behind and to the left of the stage. All were males with shaven skulls, wearing loose toga-like robes. For the next several minutes they poured out in orderly procession, each taking his precise position in the hall until a full thousand of them stood rigidly arrayed in military ranks before the stage. Complete silence reigned, except for the occasional crackling hiss of the fire lamps.

The gong sounded again, and a ripple of anticipation moved through the serried ranks. A single point of light appeared beneath the trident and spread outward in a shimmering radiance that blocked out the rock face. Through this curtain of light stepped forth a form. An electric tension gripped the assembly and held it locked onto the stage. The figure was that of a man – if that word could be used to describe the giant that advanced towards the throne. He was fully seven feet tall, with a bulk that seemed to fill the atrium. He was dressed identically in a white robe, but bordered with vermilion. The topknot of a sage crowned an immense flattened skull and from this vertical plane the features protruded with startling effect, as if from a stone relief worked on a wall: the nose long and bridgeless, perfect in its symmetry below which a curve of blond moustache joined a short spade of a beard. He carried a thick book in his hands.

The giant paused beside the throne, held up the book and deliberately placed it upon the seat. Straightening up, he surveyed the sea of rapt faces. In the utter silence, his presence was suddenly explosive: the raw, palpable force of a Moses that flashed out to bind all those in the hall to him. Except for the eyes. Where the eyes of a Biblical prophet would have blazed out at the world, this man's orbs were a pale blue, completely washed of any expression, shallow as a film of water on hard agate.

He began to speak. The voice was harsh but with a mellifluous, beguiling quality. Picked up by hidden microphones and bounced off the rock, the words rang out eerie and disembodied – coming from everywhere and nowhere at once. The cadence was deliberate, the tongue ancient Greek. The man spoke four aphorisms and in turn each was repeated by a thousand voices that reverberated like rolling thunder. Then he switched to Dari – modern Persian – speaking now direct to the gathered congregation.

'Brothers, your preparation is over. The hour will soon be upon us. Hazaras of Shia Islam, Zarthustis, Hindus, Buddhists and millions of His seed await our word – the word of the Saviour.' He pointed at the book. 'What was written long ago is now coming to pass. Less than three weeks from today, a cataclysm never before experienced will smite the world. Be not afraid of it, for you are the Chosen, chosen to go forth to the four corners of this land and carry the message amongst our people: that we are all born of Him and he returns to us in this moment of our destiny. New lines will be drawn in blood on the sand and His Kingdom established upon this earth. *Hail the Saviour!*'

The mountain shuddered with the roar of the answering multitude.

A short subterranean passage linked the big hall to another vault very like the first in size. But here all similarity ended. Where the other had pulsated to the rhythm of a dark antiquity, this one was crammed with twenty-first-century engineering: a technoscape of computer panels, flashing digital control consoles, endless arrays of stainless steel benches carrying printed circuit assemblies and electronic gear. Wires sprouted out from junction boxes on the walls and ran along the ground in thick red and green clusters like vegetation run amok. An acrid chemical odour permeated the chill air. White-coated men were scattered all over the vault: some bent over the workbenches, others typing at the consoles and still others – in what appeared to be a fabrication shop – wielding cutting torches, directing the flame carefully on spidery metal structures.

The Initiates stood unmoving, sentinels at the head of the chamber. Now and then, one of the white-coated technicians would look up at them, taking in the toga-clad figures with the misshapen heads and quickly look down again. The Initiates ignored them. Instead, their eyes were fixed to their left where two heavy pylons stretched along the width of the floor. Each carried a cut-open cylinder packed with electronic gear. Each was identical to the other: exactly 15.9 metres long and 1.35 metres in diameter. The shell was painted over in standard camouflage pattern, but the cone itself was maroon. On it, a patch of dark green formed the backdrop to a crescent moon – the flag of the Islamic Republic of Pakistan. Along the cylinder's length were six letters: GHAURI – the sub-title of the Kahuta Research Laboratories' HATF V Class Intermediate Range Ballistic Missile. The digital chronometer on the wall, calibrated to microsecond accuracy, showed the time at two minutes past midnight. It was now T minus eleven days and counting.

7

I froze with my hand on the doorknob. Faint tinkling sounds emanated from the direction of the kitchen. There was someone inside my flat. Then a switch clicked on and music soared up through the door. I drew a deep breath and walked in.

My father sat in his usual cross-legged position on the sofa. His eyes were closed, his hand keeping to the beat of the raga on his thigh. I could see my mother in the kitchen, stirring something over the stove. A picture of the dancing Nataraja of Chidambaram had appeared on the mantelpiece, adorned by the offering of a single champak blossom. Smoke swirled up from an incense stick.

They were unaware of my entry and I leaned back against the door and watched them: Neelakanta Subramania Iyer and Gowri Parvati Ammal of Chidamabaram. My mother in her nine-yard sari and my father in his spotless white shirt and dhoti. Both their foreheads smeared with holy ash. Solid. Whole. Utterly Indian. I felt the sudden, unfamiliar prick of tears; I waited, trying to get a grip on myself when my father opened his eyes.

His face spilt into a wide grin of delight and he called out, 'Gowri! Yaar vandirikan, parr' – see who has come.

We did a small aarti and food offering to the Blue-necked One and then sat down to dinner. Talk flowed easily from their side in Tamil: cricket developments of the day, news from relatives in Chennai and Chidambaram and happenings in the Sri Sankara Mutt in R. K. Puram (where they were staying to attend a residential scripture class for a week). I picked at my food, trying to appear normal, to mask the total disconnect I felt inside: like an alien from some outer planet listening in to a strange language. In parting, Gul Mohammed had repeated his warning that I was very likely under close surveillance; I was seized every now and then by a powerful impulse to jump up and go looking for the video and audio bugs that he had said were now surely planted all over the house. I tried not think about tomorrow – of what I was soon about to do. My parents must have noticed my preoccupation but my silences were nothing new to them, and after Yamini's passing they had simply decided that the best they could do for me was to just be there.

Dinner was done; my mother insisted on washing up and then it was time for them to leave. My manner was clearly worrying them more than usual, for they paused at the doorway to look at me searchingly. I said nothing, not trusting myself to speak. Then my mother reached out with both her hands and caressed my cheeks; my father nodded, and they let themselves out.

I stood there in the wake of their going and the thought that I might never see them again was suddenly overwhelming. If the devices were not there, I don't know what I would have done. Probably wept like a child in their arms, telling them over and over how much I loved them. That I had not been the ideal son they deserved, but an agnostic, cynical, bloody-minded loner. That I was determined to make it up to them. But I did none of these things; the bugs *were* there, observing me like a specimen, and the moment passed forever.

I walked stiffly back to the sofa, picked up the newspaper, held it spread wide and pretended to read. I even willed my head into some sort of automatic turning movement to mimic scanning the page. I needed desperately to think. Gul's matter-of-fact account had been like a kick to the teeth, leaving me disoriented and rudderless.

At one point in the exchange, I couldn't help but burst out in shock.

'But we're a nuclear state, for God's sake! It'll be an all-out retaliation.'

Gul's hand came out and gripped my sleeve in warning. He took a swift look around.

'You're right – up to a point. But these guys have been clever, more than clever. They know the public pressure in your country to counter-launch against Pakistan will be enormous. The only thing that will allow your government not to commit to a second strike will be two game-changing concessions which Pakistan will be compelled to make. I say compelled for good reason. The Americans will be on us like a ton of bricks; they will seize control of our nukes and inform the Indians they have done so. We will have no option but to allow it. Think of it: *Pakistan will no longer be a nuclear state.*'

Hassan said, 'And the second?'

'The second is the splitting of Pakistan.'

'Xiphos Soter. That's Greek for "Sword of the Saviour",' Gul Mohammed had said. According to him, this shadowy group formed the essential support element for the nuclear strike plan. Little, if anything, was known about the sect except that it first appeared in Pak intelligence field reports on Afghanistan around ten years ago, shortly after the destruction of the Buddha statues in the Bamiyan Valley by the Taliban in 2001. The blowing up of these two statues — amongst the great wonders of antiquity – was greeted with universal condemnation, especially from the Buddhist world. And beneath the surface, it appeared now that that single act of supreme religious vandalism had also let loose a long-suppressed mass yearning.

Hazarajat in central Afghanistan was homeland to some three million Hazaras – Shia Muslims who had been ruthlessly suppressed by the Sunni majority who had led pogroms against them over the centuries. Life had become even worse under the Taliban, and the dynamiting of the Buddhas of Bamiyan in the heart of the Hazarajat had become a turning point for these people in a way the world still had not understood. The Hazaras were not Buddhists, but the Bamiyan statues had a peculiar importance to their cultural heritage and their destruction was a shattering blow to their faint but long-held hope that they could be left to live in peace with their Sunni neighbours. Into this void of collective mourning stepped Xiphos Soter. And it promised them that which the Hazaras had only dreamed of for centuries.

Much of this I learnt later. All that Gul Mohammed had time to explain was that a mysterious ripple was spreading through Hazarajat, setting the land aflame. The message was that deliverance was at hand; a Saviour had appeared, soon to lead the Hazaras into a new kingdom to rival the great Bactrian Empire of centuries past. When I heard the story from Gul Mohammed, my incredulity must have shown on my face, but the Pakistani was deadly serious. 'You're going to have to see and hear it for yourselves. I tell you, it's happening. There's more than two million of them spread out in Pakistan and Iran. Imagine it: millions of minds lit by a single dream. And Xiphos Soter is the dream merchant.'

As far as ISI could make out, the stratagem was to have the Hazaras rise as one man within hours after the missile strike on Indian soil. From the turmoil of the aftermath, the governments of India, Afghanistan and the United States backed by the rest of the world would accede to the Hazara demand for a separate homeland – to be carved out of western Pakistan and Hazarajat Afghanistan. It was completely logical. The world over, governments would be convinced about the need to dismember Pakistan.

'And the Karzai government?'

'They will go along with it gladly if it allows them to be rid of the Pakistani threat forever. There's a high probability that the Balochis on our western borders will throw in their lot with the Hazaras. And remember the new state will be an ally – not the enemy that they face now to the west.'

I turned the page of the newspaper. The sensation of being watched was really getting to me now. Those who believe that the right to privacy is overdone should get their houses bugged. It's almost physical, the violation: your innermost space recorded and seen by some faceless creatures lurking out there in the dark.

I forced my mind back with an effort. Thanks to Meenakshi, we had pieced together a couple of things about the Sword of the Saviour – facts that Gul did not appear to know. The cult clearly was a throwback to a distant Kushan past. On a hunch, I palmed the smartphone Gul had given me and did a quick Internet search. Meenakshi had mentioned in passing that she thought the Hazaras were possibly of Kushan ancestry. It turned out she was right. Another fact jumped at me from the page. In the later Buddhist tradition of Bactria, Kanishka was revered as a great patron of Buddhism and referred to as the Saviour. It was all coming together: a still-living Kushan priesthood spearheading the cause of a Hazara homeland. It had to have an enormously powerful resonance on the Hazara imagination.

However much my instincts rebelled against it, I had to admit that there was a crazy logic to the whole thing, that I had to consider what Gul Mohammed wanted of us – however bizarre – in the cold light of reason. With one deadly thrust, the spymaster had pushed me over the edge and I was in free fall into a void without end.

The cellphone buzzed and flashed its alarm light. I snatched it up and punched the stop button. 7 am. The alarm was redundant insurance; I hadn't slept a wink all night. The hard logic of day keeps a lid on our fears but at night they creep out, like worms from the woodwork. The dark hours had gone by in a tangled skein of thoughts quivering in my head like jangling nerve ends, each bringing with it a fresh stimulus of doubt and fear. I was now half convinced the whole thing was either a gigantic scam at best or a dark conspiracy against the country at worst and my brain kept leaping about between the two possibilities in an agony of tension.

I went to the bathroom, used the loo and then brushed my teeth. My reflection in the wall mirror looked awful: a three-day stubble accentuated the grey complexion, there were bags under my eyes and my frame was positively hunched over. I pulled out some clothes from the cupboard and changed. *Take nothing extra. You're just stepping out.* Gul Mohammed had been emphatic. I was going to be spirited out of the country but I was to behave like I was going for a morning walk.

I picked up my knapsack. Took one last look at my flat, imprinting it in my memory, and let myself out. The shop shutters were down but the wayside eateries on Chandni Chowk were already bustling, serving up samosas and tikkis with cups of steaming chai to the early commuters. Cycle rickshaws and tempos carrying the day's merchandise crowded the Chowk. As I walked east, the Red Fort showed itself in gaps between the buildings, the russet sandstone walls seguing into the pink blush of morning spread over the sky.

I set a brisk pace, in the manner of one taking his morning exercise. The ISI man left me in no doubt that I would be followed. I took a casual look around, but saw no one obvious. I clamped down on a fresh wave of doubt, the edgy feeling of being manipulated. The shop came up a hundred metres to the right, a big red sign with white letters in English and Urdu: Modern Electronics. This was it. I turned, pushed open the glass-fronted door and went in. The shop was empty. Bead curtains covered the exit at the back. *Walk all the way through and get into the auto rickshaw that will be waiting.*

The auto was a beat-up old machine with canvas rain flaps hanging down the sides. I pushed them aside and got in. The auto driver gunned the engine and took off into a side alley. We were soon weaving in and out of narrow lanes, cutting

left and right at breakneck speed. It got dark as
the walls on either side closed in, blocking off
the light as we plunged deeper into the maw of
Shahjahanabad. I gripped the side bar behind
the driver as the auto whipped from side to side,
tipping and swaying like a boat on a choppy sea.

In fact, Modern Electronics had been under
observation for several hours by a cycle rickshaw
puller across the street. As soon as he saw the
target go into the shop, he brought his mouth
close to the neck mike swathed in cloth.

'Andar gaye hain. He's gone in. I repeat, he's
gone in.'

A voice answered, 'We've got him. You can
disengage. Circle round and wait at the residence
in case he has other visitors.'

The speaker was in a van, one of two men
sitting in a nondescript Tempo Traveller parked
near the gate of the Jain Mandir at the east end
of Chandni Chowk. Both wore headphones.
Electronic gear filled the innards of the vehicle.
An LED console showed a GSAT map with a blip
crawling beetle-like across the screen. One of
them hit a button on a two-way radio.

'Control One, this is Control Three. Target is
headed in a southwesterly direction. Speed forty
kilometres an hour. What instructions?'

There was a burst of static and then the answering voice said, 'Hold tight. Let's see where he is headed. Keep all transmission live. I need real-time input on this. We all stay on the target from now. Is the follow team on intercept path?'

The headphone turned to his colleague who nodded and pointed to the console and held up three fingers. He spoke into the mike. 'Yes, Control One, they are coming in behind from the Najafgarh Junction. You should see them now in three … two … one … here they are.'

Another winking beetle had now entered the screen boring down on the first from the north-west, closing in fast.

—————

The auto driver did not look back once. He hunched over the T-bar of the steering, intent on negotiating the labyrinth of gullies. A sudden square of light bloomed ahead of us, and the auto shot out of maze onto a main road. I looked around, disoriented. It took a couple of landmarks for me to realize that we were on the south bank of the Yamuna. The auto flew on, cutting directly through New Delhi, and swung onto NH 8 heading towards Palam. A flyover came up, and the driver swung onto the steep upslope of the exit. The three-wheeler whined and juddered, protesting against the thrust from the wide-open throttle. Heat waves and oil fumes billowed up from beneath the engine cowl. Just when I thought the contraption would surely seize up, we screeched to a sudden halt. Without once looking back, he motioned me out with his hand. I barely got both my feet on the ground when he was gone in another burst of smoke and sound.

I stood there in the sudden quiet. I was at the apex of the exit ramp. There were no cars or trucks crossing and the flyover had an empty, somehow menacing feel to it. Then the hum of a motor sounded to the right. It was a van, coming up from the direction of the river. I watched it come, the sun glinting off its darkened glass.

———

200 metres ahead, where the flyover hit GT Road, a Maruti Gypsy roared up the ramp at top speed. The man next to the driver had his hands held low, out of sight, holding a MM8 bolt-action assault rifle. The driver spoke into his collar mike.

'Control One, dus mein dihkni chahiye – we should have visual in ten seconds. Over.'

'Control Two, this is Control One. Target is being picked up by a van. Disrupt. I repeat, disrupt. I want both target and the pick-up vehicle destroyed. Do you copy?'

'Copied loud and clear, Control Two. We'll take them out.'

The van rocked to a stop. The door slid back and Gul Mohammed said, 'Get in.'

I stepped forward. Out of the corner of my vision, I saw a squat boxy shape breast the rise of the flyover. It shot over the top like a suddenly released projectile. A torso snaked out of the passenger seat through the window. It was a man with a head bandana and goggles, holding a black cylinder-like object. He raised it up, sighting. I stood rooted for a moment, uncomprehending, before instinct lurched me forward. I dimly heard Gul Mohammed shout in warning. There was a *phut* and I felt a sharp fiery pain in my upper arm. Gul Mohammed was half out of the van, grabbing and hauling me in. *Pop, pop, pop …* The van shuddered as if struck by hail. Gul slammed the door shut and screamed, 'Go, go!' He pushed me to the floor, knelt over me and peered over the seat. 'Kahan hain woh? Where are they?' he shouted.

The driver said, 'Bilkul aagey. Up front. They're coming straight at us.'

More staccato reverberation up close. I'd seen enough on TV to know this was automatic fire. I could feel the bullets hitting the windshield, but there was no shatter. It vaguely struck me that the glass must be bulletproof, but there was no time for rational thought; the vehicle careered about, swerving madly as more bullets hammered the front fender and then the doors.

Gul was squatting up, sighting over the driver's shoulder. 'Ram him sideways across the front fender. We'll flip him over.'

Our van roared forward in a sudden burst of energy. Horns blared out: multiple banshee wails as we arrowed into the opposite traffic lane. There was a loud *clanggg* and a shriek of twisting metal. I smashed into the seat in front and felt a spike of agony arcing up my arm. The van lifted off the ground. For one heart-stopping moment I was in the air, weightless, tipping over, then the wheels hit the ground with a jarring thump. The van bounced up, righted itself and sped down the tarmac.

'Dhire, dhire, take it slowly. We don't want all eyes on us.' Gul Mohammed was still directing the driver. He had his arm firmly pressed on my back, pinning me to the floor.

I said faintly, 'I think I'm hit.'

The Pakistani spun round. The van's floor was sticky with blood and a sour-sweet smell clogged the air.

8

Meenakshi Pirzada taught a special class on 'Power Structures in Medieval India' which wasn't part of the main syllabus. For that reason it was scheduled late in the day, into the 4–5 pm slot, but she didn't mind and neither did her students. She found teaching exhilarating. To go beyond dry facts, to bring alive the tapestry that was the past: the players, their hopes, fears, loves and hates, their politics – always the politics – that complex interplay of power and patronage, was to bring history living and breathing into the classroom. Not surprisingly, her classes were among the most popular in the university and as usual today many of her students had stayed back for discussion; by the time she got to her office it was a little after 6 pm.

She hung her knapsack on the stand by the door and dropped into her chair. She cleared the screensaver on her desktop and checked her mail.

Nothing: just routine messages. Feeling suddenly flat, she pushed the chair back and stared unseeing out the window. It shouldn't have been bugging her so much, but it did. He had promised to get in touch, but her impatience had gotten the better of her and she had called him yesterday. She listened to a recorded message that the caller was unavailable and then tried the landline. No answer. She called again this morning with the same result. Chandra appeared to have dropped off into a void.

Two days had gone by since that afternoon with Chandra, a quiet afternoon that had suddenly acquired an edgy anticipation triggered by his call that had come out of the blue. Physically, he hadn't changed much: the same baby face with the soft brown eyes, the big frame with its slight stoop, but the dishevelled hair had streaks of grey and she soon sensed that this was a Chandra who was somehow more … vulnerable, finely drawn, a man who had passed through a crucible of fire and emerged – but only just. And she'd caught his tension immediately.

The photos of the weird dead man, the thrill of pitting her wits against their mystery and breaking through; Chandra's excitement spilling over – sudden as the sun from behind a cloud: the hours had flashed by in a seesaw of unexpected emotions. They were both pondering over the fact that her discovery had only deepened the mystery, like a Matryoshka doll with new enigmas nested inside, when the policeman had come. The room had darkened, become suddenly filled with an intense apprehension. Chandra had practically pushed her out but she knew beyond all doubt that she had left behind a man who had been deeply troubled and try as she might, she could not put that out of her mind.

She was reaching for her cellphone to try him again, when it started to vibrate and flash an incoming call. She picked it up to see who the caller was but the screen was blank.

'Hello.'

'Ms Meenakshi Pirzada?'

'This is she.'

'Please hold.'

There was a series of clicks, followed by a faint hum, then: 'Meenakshi, this is Inspector Hassan.'

She sat bolt upright. 'Yes, Inspector?'

'Are you alone?'

'Yes.'

'Listen to me very carefully. Do you remember the photos that Chandra showed you on his camera? The ones of the dead man?'

'Yes, I do.'

'The victim was flung off the top of the Qutub. We don't know by whom or why, but it's important we find out. I want you to get to the top of the tower and look very carefully around. Can you do that?'

She said incredulously. 'Aren't you the police? What is this – a joke?'

'Please. I don't have time to explain. It's a matter of life and death. I wouldn't ask you if it weren't. You need to do it right away. It's very urgent.'

Hassan's voice was waxing and waning, with a hint of an echo, as if beaming in from outer space. She remembered how Hassan looked that evening and felt a sudden stab of suspicion.

'Is Chandra with you, Inspector?'

There was a long pause, then: 'Yes, he is here; but he can't talk to you yet.'

She exhaled. 'Can I speak with him, please?'

This time the hesitation was palpable over the line. 'He is injured. But not seriously. It's just that he can't come to the line right now.'

She bit down hard on her lip, quelling the spiking alarm. 'How did …?'

Hassan cut her off. 'Later, Meenakshi. Get to the Qutub in an hour. You'll be met there. Climb to the top and look for anything … anything unusual that catches your eye. I've got to go now, but I'll make sure Chandra speaks to you soon, okay?'

She took a deep breath. 'I'm sorry, but this is all highly irregular. You're a policeman, and I don't understand why you're asking me to …'

He cut her off. 'Hold on a moment.'

There was another long pause when the hum over the line undulated up and down and then:

'Meenu? Meenu … Chandra here.'

His voice was feeble with an underlying hint of strain. Her hand tightened on the instrument.

'Chandra, are you okay? Where are you calling from …?'

'Meenu, I can't speak right now. Please listen to Hassan. He knows what he's doing. Get to the Qutub *now*. And don't tell anyone.'

His breath seemed to come harsher and faster now and then the line went dead. She stared at the cellphone, aware that her hands were shaking slightly, knuckles white over the screen. She pushed off the chair, grabbed her bag and walked quickly out of the room.

***

She braked her Maruti to a halt in the car park outside the Qutub complex wall. The traffic had been terrible and the dash clock said 7.30 pm. Half an hour late. The sun had gone down; the ambient light of the June evening still had the quality of burnished silver, but she would have to hurry. She got out, cast a look around and started to walk towards the entrance gate. A shadow loomed up behind her and she spun around, startled. A well-built uniformed policeman stood there.

He did not offer a name but simply gestured for her to follow him. The guard at the ticket gate waved them through and soon they were at the Minar. The rising moon hung delicately poised over the horizon, throwing off a weak radiance that mixed with dusk light and bathed the tower in ochre, accentuating its medieval proportions: a finger of God arrowing up into the darkling heavens.

'We have opened the door to the stairs, madam,' the cop said. 'Hassan saab has instructed me to give you all co-operation. Would you like me to come up with you?'

Meenakshi desperately wanted to say yes. She was claustrophobic and the prospect of inching her way up the narrow, winding steps set her on edge. Still, some instinct told her that she would work better on her own. She wiped her clammy palms on her dupatta and said, 'No, thanks. Let me take your mobile number and call if I need you.'

The policeman had been thoughtful enough to bring a torch with him. She had visited more than her share of monuments, but there was something about these stairwells that always had her wondering what their medieval builders could have had in mind. They were all the same: narrow, tightly spiralled flights with high steps, seemingly designed to squeeze all motion out of the climber.

Perhaps it was to make it easier for a defender at the top. As she wound her way up, she felt the heat build till it was like being in an oven. The walls pressed in upon her and the feeling of being trapped in the dark womb of the tower was all but overpowering. It was only the steady beam of the torch that kept her from panicking.

The stairs kept corkscrewing up, seemingly without end and when she stepped out onto the circular space at the top, it was with a huge burst of release. She stood for a minute, wiping the sweat streaming down her face and neck, allowing her breathing to return to normal. The view was breathtaking: the sparkling haze of lights of the city winking far below and the headlights crawling along Mehrauli Road, part of a distant hustle and bustle of humanity. But here, she was far removed from it all, in a celestial firmament where the air was cool and clear and the gibbous moon shone through a gap in the clouds.

Then it struck her with sudden force that this was killing ground: a man had been thrown bodily from just this spot not long ago. She looked around quickly, as if sensing someone else on the tower, but the doorway gaped back empty. She tried to take a hold of herself, to take in the details of the place. She stood in an annular space, between an iron safety railing and the tower wall which stood a little over four feet from the floor. She ducked through the railing and shone the torch around. Nothing obvious.

For the next twenty minutes, she conducted a painstaking examination of the wall, the ground, the railing, even the doorway, and found nothing. She started again, running her hands along the brick masonry this time, probing for cracks or looseness, cubbyholes into which anything could have been hidden. Again nothing. Sitting on the ground with her back to the wall, she considered the situation. There were only two possibilities. Either the victim had planned to get to the top or he was forced here. The former seemed the less probable of the two. Entry into the tower was banned, the door probably locked and it wasn't likely that the victim was a tourist out for kicks. The second was more possible; the dead man had perhaps spotted his pursuer and managed to enter the Minar to escape detection. If so, why go all the way up? The only explanation was that the victim knew in turn that he'd been seen; that in the time left before his end, he had to …

The train of Meenakshi's thoughts broke as her eye caught a small but distinct discolouration on the floor to one side of the entrance. She took up the torch and played the light on it. It was a rust-coloured splotch, no wider than a centimetre across. She crawled over and squatted over it, touched it but it had dried up long before. Her gaze automatically travelled up along the wall and then she saw it: a small hole, offset over the top of the entrance. She stood up and poked into it carefully with her little finger. She felt the edge of something, but the hole was just the size of the finger and it was already beginning to recede further in with her touch. Reaching up into her hair, she pulled out a hairpin. Holding it like a pincer she inserted it into the orifice, pinched it close and pulled carefully. A rolled-up tube of paper slid out, clipped at the edge by the hairpin.

Her hands started to shake as she straightened it. The paper was cheap, torn from a school notebook, and the childish rust-red wiggles jumped at her from the page:

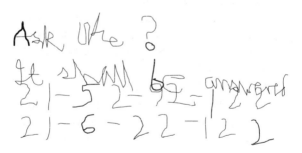

The scene flashed in front of her, vivid as if she had been there; even as the man waited here for his nemesis, he had cut himself and written furiously, dipping the stick into his blood each

time the letters began to fade, then hiding the
message just in time before the end.

A wave of emotion welled up in her: a mix
of triumph, horror and a trembling excitement.
She imagined Inspector Hassan's reaction ... and
Chandra's too. They would be so ... A bank of
clouds moved to cover the moon and an abrupt
blackness fell. She started as if struck, her heartbeat
racing to express speed. This dark pinnacle was
getting to her. She thrust the paper into her bag
and started to descend. This time, she scrambled
down the steps in a heedless rush, not pausing until
she reached the exit. The waiting cop was visibly
relieved; there was a suppressed nervousness
in his manner as he led her rapidly to the gate.
The yard outside was completely deserted. Even
the perennial hawkers seemed to have vanished.
She bent to open the door when a sudden rustle
sounded from within the car and then two coughs
in quick succession. The cop jerked back and then
slowly crumpled to the ground.

Meenakshi   stood   rooted   to   the   spot,
uncomprehending. A shadowy silhouette was
visible in the rear of the vehicle, the moonlight
glinting on the metallic snout in its hand.

9

Nalini Ranjan Pant took a sip of tea. He puckered his lips at the familiar milky flavour, overloaded with sugar. The tea in North Block had not changed since the 1980s, when he had served in the East Wing as a lowly section officer at the Ministry of Home Affairs. The beverage, he acknowledged wryly to himself, was one of those eternal verities: as unchanging as the government machine.

Pant was acting director (South Asia) in the national security council's Joint Intelligence Committee – JIC for short. The 'acting' part of his designation was by way of the fact that two of his immediate bosses had simultaneously been removed from the scene; one had been diagnosed with cancer and the other was found to have been mixed up in a delicate scandal. It had by default fallen to Pant – who was a full two rungs below the top – to step into the breach till a replacement could be found. By further coincidence, the top position in the JIC, that of the chairman, had also been vacant for some time. The appointment process was nothing if not glacial and, six months later, Pant was still de facto head of SA in the JIC, with a rare freedom from bureaucratic oversight. This time, however, the built-in inefficiencies of government had resulted in a serendipitous optimum, placing Pant in a position that was peculiarly suited to a man of his talents.

By the late 1990s India's security environment – both internal and external – presented an extraordinarily complex picture. The looming shadow of China to the north and east; the bubbling instability of the political and social cauldrons of Pakistan-Afghanistan; the internal security challenges from a fledgling but rapidly expanding Maoist insurgency, compounded by hydra-headed terror threats were but a few of the pressure points of the time. It was becoming clear that no one department or agency would have the capability to handle these challenges across multiple fronts, and the Vajpayee government responded by setting up the National Security Council in November 1998. The NSC would now be the apex body charged with directing India's national security response using all the political and economic instruments of state policy.

The JIC served as the secretariat to the Strategic

Policy Group within the NSC – where policy was actually framed – and as such was the central clearinghouse of all information received from RAW, the IB and the directorates of military, air and naval intelligence. Its analysts sifted through the mass of information that surged through its portals each day – both public and secretly obtained – on political figures, diplomatic engagements and national security developments and on economic intelligence. It was the JIC's business to separate the grain from the chaff, to see emerging patterns and present them in a coherent pattern. In short, it served as the decision support arm to the NSC, the pivot on which India's security policy edifice rested. It was an edifice that looked alarmingly dysfunctional to Pant in the summer of 2011.

He gloomily reflected on the policy group's meeting of the previous day. The political morass in the country was infecting every arm of government and the SPG was no exception. The ill-concealed public animus between the finance minister and the home minister had seeped through into the room, and though the ministers themselves were absent, their bureaucratic minions were at odds with each other on every issue. In the discussion over recent developments in Myanmar – a vital one in Pant's view – it was left to the ineffectual cabinet secretary to cajole both sides into some semblance of focus on the matter at hand. Cliques had formed in other corners: the military brass griping as usual against the defence procurement people, and then the thinly veiled insinuations of corruption all around. It was all Pant could do not to walk out in disgust.

Only the RAW group was quiet – quiet and disciplined. Venkat Rao, who headed counter-terrorism, was at his persuasive best, armed with the latest SIGINT and HUMINT reports. Moreover, his was a theme that had everyone fixed to their seats: the safety of Pakistan's nuclear arsenal.

Pant drew the thick RAW dossier marked 'JIC – Director (Eyes Only)' in large block lettering towards him and took out the latest situation reports. On 1 January and 1 July of each year India and Pakistan exchange lists of their nuclear installations and facilities under Article II of the Agreement on Prohibition of Attacks against Nuclear Installations and Facilities, signed by the two countries in 1988. During the exchange, both sides are required to indicate any changes and relocations in their arsenal during the year. RAW intel indicated that the Pakistanis were consistently cheating on these reports for the last year or more. There were also several satellite recon photos from the newly launched Indian RiSat uplink showing mobile launchers moving at random across the country – all missing from the lists supplied by the Pakistanis. Other facts and threat assessments followed: the creeping increase in the number of officers widely known to have extremist sympathies into the Pakistani strategic nuclear command; a sudden uptick in global purchases by the Pak army in NBC warfare protective gear; and SIGINT indications that something very big was afoot. All in all, it was a brilliant piece of espionage. No wonder it was making serious waves through the corridors of power.

Pant ran his eye over everything again, slower this time. He sat back, linked his hands behind his head and stared at the ceiling. Intel assessment was an art: a coupling of fact with experience. At the core of it all was intuition, that gut feel: the result of millions of neurons in the subconscious fizzing away at the synapses, analysing myriad probabilities like a sentient supercomputer. Very few possessed this faculty – this almost mystical 'feel' for an intelligence problem – but Pant was one of them. The barrage of evidence was impressive by any standards but deep down, in some hidden recess of his brain, a tiny worm niggled at him.

On an impulse, he reached for the phone and punched in a number.

'Air Commodore Jasjit Singh, please. Air Headquarters.'

'Jasjit Singh here.'

'Jasjit, this is Nalini Ranjan Pant.'

The Sikh's voice boomed out at him. 'Hello, Nalini. Aap kahan bhaag gaye, yaar? Bahut din ho gaye aapse mile hue. Long time no see. All well, na?'

'I'm fine, Jasjit. Can I take a minute?'

'Sure.'

'When were you at SFC?'

'Strategic Forces Command? Let's see now … that was until April last year. I was in command HQ for almost eighteen months.'

'During that time, how many games did you run?'

Games were simulations conducted as part of the training of nuclear forces, based on real time. Different scenarios of response and enemy counter-response were introduced into the drills, all assigned varying probabilities.

'I don't recall exactly, but at least three in ERT.'

ERT or emergency response time simulations were those that gave command crews no time for planning. A nuclear attack from one or multiple theatres was presented as imminent. Pant paused, trying to get his question exactly right.

'What was the probability you guys assigned to effective American control over Pak nuclear warheads in crisis mode?'

'Low,' came the prompt reply. 'Something like 30 percent, I think.'

'Any chance that might have changed since?'

'Nalini, let me ask you something. If you were the Paks would you place your crown jewels on the block to get neutered?'

'I guess not.'

'They will never do it ... *never*. It's their single fall-back insurance against us – against the world. We Indians feel that way too; every nuclear power does to some degree. But in Pakistan it goes way to another level. Nuclear capability to them is an article of fundamental faith, an existential part of who they are.'

'Venkat Rao and Sushil Shukla in RAW seem to feel the Yanks have their hands firmly on the trigger there. The intel is of concern, but he says they have assured him that they have it under control.'

Jasjit Singh snorted. 'You spooks. You should get your noses out of those reports; get out there into the real world and party a bit. You can get more out of a tispy Pakistani in one evening than in a month's deskwork. No bullshit, Nalini. I know: I've done it. Want to join me on Friday? There's a bash at the Russian embassy, and we've been promised some new vodka that's supposed to be something else.'

Pant laughed. 'No, thanks. You go and keep me posted. One last question. Would the Pakistanis cheat on the APA status reports?'

'I don't think so. In these days of satellites it

would be hard to get away with misrepresentation for long. The costs hugely outweigh the benefits. Unless …'

'Yes?'

'They're planning a strike.'

Pant thought about that and then asked his final question. 'Can the Americans prevent a Pak second strike?'

There was a silence at the other end. Then Jasjit Singh said slowly, 'Yes. We rated it as an eighty-plus probability that they can, and will. If the Paks fire those missiles even once, they'll never get to repeat it. They'll be defanged forever.'

10

I sat across the table from Hassan, who was trying to read the wine list by the light of the candle. The Hare and Hounds was jam-packed. Every inch of standing space was taken, especially at the bar, where bodies congregated in an intertwined mass along the counter. The chatter of voices rose and fell like a locust hum against the Pink Floyd album playing in the background.

Hassan took in the scene and shook his head as if he couldn't credit what he was seeing. The place wasn't just done up exactly like an English pub; it *was* an English pub – in name and everything else. Whites were everywhere. Plummy British accents, nasal American twangs, German, French and Italian – every nationality west of the Suez seemed to be in here. It could have been London, except this was Kabul. I had seen speakeasies like this in Baghdad which I had visited in the aftermath of the American invasion. The bars in the sealed-off Green Zone there had been much like this one: watering holes for the legions of foreign journalists, aid workers and contractors that war theatres seem to attract like flies to a carcass. And Afghanistan was the biggest conflict zone now that Iraq had wound down. It was also a Muslim country with strict rules on alcohol. The bars got around that by prohibiting entry of Afghans under the guise of conformance to local regulations. Only foreigners were allowed in and we had to show our passports to the bouncers outside.

So here we were, sitting in a patch of England in the middle of Kabul. Outside, hired Afghan gunmen ringed the building: protection against the Taliban who had issued recent threats against this place.

'What are we doing here, Hassan?' I said.

'Winning hearts and minds.' His tone was wry, but I thought I detected a real undercurrent of hostility to what he was seeing around him. He saw my eyes on him, shrugged and said, 'I chose it. Thought it'd be easier to shake Gul's minions off here. What will you have?'

'Just a glass of water, thanks.'

He flagged a passing waiter and ordered water and lemonade. We looked at each other across the table. Hassan was his old dapper self tonight. He wore a cream silk shirt and a linen suit without a tie. His thinning hair was brushed back neatly, accentuating his lean features.

I guess I must have presented something of a contrasting picture. Hassan obviously thought so.

'Chandra, it's my turn to say it: you don't look good. Are you okay? Is the arm hurting too badly?'

I said nothing. It was two days since the bullet had ploughed a furrow through my upper arm. It had luckily missed the bone, shearing instead through a part of the bicep. Gul Mohammed had stanched the wound, but had to do it roughly and I had almost passed out with the pain of it. The next twenty-four hours had been a blur: the race towards Punjab and what seemed a remote hill country beyond Amritsar, then a cross-over in the company of some local shepherds into Pakistan where a helicopter awaited us on a green meadow. Three hours later, I was being examined by a military doctor in Peshawar – 300 kilometres from Kabul. The medic – a mild-mannered man – wanted to sedate me and then get me to rest, but Gul would have none of it. And so with just sutures and dressing we were on our way again. In the jeep, rocketing towards Jalalabad on the Afghan side of the border, Gul's briefing had been just that: brief. I was to travel under my own name and profession, as a journalist doing a piece on India-Afghan reconstruction projects. Beyond that, it was up to me to manage my cover.

Gul said, 'I've given what little information we have to Hassan. There's nothing more I can tell you. Remember, we're looking for the missiles too. The moment we hear anything useful, you'll know.'

I asked him the question that had been bothering me so much. How had RAW found me so quickly on that flyover? I had followed Gul's instructions to the letter; I was sure the auto was not tailed. Gul pointed to my knapsack in reply.

'You didn't bring it with you to our meeting in Chandni Chowk. When they got into your place, they put a homing device in there too. It took me a while to figure that one out.' And Hassan? Where was he? I hadn't seen him since that evening in Ghantewala's.

'He'll call you as soon as we drop you off in Kabul,' Gul replied. 'And then you two are on your own.'

Then Gul did something uncharacteristic. He put his hand on my shoulder. 'Chandra, you're working for both countries now. May Allah show you the way.'

He handed me my passport. The Afghan visa was neatly stamped – issued by the Afghan consulate in New Delhi, as also the entry stamp of Kabul airport immigration. There was no record of my having been in Pakistan.

Now, sitting in the bar, I felt exhausted, drained. The noise and smoke were getting to me. The arm burned like it was being held over a slow fire. I didn't think I could take it much longer.

I chose not to reply to Hassan's question. Instead I said, 'What do we do next? Has Gul given you anything to work on?'

He shook his head. 'Very little. He thinks this Xiphos Soter is the key. They seem to be something else. ISI has been after them for a quite a while now, but these guys have been ahead of them every time. The undercovers they sent in came back in body bags – cut into small pieces. "Fanatic crazies who think and act with ice-cold precision" is how Gul put it. The Sword has a big cult following but a small priesthood controls everything. ISI thinks there is a single brain at the top.'

'The Saviour.'

Hassan nodded and stubbed out his cigarette. 'Gul says if we find him we'll find the warheads. Frankly, I've no idea how we're going to do that, or even how much time we have before a few million people go up in smoke.'

He was crushing the cigarette into the tray, mashing it down. His face looked pallid in the dim light, and his eyes had that haunted expression I had first seen when he had told me of his cousin in ISI. Pink Floyd floated up through the chatter, ethereal and haunting:

Us, and them
And after all, we're only ordinary men
Me, and you
God only knows, it's not what we would choose
  to do.

The talk and laughter in the bar was louder than ever but there was a frenetic – almost manic – edge to the noise. I remembered a story by a journalist for *Time* magazine who had interviewed an expat at one of these bars. She had said that it was like dancing at the edge of a volcano. You never knew when the bombs and mortar fire would erupt.

On a sudden impulse I said, 'Are you married, Hassan?'

He looked startled for a moment. It was the first time I had asked him anything personal. He shook his head. 'No. I have three sisters and they had to be educated and then married. My father died when I was very young, and I was the only son …' He shrugged. 'I guess there wasn't time for me to meet anyone.' He smiled briefly. 'I would have liked to, though. I enjoy kids.'

I said nothing, remembering that evening: Hassan and the boy outside the Nizamuddin dargah. And Yamini. That evening – so long ago. Hassan had also gone into a brown study. We sat there, the two of us with our memories, in that fake bar in Kabul, as Pink Floyd sang:

Black and blue
Who knows which is which and who is who.

I drained my glass and got up. 'Let's go.' Hassan paid the bill and we threaded our way out. The warm muggy air hit us like a blast after the air conditioning. My legs suddenly buckled and I fell against him. His arms were around me in a flash, holding me by the waist, careful of my wound.

'Easy now, Chandra. Lean on me. We'll get to the hotel soon and you can get a good night's sleep.'

The pain really hit me now, a fiery blaze right through my arm, and at the same time, a thought.

I whispered, 'Hassan, lift me up.' He propped me up. I looped my right arm over his shoulder and said into his ear, 'The murdered man was at the top of the Qutub for a reason. I think you should get someone to go up there once more.'

'But we've done that. Our guys took a really good look around.'

'Maybe not good enough. We should send Meenakshi.'

11

Meenakshi's blood rushed to her head. She opened her mouth to scream, when she found herself looking at the bulbous tube of a silencer thrust through the window.

'Don't do it,' said the voice from the rear. 'Get in and drive. I'm not going to hurt you, but if you make a noise I will be forced to.'

A car door opened nearby and she noticed for the first time a white Ambassador, parked about twenty yards away. Two men got out and walked purposefully towards her. She took a reflexive step back and her foot hit something soft. She gasped as her foot touched the body of the cop on the ground beside her.

The man in the car said, 'He's not dead: just tranquilized. He'll be taken care of.'

The two men came up, lifted the body and began to carry it back to the car. A small pool of blood stained the sand where the man had lain. She stared at it, stricken.

'Get in, *now*.' The voice hardened, the menace unmistakable. She got in and sidled into the driver's seat.

Fifteen minutes later, she was seated in a room at the Qutub Hotel. Three men – apart from the one in the car – faced her in straight-backed chairs. One was thin and bespectacled with an academic air; the other two were fleshy, with pasty indoor complexions. All wore safari suits. The man who had held the gun to her stood to one side. He had reddish hair and splotches of luekoderma on his face and arms. Large buck teeth protruded between closed lips. He had the look of a simpleton, except for the malicious, calculating eyes that regarded her now with obvious enjoyment.

The group studied her in unnerving silence, then Red Hair said, 'Miss Pirzada, aap samajhdar ho. You are an educated woman. Please understand you are in serious trouble. What were you doing at the Qutub?'

Meenakshi felt the fear bloom anew. With an effort she held herself together and whispered, 'Who … who are you?'

'We'll tell you. But first: what were you doing in the tower?'

She said in what she hoped was a steady voice,

'You murdered that man – a policeman. In front of me as witness.'

'He was not a policeman. That was a foreign agent. And I told you: he's just drugged – tranquilized. I'm asking you once again: what were you doing at the Qutub?'

'Go to hell.'

The man with the spectacles turned and nodded to Red Hair. 'Tell her.'

Red Hair said, 'You think we are some kind of goondas? Some criminal gang?' He walked right up to her, bent down and looked into her eyes. 'We work for the Indian government.'

'Indian … what?'

'The government. We're part of internal state security.'

The incredulous expression on her face spoke clearer than any words. The man who looked like a professor cleared his throat and said mildly, 'Ms Pirzada, we work for RAW. The Research and Analysis Wing of the Cabinet Secretariat. You don't have to take our word for it. Please go tomorrow to police headquarters at ITO and ask for Police Commissioner Sahay. He will meet you personally. You'll have proof enough that we are what we say we are. He will also brief you about Inspector Hassan.'

'Inspector Hassan!'

Her interlocutor leaned forward and looked

at her intently. 'Ms Pirzada, what I am about to tell you now is a matter of national security. No word of this will ever leave this room or the consequences for the country ... and you ... will be severe. Am I understood?'

She said nothing. The man kept his eyes on her for a while then said, 'I am going to take your silence for consent; you'll know soon enough that what we speak is the truth.'

His quiet demeanour and the calm way in way he spoke shook her. 'You just killed a man, for God's sake! I saw it myself.'

Red Hair said brusquely, 'He was a Pakistani agent working for Hassan. A minute longer and he would have got you.'

'Hassan is a ...?'

'He is a top Pakistani spy. We've been keeping an eye on him for some time. And he's hooked your friend Chandrasekhar.'

She blanched. 'That's impossible! Chandra would nev ...'

Red Hair gestured to one of the other men who pulled out a brown envelope and threw it on the table in front of Meenakshi.

'Look at those before you say anything more.'

With shaking hands she opened the cover. Inside was a *Times of India* photograph accompanied by an article. It was dated about a year ago. It was a picture of the Pakistani president at a function in

Karachi with the chief of army staff. The caption named them as also the man next to them: Salman Qazi, Director General, ISI. And just behind them, standing partly in the shadow ... was Hassan. She stared at the photo, mouth dry and breath tight in her chest. He wore nondescript civilian clothes, but there was absolutely no doubt. It was Hassan. Unless the photo was doctored. She took it up closer and scanned it carefully.

The professor said, 'Check the *TOI* archives. Even we can't alter all the editions that came out that day. And go to the police station tomorrow. The IGP will tell you a bit about the man we have been laying a trap for.'

She laid the cutting back on the table. 'And Chandra ...? How is he involved with Hassan?'

'We don't know,' Red Hair said. He shrugged. 'Perhaps he's been bought by the enemy.'

'Are you saying Chandra's turned traitor?' She looked at him in blazing contempt. 'I don't care who you people are, but if that's what you think, you know nothing about him.'

Red Hair smiled cynically but it looked more like a grimace, lips pulled back over the protruding rabbit incisors. 'Everyone has a price.'

Meenakshi shook her head decisively. 'No. Not Chandra. You can kill him, but you cannot force him against himself ... the country.'

Red Hair said very softly, 'He has parents, no?'

She looked at him, horrified. He nodded and said in a chillingly conversational tone, 'Yes, madam. Anyone can be purchased. Only the price will be different.'

The man with the glasses said reasonably, 'Look, we're not saying it's only that. Hassan can be very ... persuasive. It's more than possible he's convinced your friend that whatever he's working on is important for this country.'

Without her knowing it, she was hugging herself with both hands, struggling to control the tremors through her body. She whispered, 'Where are they now? What is Hassan involved in?'

'We can't tell you that. All you need to know is that Hassan – which is an alias by the way – is the mastermind behind a plot to damage the country seriously. Now, what were you doing at the Qutub?'

They kept at her, hammering home the fact that the longer Chandra remained tied to Hassan, the greater the danger to him. Despite her overmastering fear, Meenakshi reached deep inside herself to refuse them further information till she met the commissioner of police the next day. Finally they agreed to let her go, but not before Red Hair indicated that he would be waiting for her at the police station the next day.

This further indication that these people were who they claimed they were shook her.

The reaction set in as soon as she got home. She sat on the couch, staring straight ahead, her mind a frozen blank. As the minutes went by, slowly, the evening started to seep back into her consciousness. The *phut* of the silencer and the cop folding beside her, her first glimpse of Red Hair in the rear of her car and then the long, painfully drawn out interrogation filled with one shock after another.

Hassan – a Pakistani spy. Holding Chandra – willingly or unwillingly – a hostage. She couldn't believe it; she told herself again and again that it all had to be some gigantic mistake, that there had to be a simpler explantion for it all. A simple – if highly unusual – request had snowballed into a bizarre, surreal three hours, full of frightening portents. What if the commissioner of police confirmed all they had said about Hassan? She couldn't even begin to think about what she was going to do.

The next day, on her way to Parliament Street, she stopped off at the *Times of India* building at ITO and visited their archives, where old editions were stored both as hard copies and on microfiche. Even after she had scanned it several times over, it took her a while to accept the fact that the photo was authentic. The meeting at the police station proved even more unnerving. She was expected and had been immediately shown in to the PC's chamber. The city's top cop was polite, and blunt. He confirmed that Hassan had been tagged as a spy for Pakistan almost a year ago and that he was engaged in a massive conspiracy against the country.

'I'd seriously advise you to co-operate with the people who have arranged this meeting, Ms Pirzada. I need not remind you that you are an Indian citizen with a bounden duty to your country.'

When she emerged from the office to find Red Hair waiting for her just outside, she decided she had no choice but to co-operate. The man insisted on debriefing her in a separate room right there in the station. She told him about the call from Hassan, her trip to the Qutub and her discovering the paper there. Red Hair almost snatched it from her hand and gazed at it for a long time. There was a huge tension about him now, as if he was trying to literally prise out the meaning from the crumpled sheet. He turned and looked at her searchingly.

'What do you make of it?'

'Nothing. It's gibberish. It's probably some child that did it, maybe in the days when the tower was open to the public. I can't think of any other remotely possible explanation.'

'Yet Hassan sent you there. You're sure there was nothing else?'

His malevolent eyes were on her, intent. She shrugged and said, 'No. Nothing. I looked everywhere, but Hassan gave me nothing to go on. I didn't even know what I was supposed to be watching out for.'

Red Hair shoved the paper into his pocket. Then he gave her a blank ivory card with no name, just a single number printed on it. 'Next time either Chandra or Hassan get in touch with you, find out where they are. It's very, very important. Then call this number and ask for me: Shukla. Is that clear?'

He walked away, then turned around. 'Don't try to move out of the city. We may need you any time – day or night.'

She nodded, trying to keep the distaste out of her expression, wondering if all RAW types were chosen for their unpleasantness. This Shukla was a boor and bully and the other one with the glasses had been cold as a fish. But there was no room for personal feelings now. The earth had shifted under her feet; Hassan was an enemy and Chandra was somehow involved with him.

12

Afghanistan as a country shows up relatively small on the world atlas, due to the peculiarities of the azimuthal projection system used to depict a spherical Earth on most maps. In reality its landmass covers over a quarter million square miles. 80 percent of this immensity is arid mountainscape. The plateaus and peaks of the great Hindu Kush range slice through the country across a northeast-southwest axis as do the Pamirs at the northern extremity of the country, making Afghanistan one of the most inhospitable terrains on the planet.

It is also a country wedded to the idea of war since the beginning of time. It was, and still is, said of the Afghan that he is never happier than when he is fighting. Fiercely proud and independent, the people of this country have resisted every invader since Alexander the Great.

That martial tradition has continued well into the late twentieth century; these seemingly primitive tribesmen have time and again managed to force back such formidable and well-equipped armies as that of erstwhile Soviet Russia through mastery of sustained insurgency and attrition warfare.

The war on terror that began in September 2001 has today morphed into a relentless seesaw battle of attrition between the Afghan and Pakistani Taliban and tribes allied to them and NATO and US forces (with their own tribal cohorts) that have effectively turned this country yet again into an enormous, complex theatre of war.

It was through this dangerous, fractured country filled with warring tribes and treacherous, ever-shifting alliances that Hassan and I had to pick our way towards obtaining the smallest clue that could point the way to the lair of the Sword of the Saviour. The odds in our favour were, as we both knew, laughably small. If a formidable machine that was ISI was making no headway, what chance did we – two lone individuals – have in this trackless wasteland?

Hassan's idea to get Meenakshi to revisit the scene of the crime on the tower was, we both knew, a long shot and would most likely yield nothing. Any pointers we could expect would emerge only here in Afghanistan. And we would work utterly on our own, steering clear of any contact with

Indian or Pakistani officialdom. India, for reasons that were clear already; Pakistan, because Hassan had reservations about Gul Mohammed.

'Gul's ISI, Chandra. I don't trust him anymore – not entirely anyway. Maybe it's all true, this stuff about the nuclear warheads, but it's possible it's just a smokescreen. Let's keep to ourselves and not a word to anyone.'

Oddly enough, I had felt a lot better when I heard him say this. We had booked into a double room at the Falak Hotel and, as I badly needed to rest, we turned in, resolving to discuss our next moves at the crack of dawn the next day.

I woke up with my arm feeling tight and swollen, and a dull ache that spiked sharply when I moved it. I looked around, disoriented. The room was spacious with a high wooden-beamed ceiling from which a colonial-era fan revolved slowly. Hassan, showered and shaved, was sitting on the chair and poring over a map spread out on the table. Sunlight streamed in through the large windows and I could see the flat lime-washed roofs of the city stretch away into the distance. Far away, a few gaily coloured kites dotted the azure blue sky.

The memory of last night came flooding back. I sat up and swung my legs over the side of the bed. 'What time is it?'

Hassan's reply was a shock. 'Almost noon.'

'My God … noon. We've lost the morning. You should have woken me up, Hassan!'

'Take it easy, Chandra. You were in no shape last night. It's going to be very stressful for us over the next few days, so I figured you should get the rest you can. The last thing I need is for you to fold up physically. And I also needed some time to think.'

'Give me a few minutes to get ready.'

When I joined him, he was still bent over the map. It was a 1:250000 physical projection. The country looked wild and forbidding, even in compressed mode, ridges and ripples of mountain and valley spread everywhere like leathery scales.

Hassan said, 'Well? Any ideas?'

'Hazarajat,' I said. 'Isn't that where the uprising is supposed to begin? It might provide the best cover for a missile site.'

He nodded approvingly. 'My thought exactly. The problem is that we are still looking at a bloody big area: ten subdivisions spread over close to 200,000 square kilometres. But let's not forget they're going to have to launch from inside Pakistan. That means from just across the Af-Pak border somewhere along the Durand Line. We're looking at mobile launchers. Driving them cross-country with the Talib, ISAF and Pakistanis crawling all over the place is a huge risk. I think east Hazarajat is our best starting bet.'

'Can't they launch from deep within Afghanistan?'

'They could, but the chance of discovery is higher. The American spy satellites are very active overhead. Remember, they have to prove to the world that the missiles were launched from Pakistan.'

He stared some more at the map and stabbed his finger. 'I think we should head toward Ghazni, southeast of here. It's a provincial capital with a big mosque to the south of the city. It's a religious centre and also where community leaders congregate to discuss anything of importance to the Hazara nation. Remember this rumour Gul spoke of … on the Hazara nation-to-be? I think we'll pick up the threads there. Maybe something that'll give us a clue to Xiphos Soter.'

'How do you know about this place?'

'I've been doing some reading en route to Kabul. By the way, can we try Meenakshi? Might as well get that out of the way before we start.'

I pulled out my Nokia. It was the same one that Gul had given me. Apparently it was programmed to work anywhere in the world and calls in and out from the phone were automatically scrambled. Before I could punch in the number, Hassan said, 'No, Chandra.'

Our eyes met. He said, 'It's probably traceable. If I were ISI, I'd be keeping very close tabs on us. Make the call on the hotel phone.'

'Won't that be traced also?'

'I doubt it. I chose this hotel at the last moment after getting into Kabul. And,' he shrugged, 'We have to take some chances in this game.'

I picked up the room phone and placed the call through the operator. It came through immediately and, by a miracle of modern technology that never failed to amaze me, Meenakshi's voice sounded as clear as if she was in the room.

'Hello?'

'Meenu, this is Chandra. How are you, Meenu?'

There was a silence, then her voice came back, low and anxious. 'Chandra, are you okay? You sounded bad yesterday.'

'I am fine, Meenu,' I replied loudly, trying to be reassuring. 'I had a little accident, but I am quite alright now.'

There was an audible exhalation of relief over the phone. I was oddly moved. It was very likely my imagination but I was conscious of a sudden warmth coming through the line, separated though we were by hundreds of kilometres.

Then she said formally, 'Where are you?'

It didn't feel right. The quickening I had felt on hearing her voice faded.

'I can't tell you that yet, Meenu,' I said guardedly. 'Are you alone? Can we speak?'

'I'm alone. Is Hassan with you?'

'Yes, he's here.'

'Chandra, he must not see you when I tell you this. Can you get away from him?'

I tried to keep my voice normal. 'No that's not possible. We're about to leave now and I'm not sure when I can talk next. We both wanted to know if you found anything at the Qutub.'

There was a long silence. The line was clear enough to carry the sound of her soft breathing. Then she said, 'Chandra, listen to me very carefully. I had a visit yesterday from some people who work for the government; it's some national security thing. They met me at the Qutub. Hassan is a spy; he works for Pakistan. They say he's behind a major plot against India. They wouldn't say what, but it seemed like something very big.'

I felt my chest constrict so tight I couldn't breathe. I turned as casually as I could and hunched over the instrument, holding it tight to me as if I couldn't hear her very well.

'Chandra … are you there?'

'Yes, go on.'

'I went and met the commissioner of police at the police HQ in ITO and he confirmed it. 100 percent. There's no doubt, Chandra. They showed me a photo of Hassan with some Pakistani top brass and it checked out at the *TOI* archive. You've got to come in, Chandra, and bring Hassan with you.'

I glanced over at my shoulder at Hassan. He was looking at me intently. I mouthed meaninglessly to him, as if I was barely following her, and then slumped low over the phone and said:

'Meenu, what was that … you have to speak louder.'

'You have to bring in Hassan. Or tell me where you are. *Now.*'

'Did you find anything at the Qutub?'

'I'm telling you …'

I raised my voice and said deliberately, 'I am fine, Meenu. I said I'm okay. What did you find?'

Another long hesitant moment, then she said coldly, 'Nothing. There was nothing there.'

I knew she was lying. I said curtly, 'Okay, Meenakshi. I've got to go now. Either Hassan or I will be in touch soon.'

Her voice rose up in a sudden wail, as if a dam had burst. 'Chandra … no. Please listen to me. You must come back. Turn Hass …'

I placed the receiver back in its cradle. Hassan was waiting with an expectant expression on this face.

I shook my head. 'Nothing. She found nothing.'

He kept his eyes on my face. 'She seemed to have something to say.'

I made a face. 'Mostly she was blabbing on about my health. It looks like you managed to alarm her yesterday. She wanted to know where we are.'

Hassan suddenly exclaimed, 'Your arm. It's bleeding.'

I looked down and saw that the bandage was completely soaked. When the first shock of her words hit me, I had unknowingly transferred the phone to my injured arm. Hassan rummaged about in his duffel and came up with a small roll of field dressing with some antibiotic powder. He held it up. 'Pak army issue, courtesy ISI. I'm supposed to dress you up as we go along.'

I let him unroll the blood-soaked cloth and re-dress the arm. The pain was intense, but it helped mask the turmoil inside. Cops and journalists are hard-bitten professionals with much in common. They work mostly on people; over time they acquire an instinct for reading people, for sensing the truth buried beneath the layered complexities of human behaviour. Hassan had said he had a gut feel for people; what I didn't say then, but what had kept me going along with him, was that same instinct. The instinct that told me that Meenakshi was lying a moment ago when she denied finding anything at the Qutub, but which also had lent truth to Hassan's words that first evening in my apartment; which told me that, last night at the bar, we had moved closer in some undefinable way.

Till now. *Hassan: a Pakistani spy.* I grit my teeth and the sweat broke out all over my face.

I pretended it was my arm, but it really was the mayhem inside, a complete and utter sense of an imminent mortality, like a fish that has been hooked and tossed out on land thrashes about as its life ebbs away.

13

Work in the clandestine chamber deep in the mountains had gathered pace over the last few days. The project handlers had stepped up the pressure; technicians worked in day-night shifts and the two cylinders grew like silk cocoons, acquiring new layers of guiding, sensing and fuel control equipment.

The HATF V is an Intermediate Range Ballistic Missile or IRBM. Developed by Pakistan's Kahuta Research Laboratories, in its first version, named Ghauri I, the projectile was designed to carry a payload of almost 700 kilograms over a distance of 1500 kilometres. The missiles here were an advanced version – Ghauri II – based on the design of the North Korean Nodong 2 IRBM. The enhanced liquid fuel propulsion system and lightweight carbon fibre shell of Ghauri II allowed an increased payload of almost 1000 kilograms or one metric ton to be delivered to a target 2600 kilometres away. The inertial navigation guidance system with GPS controls was equipped to guide the missile to its target with an error of less than 200 metres.

At the design speed of approximately three kilometres per second, the Ghauri II will traverse the southward arc from its launch point on the western border of Pakistan to Mumbai – India's commercial capital and a distance of almost 2000 kilometres – in a space of 650 seconds, a little under seven minutes. Ten seconds from the end of mission, the warhead detaches itself from the missile and fall away on a trajectory towards the detonation point. When it goes off, a nuclear explosive of this size – around one ton in weight – generates the explosive force of around four kilotons or four million kilograms of TNT. However, all comparisons with a conventional bomb beyond this are meaningless. If the explosion took place at a low altitude – from 200 to 500 metres above ground – the blast itself will take up around half of the energy released. The area in the immediate neighbourhood will rise within seconds to a temperature of several million degrees. Physical matter in the vicinity, both inanimate and animate, will receive a thermal radiative impulse which will take its temperature up instantly to that released by the thermonuclear fission. Biological life within one kilometre of the blast centre will be vaporized and all buildings within a two-kilometre radius will be reduced to fine rubble.

Within three to four seconds, the thermal radiation morphs into kinetic energy by way of an intense shockwave of gamma rays, resulting in the familiar mushroom cloud which the world so closely associates with the atomic bomb. Blast winds at speeds of upto 800 kilometres per hour will race out from the epicentre, spreading out in a roaring wall of flame over the city. A human body even at a distance of four kilometres from the explosion will suffer first- to third-degree burns, severe pulmonary embolism, lung haemorrhage, eardrum shatter and retinal burn.

Electromagnetic pulses and ionizing radiation will spread rapidly over several kilometres, aided by the prevailing wind. Here they will linger for decades, causing widespread acute and lethal radiation syndromes. The estimates vary, but the total death toll within a densely crowded city such as Mumbai consequent to a four-kiloton device exploded at 500 metres above Dharavi slum were placed by most studies at two to four million people.

Eight persons sat around the conference table in the operations control room. Six – one of them a woman – wore white technician coats. All their attention was towards the head of the table, where the two men who had just flown in from India were seated. The man who wore old-fashioned horn-rimmed glasses and had a professorial air was called Venkateswara Rao; the other, with buck teeth and a horsey face topped with thick red hair was the man who called himself Shukla.

One of the white coats cleared his throat nervously and said, 'We are ready for the status update.'

Shukla said in his grating voice, 'Shuru mein hi bata deta hoon. One thing before you start. This meeting is important. We don't want to hear questions or any other nonsense. You're to listen and obey. We have your families. You know that. The least sign of ghadar *from anyone of you* and we will send each of you their body parts: one each day.'

The fear in the room was thick, palpable. The scientists sat rooted, like hypnotized deer caught in the glare of headlights.

Venkateswara Rao polished his glasses and said in mild rebuke, 'Shukla, there's really no need to threaten them like this. I am sure it's not necessary. They are happy knowing their families are safe, that they will continue to get a chance to speak to them twice a week. Am I not correct?'

There was no answer. Rao expected none. He

simply held each of them in his gaze till their heads dropped one by one, unable to meet his eyes.

Rao steepled his fingers and said, 'Please proceed, Dr Sastry.'

The projector came on with a PowerPoint slide. For the next thirty minutes the scientist, who was the Technical Leader (Operations) took the two visitors through the presentation. He dealt with the readiness of the mainframe structure and then the sub-systems – the inertial guidance and gyros, fuel controls and radar fouling instrumentation – before finally coming to the warhead itself.

'As you are aware, the payloads are ready. We have pre-calculated the yields at four to four point zero three kilotons per warhead. The final assembly awaits only the arrival of the triggers.'

He paused, the question unspoken. Shukla said shortly, 'They've crossed the border. ETA at site is eighteen hours from now, maximum.'

'Very good. We will start the pre-launch calibration and testing thoroughly on site to eliminate the possibility of any resets in transit. We will need target co-ordinates now to start the flight path programming.'

Rao reached into his briefcase and came up with a folder. Without a word, he pushed it across the table to Dr Sastry. The scientist picked it up and started to read through the single A4 sheet inside. His eyes widened suddenly; he read through the sheet once more, as if he couldn't believe what was written there. When he looked up at Rao his face was white with shock. The paper trembled as he held it up.

'But ... but this says ... that the target is ...'

Shukla said, 'Yes. Mumbai. And the second target is Urumqi in China.'

The chamber was Arctic cold, but the visitors from India were actually perspiring. There was something about the titanic figure that inspired extreme dread. Close up, the skull was the size of a flattened boulder. Each of the washed-out eyes that bulged slightly from beneath the forehead seemed to have an independent life of its own, holding the two of them simultaneously in its gaze. The effect was eerie, unnerving; it dominated the two men totally. The creature had been listening to them, unmoving, for the last several minutes. There was a brooding hiatus when they finished, one that neither of them dared to break. Then the voice came, deep as rolling thunder, speaking a thickly accented English:

'It is good. Then the hour approaches as foreseen. Meantime, word of the Saviour has been spread throughout Hazarajat. Millions will rise and we will see our nation reborn.'

Rao cleared his throat and said, 'We respectfully

request that you wait for our word, Excellency. It is *most important*. The uprising will have to be timed exactly; a little too early or too late will be fatal for the Cause.'

'The Cause cannot fail. It is ordained.'

'Excellency, I agree. But still I urge caution. The enemy is active; they begin to suspect – even if they have no proof. As you know, one of the Initiates was turned. It is only by your own extreme vigilance that we caught up with him before it was too late.'

Something feral flared momentarily behind the askew eyeballs. 'That will not happen another time. The Saviour will be with us: he will not allow us to fail.'

Rao and Shukla exchanged looks. Shukla said, 'You know the enemy has sent spies against us in the past and ...'

The giant cut them off with a chopping motion of his hand. 'And you know what happened to them. You know what happened to one of our own who dared to think he could go against us.'

'Yes, yes ... of course. Now we think two more are on their way. They may have reached Kabul. Fortunately we have their descriptions. We want your Initiates to put out the word into Hazarajat, among the people. The reward will be great for whoever brings them in alive. We need them alive to be questioned.'

The figure rose, filling the room with the sheer power of its presence. 'It will be seen to. We will send you word when they are in our hands.'

The minute hand of the wall clock in the warhead assembly area crossed the twelve-hour mark. It was now T minus six days and counting.

14

In a world that was increasingly dominated by instant news, manufactured to titillate rather than to inform, penetrative investigative journalism was fast becoming a rarity. Most of the younger crowd had little taste for it. The long, lonely hours on the beat: hours spent casting for leads, then fruitlessly chasing them into dead ends, hours coaxing reluctant witnesses to talk, the intense struggle to connect the threads, unsure of what – if anything – lay at the end of it all. More often than I cared to admit, it all came to very little in the end. A petty scandal perhaps, one in a drowning mass of them, or a tawdry nexus between a babu and his political master. On occasion though – not often – I would stumble upon something; what started as a mundane incident or perhaps an innocuous meeting would take me down a sudden unexpected turn. And there in a dark alley I would see – outlined faintly in the murk – the contours of a headline break of huge magnitude. In such cases, almost without exception, the leads I pursued were elusive, informants lurked in shadows and the truth could never be confronted, but rather approached only obliquely and teased out of the dark underground where it rested. And then the trail utterly consumed me so that I lived in a sort of twilight zone where nights morphed into days without end and all sense of time was lost.

The next four days were like that. The ends I sought were starkly simple: the whereabouts of Xiphos Soter and truth of Syed Ali Hassan. Yet never was a goal more mysterious, more like a mirage that receded faster than I could move towards it.

From the very first day of our quest, as we travelled south to Ghazni on the bus, Hassan was like a man possessed. His face became even thinner, the skin stretched tight over its contours as he cast about obsessively for signs. This was the first time I had the chance to see him in direct action, and it hardened the seed of suspicion that Meenakshi had planted. The man was a consummate actor. He had a knack for striking up conversations with anyone and everyone – on the street corner, in shops and in the mosque – all in a perfectly casual and natural way. His eyes were everywhere, darting about like a crow's, seeking out anything or anyone out of the ordinary. When he saw someone he wanted to approach, his manner shifted with the rapidity of a chameleon. In no time, all his tension melted away as if it had never been; he would hail the man cheerily and soon they would be in animated conversation. It was at this time that I was astonished to discover that he spoke both Dari and Pushtu with seeming fluency. When I queried him on this, he was offhand, saying that languages were his area of interest. But seeing him in this Afghan milieu I was convinced this was familiar territory to him, that he had been here many times.

In the evenings we would repair to the mosque. The huge courtyard was filled with worshippers, mostly of a distinctive Asiatic cast with oblique eyes and high cheekbones, very different from the sharp-featured Kabuli. It was easy to see them as descendants of the Kushan Yuezhi of the Chinese steppes.

We would put on our knitted kullas and kneel in prayer with the congregation. Afterwards, Hassan circulated freely among them, threading his way through the courtyard like a man who had lived here all his life. He would work the crowds in this way till it was late and the mosque had emptied, leaving just the two of us beneath the onion dome and elegant minarets etched against a darkling sky. We would get back to the hotel.

There he would bolt down some food and leave immediately, saying that he had more work to do. I never knew if he came back at night but when we took to the streets the next morning, I saw from his wan look and the bags beneath his eyes that he had had little sleep.

According to Hassan, the Hazaras are a friendly, engaging people. But there was a new wariness to them now. Each time Hassan tried to steer the talk to politics, they clammed up. No one was ready to talk to a stranger except about the most mundane things. Still, over four days of incessant mixing he had established certain facts beyond any doubt. The Hazaras were readying for freedom. The Saviour's coming was nigh as was Tofulu's, they said. Tofulu seemed the name for their new country-to-be. Hassan said that this euphoria was almost as tangible as the air around us. The problem was that no one, *not one*, could tell him when and from where this Saviour would come. They just did not know; all they knew was that the promise of centuries was at hand. It was as if the Hazaras had been enveloped by an elemental force, a gravitational field that had no explanation. It just was.

After four days and nights of this, I could see he was at the end of his strength. For my part, I felt less than useless. The game was altogether too deep and I could see no way forward of my own in this huge, unfamiliar country. My one aim, the strategy I had determined for myself, was to hang close to Hassan and when the truth – whatever that proved to be – showed itself, I would get it out as quickly as I could to Meenakshi and then give her our whereabouts.

On each of the three nights after Hassan had left, I tried calling Meenakshi – if nothing else to listen to the sound of a familiar voice – but there was no answer. Then on the night of the fourth day, as I lay on the bed with my throbbing arm, feverishly trying to find some way out of this labyrinth I found myself in, she called.

'Hello, Chandra?'

I felt a huge rush of relief. Her voice was warm as honey, but had a hurried undertone.

'Wait,' I said. 'Can you call me on a landline?'

'Where are you?'

'In a hotel in Ghazni, Afghanistan.'

There was silence, then: 'Give me the number.'

Two minutes later the hotel instrument shrilled. The first thing she said was:

'I am calling through Skype. I think it's safe to talk. How are you, Chandra? I was really worried the last time we spoke.'

'Sorry, Meenu. Hassan was right there so I couldn't risk it. But I've been trying to get through to you these last few nights. Your phone's been ringing.'

'I know, I know. It's tapped – in case you call. And they're tailing me everywhere. I'm calling you from the STD booth of my campus restaurant. Chandra, first I need to know: are you okay?'

'I'm fine. Someone shot me in Delhi, but it was only a superficial hit. I guess when Hassan called, I'd lost some blood and sounded worse than I was.'

'Oh my God. Shot ... shot by whom?' she said in a horrified whisper.

'I don't know, but I think it might be someone on our side of the fence. They were tailing me the whole time. But I don't really know; this whole thing is so damn mixed up that ...' I stopped abruptly and said, 'Anyway, I'm okay, Meenu. I really don't want to talk about it now.'

She exhaled. 'Okay ... at least you seem alright. What are you doing in Afghanistan, for God's sake?'

'Meenu, I can't go into it. Hassan can be back any time. All I can say is that Hassan convinced me it was a matter of vital national importance that I come here with him.'

She processed that for a bit and then said, 'I lied to you. I did find something at the Qutub.'

My heart leapt into my mouth. 'What ...?'

She continued hurriedly, 'I was really conflicted

for a while … I guess I still am. I mean, these people … I'm sure they are who they say they are … but …'

Her voice trailed away. I waited.

'The whole thing bothers me. These RAW types seem to be so hard … cruel would be a better word, I guess. But it isn't just that. The way they shot the man Hassan sent to help me at the Qutub … so casual, like swatting a fly.' I could almost imagine her shuddering as she said it. 'I somehow can't believe they're the good guys, Chandra. So I've come to a decision: the only one I can trust is you.'

I said, 'Meenu, what did you find?'

She didn't reply. Instead she said, 'What are you doing in Afghanistan?'

I understood she was looking for some reassurance; in a way we were both exactly in the same position, lost and alone in a world of smoke and mirrors.

'Meenu, you just said you trust me. Do you mean it?'

'With all my heart.'

'Then listen to me. Hassan may or may not be the enemy, and we may even be on a cooked-up wild-goose chase but if what we have been told is true, millions of lives are at stake. Some sort of nuclear strike is being planned on Indian soil and …'

Meenakshi gasped. 'What …? What are you …?'

'Meenu, listen to me. We don't have much time left. Hassan could be back any minute. Tell me what you found, okay?'

She paused, obviously struggling to get a hold of herself. Then she said in a low voice, 'It's a piece of paper.'

I listened, riveted, as she went on to describe the squiggles, written in blood, on the torn page. She had given it up to the RAW agents, but not before she'd copied them down.

It seemed that the night at the Qutub, and then the encounter with these men, had triggered a powerful reaction. For almost two whole days she had obsessed with it, tried to come to terms with it. Except they would not let her. She had a strong feeling of being watched. It didn't help that Shukla called her almost every few hours to check if I had made contact in any way. It was in this state of high nervous tension that she had a sudden spark.

'I was giving a lecture when it struck me. The paper said: "Ask the question and it shall be answered." Chandra, have you heard of the Milindapanha?'

'No. Should I have?'

'I should think so,' she said tartly, the old Meenakshi showing through for a moment. 'It's a classic treatise from the first century BC called "The Questions of King Milinda". Milinda, or Menander, to give him his Greek name was an Indo-Greek monarch who converted to Buddhism 400 years before Kanishka. In many ways, he is the spiritual and temporal inspiration for much of what the Kushans achieved later.'

'And for someone like Xiphos Soter.'

'Exactly. I went straight to the Rhys Davids translation which is the standard one. Guess what the numbers were?'

My heart was thumping painfully in my chest. I could feel the blood surging through my arm, setting it on fire. 'Page numbers?'

'Chapter, section and line numbers – in that sequence. Each word I traced is in turn a number. Except one – the number 6.'

'Do you have them?'

'Sure,' she replied promptly. 'Do you have a pen and paper?'

I grabbed at the pad next to the phone. 'Go ahead.'

I wrote it down as she read it out to me: 34836782.

'What do they mean, Meenu?'

'No idea. I thought you might know.'

I stared at what I'd jotted down. It was definitely no co-incidence that all the located words in 'The Questions of Milinda' were numbers. They had to mean something. I felt a faint tug somewhere deep in my subconscious; the numbers were telling me something, but I couldn't put my finger on it.

Her voice was low, laced with a real fear. 'Chandra … this nuclear thing. I …'

I cut her off quickly. 'Meenu, we can't talk about it on the phone. It's too dangerous. There are reasons why we cannot go to the people even on our side. I have to do this alone.'

She said nothing. My watch said 10 pm. It was time to stop. We had been talking for too long already but I found I was reluctant to cut the connection. I sensed so was she. We had reached out and found each other, perhaps for no more than a fleeting moment, but one that we clung to over the void.

'Meenu, I just wanted to say … well done. You're sitting in Delhi, but you've done more – far more – than Hassan and I put together.'

She half laughed. 'You Madrasis and and your stiff upper lip. But thanks.' Then her voice had a catch in it. 'Chandra … just come back safe. I'll be waiting.'

'I will. I promise,' I said with a confidence that I was far from feeling. I replaced the receiver and sat back in the chair. The warm afterglow of the call filled me. I thought back to the time when I'd called her on impulse. When had it been … eight, no … seven days ago. Just a week! I couldn't believe it. It felt more like an aeon on this deadly rollercoaster, barreling through loops and twists, being turned inside out each time.

It hit me just as I got out of the chair: I knew why the numbers were so familiar.

15

Nalini Ranjan Pant disconnected the call and swivelled his chair around. Through the large bay window to his left, Lutyens' Delhi stretched away in all its majesty: from the magnificent pile that was Rashtrapati Bhavan at the head of Raisina Hill, the Rajpath flowed arrow straight between the North and South Blocks towards the delicate cupola of India Gate under whose canopy the eternal flame commemorated those who gave up their lives in the defence of their motherland. It was a view that he never tired of no matter how many times he viewed it; each time it renewed him, gave him strength.

Counter-intelligence was, in many respects, a front line of defence against the enemy. It was an amalgam of many things. Poring over papers behind a desk; directing spies in the field and analysing the HUMINT that came in at such risk; scanning the global electronic chatter, the satellite images; getting under the skin of those who would do the country harm and to think as they would. And then connecting the dots. That was the essence of what he did. And if he did it right, lives could be saved. Not just on the frontier, where troops placed themselves in danger each day, but also in that anonymous, shadowy world of espionage where his agents and spies fought a phantom war with the enemy. It was a responsibility that consumed him.

A knock sounded on the door and a bespectacled face poked through. Pant waved a hand, beckoning him in. Rao walked in, followed by Shukla.

'Thanks for coming in at such short notice, Rao. I really appreciate it.'

'Don't mention it, Pant. You've been to our office many times. The least we can do is reciprocate.'

Pant nodded. 'Thanks anyway. Kuch chai ya coffee?'

'No, thanks. We actually have another meeting set up in half an hour.'

'Okay, then I'll get to the point. The HM wants an update on this business with the Pakistan SCC. You recall RAW had raised some real concerns.'

They went quiet for a moment. Shukla said in his rasping, unpleasant voice, 'But we didn't get any ...' when Rao cut in. 'Well, there's no change in our assessment. Extremist control over their arsenal cannot be ruled out in the future, and while …'

Pant interjected, 'Look, Rao. You've been saying this for a while now. How imminent is the development? I mean, should we start counter-action now, immediately?'

Shukla shifted in his chair. Rao shrugged. 'We have no means of exactly assessing the extent of penetration of the SCC by these people. That kind of intel takes a while to build up, and even then is likely to be speculative to some degree. All we can point to is an accelerating trend.'

Pant kept his eyes on the two men. He said sharply:

'It's a trend that you've been pushing hard for more than two months now. It's got the cabinet quite worried. If the threat level has escalated significantly we need to act.'

'What do you have in mind?'

'Two things. Let's pull the NTRL into this. We need to really step up the electronic surveillance on the SCC there. Saturate their airwaves. The second is what I've been suggesting for quite a while now: to get the Americans and the Chinese on board. They're the ones with the levers. Let us match the intel between us and move together on this one.'

The RAW duo exchanged glances. Rao said carefully, 'I agree, Pant. Why don't you call NTRL and we'll bring in the Americans and the Chinese. We'll move to set up the meeting ASAP. I'll keep you posted.'

Pant said, 'When? I'm really under pressure on this one.'

'We'll set it up within the week.'

When they had gone, Pant removed his thick glasses and rubbed the bridge of his nose, a habit he had whenever he was processing information.

Item: he had made just a suggestion and they had immediately agreed to come to his room. A small but, for RAW, a pretty tectonic shift in behaviour. Even in the savage turf wars within the intelligence agencies, RAW was notorious for its stand-offishness. If you wanted to see them *you* went to their offices; it was never the other way around.

Item: he had raised his voice deliberately, something that normally would have got them bristling. But today's reaction was all sweetness and light.

Item: the government had recently set up the National Testing Research Laboratory to co-ordinate electronic eavesdropping strategy. RAW had been furious at this clipping of its wings and they'd gone after the NTRL people with a vengeance. Now when he'd provoked them with the suggestion to bring in NTRL, there was not the slightest sign of rancour: nothing but a totally professional response.

Item: the thing about the Chinese and the Americans. Rao and Shukla had insisted for several meetings now that it wasn't necessary to bring them in. Why the sudden volte face?

Item: Pant had thrown them a bait on the timing and they had taken it. The operative time frame had narrowed down to one week.

He was watching the RAW men closely without appearing to. There was something about their body language – their relaxed physical posture, so completely at odds with their usual in-your-face aggression – that hinted at an explosive tension within. He was conscious of a faint uptick in his pulse as hunches began to coalesce into certainty He picked up the phone and punched in an extension.

The voice on the other side said, 'Yes?'

'I think you're right. Any news from our man there?'

'No, nothing yet. It's proving to be tough. But something big is going down: everything he's experienced the last week confirms it.'

Pant disconnected. He was a hard-headed man, ruthless even. Emotion was not something he could afford to indulge in in his job. But he was suddenly conscious of a severe disquiet, an almost physical distortion of space-time in his immediate vicinity. It was as if he was in a lift and the cables had suddenly snapped: as the cage goes hurtling down out of control, the walls suddenly start to close in.

16

The GPRS on my phone didn't work in Ghazni and I had no way to check if my hunch about Meenakshi's numbers was correct. I stayed awake through the night on a diet of adrenaline, and furious thought. After seesawing for hours between the pull of my own instincts and the push of what seemed to be Meenakshi's cast-iron proof, I had come to a fateful decision: I would have to lose Hassan. It was a resolution that left me in an agony of self-doubt. For the first time since that morning at the Qutub, when my life started to unravel, I would be striking out on my own. I was used to working alone, but on reasonably familiar ground, among people I could connect with. This was Afghanistan; war and conflict were inseparable with the rubric of this country. The Taliban were everywhere and a lone stranger would be an easy target for the kidnapping gangs that were said to roam the countryside. But I told myself again and again that I had no choice. If the numbers were what I thought they were, I couldn't chance them falling into his hands. Even as I made the decision, however, I was conscious too of a certain guilt, a sense of committing an act of betrayal that no amount of rationalization was able to dispel.

At the first light of dawn, I exited the hotel through the rear. I wanted to put as much distance as I could between Hassan and me, so I headed straight for the north end of town. There I sat in a small eatery in the market, sipping thick Afghan coffee, waiting for the local Internet café to open.

By ten o'clock, I was hunched over an antiquated desktop that still ran Windows 98 and connected with an excruciatingly slow dial-up. I brought up Google Maps and punched in the numbers: 34.83 latitude and 67.82 longitude. I kept my eyes locked on the screen, almost as if I was willing the answer out of it. The seconds crawled by; the map started as a fuzz of pixellated dots and then spread itself over the screen like moss. My mouth was dry and the hair stood up on the back of my arms as I recognized the map of Afghanistan. The map shrunk itself slowly, zeroing in on the co-ordinates, and then stilled. I hit the satellite photo icon and waited once more. The screen shifted into the physical map mode, showing up rugged mountains and valleys; the orange balloon marker appeared and digitally pinned itself to the location I had entered. The text on the map just behind the marker said it all. *Bamiyan.*

I took a quick look around the shop. The place was empty. I cleared the screen and waited, trying to get my breathing to normal. Without any question, Meenakshi Pirzada had handed me the biggest break of our quest thus far, the vital pointer both Hassan and I had been seeking. The Bamiyan Valley. This had to be it: the site of the clandestine missile programme. Bamiyan was at the very heart of Hazarajat, nestled among the Koh-e-baba spurs of the Hindu Kush. I recalled there was supposed to be a large reconstruction project there centred around the Buddhas. *Led by the Archaeological Society of India.* It was all starting to come together.

The map showed no major road from Ghazni to Bamiyan; I was going to have to travel north to Charikar via Kabul and then westward: a dogleg of over 500 kilometres. There was no time to lose.

I went over to the man at the counter and tried some broken English. 'Need taxi. Where get?'

He replied in passable English. 'You from Al Hind?'

'Yes.'

Instantly he grinned and thumped me on

the shoulder. 'Aha … I like. I like very much. Amitabachan. You know him?'

'No, not really. Can get taxi?'

'Where go?'

'Bamiyan.'

'Ah, you go see Buddha, no?' He shook his head mournfully. 'They gone. But smaller No. 3 Buddha there. Wait here. I call my cousin. He take you.' He yanked out a cellphone and started jabbering in glottal Dari.

I kept a lid on my feverish impatience and looked around, checking automatically for Hassan. Knowing he couldn't be here, but the wash of relief still touched with that lingering sense of regret I couldn't throw off. I forced myself to relax, to take in my surroundings for the first time. Except for the stony mountains ringing the horizon – part of that stark immensity that all Afghanistan seemed to invoke – I could be back in any small town in India. Men in loose jubbas and pyjamas wandered among the petty shops or squatted by the roadside, engaging in idle talk. Across the dusty street, a group of women walked in a tight bunch, protective of each other, the wind whipping up their black abayas. And here was my taxi tout, almost certainly getting ready to gyp a 'foreign' tourist exactly as his counterpart would back home in Delhi. We are all so alike, I thought as I waited. Why are we caught up in conflicts without end?

When the car trundled up, my heart sank. An old beat-up Ambassador. I hadn't ridden in one since a trip to Calcutta four years ago, and this one seemed even more ancient than the Calcutta rattletraps, if that was possible.

My new-found procurer was watching my reaction like a hawk. He clapped my shoulder and said heartily, 'No worry. Your country car.' He made a thumbs-up sign. 'Fitted with brand-new Benz engine. Go very very high speed.'

All the while he was propelling me gently but inexorably towards the jalopy. Just before being practically pushed inside, I got in a word:

'How much?'

'Listen, my friend. You from Al Hind, okay? Like my brother. Take no extra. My cousin tell you on the way, okay?'

I gave up. The driver engaged into first gear and we shot off in a cloud of dust.

We bounced along the mosaic of tar and dirt that passed for the highway to Kabul. There were times when even this rutted road thinned and petered out into the desert like some lost river and then we were onto a trackless wasteland. The Ambassador's 'very very high speed' was all of fifty kmph. On the few occasions when the driver could be persuaded to floor the accelerator, it rattled and shook so much from every joint and limb that I feared the worst.

At this rate it would take us at least twelve hours to Bamiyan, but there was nothing I could do but wait it out in this contraption. Nothing. I had been twitchy, every nerve on edge, raging at my stupidity to have got conned into this crate. But now, as I looked out the window, it struck me how the car must seem to a distant observer: a beetle inching its way across a vast sandscape capped by cerulean sky.

Perhaps it was the effect of this infinite canvas where the earth stretched away into the limitless horizon and where all feeling of time and distance seemed subsumed into the here and now; perhaps too I realized the futility of fulminating at something I could do nothing to change. Whatever be the reason, I became calm. And with that acceptance came a new tingling of resolve, a sense of purpose as it came home to me that my days with Hassan, so filled with angst and helplessness, were over. Whatever the future held, I had retrieved myself. I was once again a reporter on the trail of a story – without question the biggest story of my life, but one laced this time by the sobering realization that upon my success or failure perhaps depended the lives of millions. There was also fear, the gut-wrenching fear of going up against an implacable, shadowy enemy; but fear by itself was an old companion and I could deal with it as long as I was in control of my own actions. I realized now that it was this loss of mooring, this being cast adrift upon waters beyond my ken, that had got under my skin ever since that fateful day at the Qutub.

I leaned back on the lumpy seat, letting the miles crawl by steadily, and deliberately turned my mind to what might lie in wait for me at Bamiyan – at the contour marked by the pin on the screen. The Buddhas were being reconstructed at the site under some sort of an international effort sponsored by the UN. India's ASI was in the lead in keeping with the fact that it had been involved with the restoration of Afghan monuments for many decades now. I thought about it; the organized chaos of a construction site typical of any the world over: cargo containers converted into prefab project offices, filled with archaeologists, scientists, technicians; the cranes with their booms; people – Indians – hurrying around everywhere; trucks, trailers, vehicles of every description, roaring in and out of the place in a constant stream. Could this din serve as an unwitting camouflage for a much deadlier purpose? I really had no idea, but it seemed as promising a cover as any I could think of. That note had been written in blood and it had clearly pointed to something. What could it be if not the location of the missiles?

I blessed the serendipitous impulse that had impelled me to call Meenakshi that evening in Delhi – just before my whole world had exploded. Without her I'd still be groping around. 'The Questions of Menander' – the Milindapanha. Not in a million years would I – or most people – have cracked that one. What were the odds that a historian, and one sharp as a knife, should have been at hand exactly when I needed her? I had always been dismissive of the notion of taqdeer, of a pre-ordained destiny that lies in wait for us. But now, in the loneliness of my solitary quest, it provided me a ray of comfort to know that luck – such as it was – had worked in my favour.

I hadn't slept at all the previous night and must have dozed off for when I woke with a start, the scenery had changed; the arid land had begun to green, with patches of cultivation on either side of the road. The stalks were waist high, fanning out near the top into long, delicate leaves that drooped. Soon the fields blanketed the ground, stretching away as far as the eye could see. I was astonished at the rapidity of the change: from desert to fecund farmland in the space of less than a half hour.

'What crop is this?' I asked in Hindi. The driver – as taciturn as his cousin was voluble – merely grunted one word. Afeem. *Opium.* These were poppy plants. I stared at this sea of green rippling in the breeze; these were the true killing fields of Afghanistan, protected by powerful local warlords and politicians, and the source of three-quarters of the world's supply of heroin.

Another hour of this and the road debouched into another valley and the land was sand and rock once more; clearly, what we had passed through was some kind of a river valley. But now, I started to notice a gradual increase in traffic. A stone signpost – the only one I had seen on this road so far – said 'Bamiyan 50 kilometres'. Eateries and chaikhanas began to pop up at regular intervals with cars and vans parked in front. Vehicles poured onto the highway from side roads, and soon we were in a bumper-to-bumper crawl. Now and then tippers, mechanized shovels and other off-roaders trundled alongside the highway like outsized monsters, throwing up dust clouds. Hoardings for hotels and other tourist trap-sounding names sprouted like trees on either side. The road took a dogleg and we were in a bluff, between twin rock ridges guiding us in.

'I take you hotel?' the driver asked tersely.

'No. Straight to the Buddhas, please.'

A red sign said 'Parking for Bamiyan Buddhas' off to the right. The driver spun the wheel, swung the Amby into a big parking lot and cut the engine. It was a blessed relief to get out of the car. My joints were stiff and my arm felt swollen as I stretched it. My bandage had red splotches where the wound had leaked, and I felt a buzz in my head that was usually a sign of fever. In my hurry I'd forgotten to take the pills the doctor had given me back in Peshawar; there was nothing for it now but to go on. The driver quoted what I was sure was an extortionate fare but I hadn't the strength to argue. I paid him in silence, shouldered my bag and started to thread my way through the parking lot. The air was fogged with fine dust that came off the moving vehicles. I crossed the road, came around the back of a large luxury coach and stopped – rooted to the spot.

Spread before me was a panoramic expanse of valley. The level plain on which I stood stretched dead ahead for almost a mile before terminating in a horseshoe curve of a cliff. This monolithic wall rose sheer from the base and joined the earth with the sky hundreds of feet above: a vertical bridge to the heavens. The cliff was riven by the wind and rain over aeons into vertical channels to produce a living, almost flesh-like effect, accentuated by pockmarks spread all over its face.

From where I stood, two giant rectangular grottos could be seen, carved deep into the hillside, like guardposts looking down the valley. I didn't need to be told what they were. Till March 2001 – when the Taliban had declared them 'un-Islamic' – two of the greatest monuments of the ancient world stood within them: the Buddhas of Bamiyan.

The view was awe-inspiring in its historical sweep. The Valley of Kings in Eygpt, Mohenjodaro in Pakistan and Machu Picchu in Peru; I could think of few other sites I had seen that captured the extreme grandeur and mystery of a lost civilization. Here, amidst the arid mountains of Central Asia, Buddhism had flourished for more than a millenium before being overrun by a wave of Islam from the west.

The signs of construction were everywhere. A wide cordon was drawn around the approach to the cliff, the single entry point being a makeshift gate with a security cabin. Beyond, in the work area, a wooden stairway snaked up the cliff onto a low platform near the Buddhas, where workers were crawling like ants over the lattice of scaffolds that were set up where the statues were – or had been.

In the half a minute it took for me to register all this, the wonder of the place was already fading, replaced by intense anxiety at the scale of it all. The Google marker dominated my mind's eye, and the sinking realization that I had completely underestimated my task. The co-ordinates were limited to degrees and minutes; it didn't go beyond that. The marker could be off by several kilometres – in any direction. In the initial excitement – euphoria even – I had missed this.

The valley itself was a few miles across, but it was just a small fraction of the convoluted mountain mass of the Hindu Kush all around. And I had no idea what to look out for, no clue about what a missile assembly would look like. A hangar perhaps, or an engineering workshop innocuous enough to be buried in the flurry of reconstruction all around? Or was it some underground factory in some wild, remote section of this range? Wherever it was, it would be heavily camouflaged to escape all but the most detailed inspection. The old sense of being overwhelmed began to creep up, but I held fast to one thought: there were plenty of Indians here, and they would be my starting point. If I worked carefully and probed deep enough, I felt I had a chance of getting a break.

Minibuses were ferrying visitors into the valley. I got into one filled with a bunch of white tourists and what appeared to be a flamboyant Italian guide. As we trundled off, I gathered from the talk around me that the ISAF – a euphemism for NATO and US combined forces – had cleared this area of the Taliban a year ago, which accounted for the recent tourist influx. Just how much became even more apparent as we approached the cliffs. Tour groups, school children on excursion, Buddhist monks: the swarm of people was amazing for what was supposed to be a war-torn country.

The bus stopped, we got off and moved to a vantage point close to the cordon. The guide spun around and threw out his arms. 'Ladies and gentlemen, welcome to the Bamiyan Valley. For the next three hours I will present to you a centrepiece of one of the greatest sites of the ancient Buddhist world. Here we stand: possibly at the very place where the celebrated pilgrim Hiuen Tsang stood more than 1500 years ago, meditating upon the Brihad or colossal statues of the Buddha that gazed silently across the valley. Alas, they gaze no more.' He removed his straw hat and hung his head as if caught up in a solemn moment.

It suddenly struck me that the group tour would be the perfect cover to do a recce of the place. I took out my press card on its ribbon and slipped it around my neck, then opened my notebook and stood poised expectantly. The guide eyed my press card and his solemnity vanished, replaced by a sudden expansiveness. Pointing triumphantly at the work behind him he said, 'But, my dear friends, do not lose heart. They will rise again from the ashes. What you are seeing is marvel, marvel of modern technology. Our scientists, many of whom are from Roma by the way, are using a technique called anastylosis to restore these great statues. First, we use a laser projection to ...'

I tuned out, pretending to take notes, but looking around as carefully as I could. We had been walking steadily towards the cliff and the coffin-shaped recess loomed up as we got closer to the western end. We came to the rope barrier and stopped, struck dumb by the extraordinary sight. The grotto, if it could be called that, had been cut some thirty feet deep into the mountainside, then soared up the cliff face, an enormous vault that took my breath away.

'175 feet – fifty-three metres high, cut from living rock,' the guide said in reverential awe. 'A colossus of Rhodes of the Buddhist world. One kilometre away is its counterpart and between them are the caves of Bamiyan: home to Buddhist monks since time immemorial.'

The presence of the destroyed statue could be almost physically felt, so powerfully was it suggested by the shape of the niche and by the faint traces of the figure itself still left against the stone from which it once sprang. We looked on silently, with that wonder that comes when one is faced with true grandeur – often from a work of nature, but sometimes also from the work of man.

Wooden platforms had been set up at various heights within the niche and from these teams of workers were taking measurements. Sized stone blocks had been piled up at the base, and I could see one of these had been pre-cut to the shape of a giant foot. Clearly the rebuilding of the Buddha had begun.

To our right, some monks sat on the ground absorbed in meditation, seemingly undisturbed by the hustle and noise all around. So caught up was I in the prospect before me that I was unaware that one of the seated figures – face shadowed by a cowl – was watching me intently.

17

Meenakshi was brushing her teeth when she heard the ping of an incoming SMS. She rinsed quickly and went into her bedroom. The words jumped out at her from the backlit screen.

Hassan in the clear. Actually working for us. Trail getting hot. Pls urgently call Delhi 8356537231. C

She read it again, then sank down limply on the bed. She stared unseeing at the window opposite. The hours since her last conversation with him had been anything but restful. She could think of nothing else but his call and the ominous nuclear threat that he had spoken of so briefly. The next day had sped by in a distracted blur; she could remember little of class and the staff meeting that had followed. She had gone through the motions like an automaton, her whole being intensely distracted by threatening portents at every side. She felt like a frog being slowly boiled in water.

Shukla ... Indian intelligence ... had placed incontrovertible evidence before her that Hassan was an agent for Pakistan. And that he somehow had Chandra in his power. She had believed them – till Chandra's call. Though Chandra had made it clear that he was still with Hassan, and had been tense on the phone, she had a strong feeling he was acting alone, that he had taken her warning about Hassan seriously. So, despite Shukla's threats she had given him the numbers. She was now directly complicit in an act that could – and would – be held by her interlocutors as directly aiding and abetting the enemy: the act of a traitor. It was a feeling that ate at her like acid.

Now, seeing the SMS, she didn't know what to think. Chandra had obviously discovered something. Something that had convinced him of Hassan's bona fides. But why didn't he call to explain? She knew he was now engaged in some sort of a desperate mission, a race against time and ... this immiment nuclear threat. It was more than possible that he was in no position to call in.

She wrestled with it for a while; she wondered if the SMS was a trap, sent by someone else. The message had no number ID, but Chandra's phone was encrypted to mask the sender. She clicked on Skype on her cellphone and punched in the number.

The guide cut the tour short a full hour earlier than he was supposed to. A storm warning was out: one of those freakish squalls caused by rapidly moving air currents over the Hindu Kush. The westerly sky was clear, the dipping sun bathing the crags in shimmering ochre as the stone soaked up the angled light. But clouds were moving in from the north: purple, heavily pregnant nimbus banks bunched tight together.

The tourists and construction crews had dispersed to the town, and the off-road tippers and dumptrucks had been pulled back to the valley perimeter. Apart from a few monks about, I had the place pretty much to myself. A quiet lay over this ancient valley, but this was a quiet that presages a storm. Perhaps it was the predicted weather shift, but an oppressive feeling had been slowly but steadily been growing within me the entire afternoon, a sense of impending doom, and no matter how much I tried, I couldn't shake it off.

I had covered much of the valley floor from end to end, some of it with the tour group and the rest on my own. Finding nothing useful, I now decided to try the construction camp set to the eastern side of the bluff. Several of the security guards on the perimeter were Indians, and happy to talk to a fellow desi. My press card worked well and a bunch of them gathered around. It turned out that the ASI was indeed here in strength as part of the international effort, and the Indian government had contributed its share of security cover by way of a CISF contingent.

With a bit of friendly persuasion, they let me wander about with the warning to make it quick what with the coming storm. The camp was big, at least fifty to sixty tents spread over around a thousand square metres – all neatly stockaded into sections. One area contained the tented workshops. I took each by turn. They were basic in purpose: electric stone-cutting and -shaping tools, some electronic gear by way of measuring instruments, generator sheds and miscellaneous stuff; after pretty much covering them all I could see nothing that could even remotely be connected to a sophisticated missile programme.

I waved to one of the guards. He came up, smilingly cheerful. I saw his well-oiled hair, the thin pencil of a moustache and made a snap association. I said in Tamil, 'Oru kelvi.' One question.

His smile broadened. 'Ninga enda ooru?' Where are you from from?

Chidambaram once, but now Delhi, I said.

He nodded and smiled again, happy as most

Indians are to see one of their country cousins. 'I'm from Pudukottai, saar. Evalo venalum kelungo.' Ask all you want.

'There must be many Indians working here?'

'Yes, many. Mainly ASI people. They are all over the site.'

'Where do they stay?'

'In Zuhak Hotel. Our fellows fully there only. So many of them and they all want home food, no?'

'And all of them work here? No other construction and any other projects close by that you have seen?'

He shook his head. 'No, saar. I took jeep rides all over the mountains. All here only. But you can ask at Zuhak Hotel again, if you want.'

'Everyone is staying there, right?'

'Yes.'

I thanked him and turned away. As I started off towards the taxi stand at the mouth of the valley, he said, 'Only few technicians are staying up in the caves.'

I tried to keep my manner casual. 'Caves. You mean the caves up on the cliffs?'

He shook his head. 'Not the regular ones to the left.' He turned and pointed directly up. 'Those. The new caves, just above the small Buddha's head.'

'What are they doing there?'

He shrugged as if it was of no consequence. 'Some special thing, some measuring on the rock. Mad fellows. They never come down even on weekends; eat and sleep there only. Don't talk to anyone.'

'Maybe I'll interview them tomorrow.'

He smiled. 'You can try.' He tapped his temple and shook his head again. 'Crazy fellows. Won't be surprised if they're still up there, in this weather.'

———

I stood behind the scaffolding at the base of the cliff. The guards had long since made off to the Nissen huts that made up their living quarters. The sky was dark now, and starless, muffling the valley in gloom. Lightning sputtered intermittently from the heavy bank of cloud overhead. A single sodium vapour lamp beneath the grotto was no more than a small pinprick of light, its rays sucked up and swallowed by the dark maw of the Buddha hollow.

The caves of the Bamiyan cliff-face were well known as residences of monks for centuries, but I'd only just learnt from the guided tour that, when the Taliban had blasted the statues, other – and till now secret – caves were revealed behind the figures, hollows hidden away from human eyes for a thousand years. It was to the ones uncovered near the head that the guard had referred to.

The black void was covered by bars of scaffolding and looked like a prison designed to hold a giant. The lightning forked again, more vivid and intense this time, and by its metallic glow I saw the lattice of poles snake upwards into the dark. Thunder rumbled across the valley and the cliffs answered, throwing the sound back in a sonorous roll of drums, deep and threatening. I felt a sudden sting on my cheek; it was a heavy drop of water striking me on the face with the force of a small projectile. Then the sky opened up above me.

I stood there, soaked to the skin. The rain sheeted down in a solid, coruscating, diamond-hard hail, smashing into me with bullet force. The arm, to which I had paid scant attention during the day, was ablaze with fire and I felt dizzy with the agony of it. But whatever was up there was waiting, drawing me towards it remorselessly, and I was set upon a path from which there was no turning back. I shuffled forward, put my good hand on the pole and hauled myself up the first rung.

Deep inside the mountain, the boom of the mobile crane was poised over the long cylindrical tube. It inched down, jaws wide open to grip the metal brackets welded to the shell. Slowly, operating with delicate precision, it picked the projectile and moved it to the wide-bodied TEL trailer and the hinged hydraulic frame that was designed to receive it. The same operation was repeated, and the second cylinder set upon a separate trailer lined up in the bay. Dr Sastry, who was watching the entire operation carefully from the control cabin, made a time-out gesture and then rotated his fist. The operator raised his hand in acknowledgement. There was a hiss of escaping compressed air and then silence as the crane stilled.

The project director picked up the red phone and punched in a number. 1500 kilometres away, the man in the anonymous office off Lodhi Road answered the call. It was Shukla.

He listened in silence and then said, 'Good. Have the vehicles ready to move out on my word. You'll hear from me no later than IST 1600 hours tomorrow. Destination instructions will be given at the same time.'

Shukla disconnected and then redialled. 'It's me. The trucks are ready. We're ready to flag them off at midnight tomorrow as planned.'

The voice at the other end asked a question. Shukla said, 'Yes, we got the tip-off from Ghazni and we've been tailing him since. The woman's got to be the source; she must have broken the code on that paper. He got into the valley yesterday.'

The squawk over the line became more urgent. Shukla said, 'We're not underestimating this one; we're assuming he will find us. I'm leaving tonight to oversee the transports and I've personally briefed the teams there. They'll be ready. And just one more thing: I'm leaving the questioning to the big man.'

There was pause on the other side, then a question. Shukla's lips parted over the horse teeth in a vicious grin.

'I've sent a guy over just now. The bitch is taken care of.'

He glanced at his timepiece and compared it to the one on the wall. 1954 hours, 7.54 in the evening of T minus four days and counting.

18

Meenakshi Pirzada had just called the number which had come to her on SMS when she heard the doorbell chime. She hesitated, caught momentarily between two states. She heard the number ring briefly before she disconnected and walked out into the hall.

The bell sounded again as she approached the entrance. 'Haan, haan, aati hoon …' she called out. At the door, she put her eye to the glass peephole. It was the delivery boy from the local store with her order. She unlatched and pulled the door open.

'Salaam memsaab,' he said, sketching her a salute. 'Aapke liye.'

She took the bag of groceries, checked off the items on the list and paid him.

She shut the door and was turning towards the kitchen, when she heard a faint click to her right. Of late her senses had become much more acute. Possibly it was this awareness of being under constant surveillance, that and her own heightened fears, but she found her senses operating to an excruciating pitch of alertness. She was literally beginning to shy at shadows.

She stood still now, seeking the source of the sound. The curtains across the bedroom entrance billowed out, then stilled as if buffeted by a momentary gust of wind. She was puzzled for a moment, then froze. She had shut and bolted all the windows when she had left in the morning and they had still been that way when she'd got back. Someone or something had forced a window and was now in her bedroom.

Shock, then raw fear lanced through her, sending her pulse into overdrive. Her first impulse was to open the door and run out. The sense of being totally exposed out there in the living room was overpowering. She was reaching for the doorknob when, with an enormous effort, she controlled herself. She reached into the hip pocket of her jeans and pulled out something short and squat. Keeping along the living room wall, she sidled quickly along the wall to the bedroom curtains. Then she flattened herself by the doorway and waited.

The seconds ticked by, each beat a lifetime. Her breasts rose and fell infinitesmally, breathing all but suspended, her senses totally focused within the bedroom. One minute ... two ... A hand pushed through the curtains, holding a gun, a silenced pistol exactly like the one she'd seen before. It extended out, probing the air, like the snout of some obscene animal. Ever so slowly, the curtains parted. Then, as the body emerged, she struck. Her hand whipped up, the spray hissing out in a high-speed jet, catching him full in the face. He screamed and reeled back, the gun falling from nerveless fingers, hands clawing at his face, seeking to rip away the raw flame of the ChilliGuard. She went after him and hit him with another long burst at three inches from his face. He yowled again, then his eyeballs rolled up, his legs folded and he hit the ground with a thud and lay still. Meenakshi clutched at the doorjamb, chest heaving, moaning softly as the reaction set in. She pushed herself off the wall and wove her way on rubbery legs to the front door. She leaned against it yet again, almost overcome, then fumbled with the latch and let herself out. She paused awhile, drawing in great gulps of muggy night air, then a fresh wave of terror consumed her and she raced down the steps and onto the road.

How long she walked, she could not say. At length, she saw a DDA municipal park ahead. Pushing past the turnstile, she went in and flopped down on a bench. Acting on pure reflex, she looked at her watch. Fourteen minutes past midnight. She leaned against the back rest of the seat, limp now with the reaction. The park was empty of people, but a stray dog came up and nuzzled her hand. She listlessly reached down to stroke it, when a buzz sounded against her thigh. She pulled the cellphone out. No caller ID.

With trembling fingers she pressed the answer button. 'Chandra …?'

The voice that answered was calm, measured, yet laced with a powerful urgency. 'Ms Pirzada. I beg you, do not hang up.' Then, as if the caller was sensing her surging panic, said tautly, '*Do-not-hang-up*. Please. I know you've just escaped an attempt on your life. I am on your side … and Mr Chandrasekhar's. He's in great danger. If you value his life, and yours …. please.'

Her finger hovered over the red disconnect button. She felt a wave of nausea. She wanted to crush the call, then fling the phone from her as far as she could; to end this nightmare once and for all. But she could not; the phone was her only lifeline to Chandra.

At long last, she said whispered shakily, 'Who is this?'

'My name is Nalini Ranjan Pant.'

The storm howled like a banshee around me; skies riven with lightning and thunder released water in sheeting waves that hammered at my vision. The roaring hurricane was filled with poltergeists that seized the scaffolding and shook it furiously from side to side. My left arm hung useless by my side; I dared not bring into play. Instead, I had to use the fast-fading strength of my right hand to haul me up the swaying stairs of wood and iron poles.

Through it all, another ghoul sat on my shoulder like a vetal, whispering malignantly into my ear, conjuring up dread images of the flattened skull, the frozen death mask. Each heave brought me closer to the creature's lair where more of its kind waited, perhaps forewarned, an ancient evil in the dark. And I was alone – utterly, completely alone.

It went on ... square by hellish square, a torment of one slippery rung after another. I jumped, hooked my arm over the next bar and pulled myself up. Hook, jump, haul ... hook, jump, haul; I inched up those monstrous stairs. My body was a leaden, bloated corpse that threatened to drag me down with each movement.

I became vaguely aware that my right arm was starting to distance itself from me. It felt puffy, filled with stings, like a pincushion pierced by needles. I raised it, flung it over the next pole and pulled myself up. And slipped.

In panic, I brought up my left hand and locked it over my right. My feet scrabbled for a hold on the lower rung but could not find it. I cried out in an agony of fear, clinging to the bar like a ragged doll, suspended between earth and sky, stuck fast in an elemental firmament.

My arm was being stretched on a rack, slowly torn from its socket. The pain was intense and I knew I could stand it no more; perhaps my inner self had begun to prepare itself for the end for I felt a grey blanket spread over my mind, shutting down thought and feeling.

I felt a faint judder through the frame, a vibration through the soles of my feet. It barely registered upon my fading senses, when it repeated again: stronger this time, closer, somehow not of the storm. I looked about foggily, then cast my eyes down. A figure was crawling up toward me, clothes flapping out, like the wings of a great vampire bat. Silver light flashed again through the sky, throwing the face into cold, chalky relief. It was Hassan.

For one heart-stopping moment I was sure it was a ghost, a spectre from a nether world. My mind utterly rejected what my eyes were registering. *Hassan. No ... it couldn't be ... not here ...* Then the figure opened its mouth and screamed something, but the words were whipped away in the wind. Horror bloomed, filling me with an inhuman strength. I started to scramble up the poles, flailing both hands in a frenzy.

A stone ledge jutted out from the rock face less than ten feet up. I edged up to it, kicked off from the poles and rolled over on to the floor of the slab. I lay there, dead to the world. The poles rattled and shook, pulling me out of my stupor. The creature was coming after me. I looked around frantically and spotted a length of broken pipe propped up in the corner against the wall. Snatching it up, I staggered to the edge and peered down.

He was almost level with my feet, reaching out to grip the ledge. I swung my arm back to strike at him. He looked up at me; his face was white with exhaustion, stretched tight over the bones. My arm was drawn back to its limit. I tried to bring it down, to smash the tube into Hassan's face and send him toppling into the depths. But I could not. For one long moment we held our positions, me with my arm raised for the strike and Hassan with his raised protectively over his face: a frozen tableau against the cliff.

Then my shoulders slumped and the pipe clattered to the floor. Whatever the consequences, the die was cast now. I could not send another human being to his death. I staggered back with a moan; my left foot stepped on a loose stone and buckled suddenly, throwing me off-balance. I lurched forward, scrabbling my hands frantically into the air to regain my footing. But the surface of the stone was slick with rain and my right foot slid over it in a deadly skate and tipped me over the edge.

I fell forward head first, plummeting down past Hassan – and jerked to a dead halt upside down. Hassan had caught me by my belt. I swung there, corkscrewing like a pendulum gone awry. The darkness stretched away below me, a black void without end. Terror lent me a preternatural awareness; every sense was at an intensely heightened pitch. The rasping of Hassan's breath filled the night, the ragged susurration of a man barely in control. And then his grip started to slip.

He shouted, 'Don't move. Don't move, Chandra.'

My panic was absolute: my body one giant jangling nerve – stretched to breaking point. I dimly heard his voice and, with a gigantic effort of will, fought myself to stillness.

Hassan cried out again, 'See if there's a bar you can catch. Do it *slowly*. Don't jerk!'

I tried reaching out for the vertical pole parallel to me, but it was a good foot away from the tips of my fingers and I hadn't the leverage. The sweat was pouring off me, running into my eyes, stinging, blinding.

'Have you got it?'

'No, too … far …' I croaked.

There was a silence, then his voice came back, taut with a desperate strain. 'Hold on.'

The ladder shook; I swayed, felt my trousers rip at the crotch seams, dropping me by a few inches. The cloth was beginning to come apart: Hassan wasn't going to be able to hold on. I swayed again; realized what he was trying. He was working his way laterally to the right, to get me closer to the next vertical pole. Each step he took, the seams tore some more. An inner awareness told me of his desperation. I locked my entire awareness around the pole. Time, space, the universe: all shrank to that pole. Nothing existed beyond it, the absolute, total terror of it. I was beyond the storm and the rain and the dark, my precarious position high above the rocky earth, beyond even the fog of pain and exhaustion. All sense of time and space faded, replaced only by one thing: that pole.

Hassan shouted out, a wild despairing cry, *'Catch it, catch it. Now!'*

I felt the cloth come apart. As I dropped I flailed my arms towards the pole in one savage lunge, putting everything I had into it – and caught it. I hugged the bar to me; my inverted body toppled over sideways, my feet scything down to hit the scaffolding with a thud, almost wrenching my arms from their sockets. Flesh ripped over the wound on my bicep and I almost passed out. Through the fog of pain, I thought I heard Hassan's shout from far up, but it was all fading now. I felt my body slacken and then it all went black.

Someone was slapping me. Tossing water onto my face. I felt fingers painfully pinching my upper lip. I wanted to protest, but hadn't the strength.

'Chandra, come on. Wake up.' The voice was insistent, the slaps sharp and stinging. I opened my eyes. Hassan was bent over me. I thought I saw a swift relief pass over his drawn face.

'What … what happened?' I whispered.

'You almost finished me off, is what happened,' he said with a tight smile. 'You passed out. I managed to grab you just in time and haul your fat arse up here. So we're even now.'

I said nothing. He read the question in my eyes.

'It's time for some explanations, Chandra.'

It was suddenly too much. The torpor was back with a vengeance and I didn't want to listen, wanted nothing more than to just lie there and let myself drift away.

'Chandra, come on. None of that, now. I need you.'

Hassan was squatting on his haunches. I noticed with a kind of hazy surprise that he showed none of the after-effects of that hideous time on the scaffold and his escape from certain

death at my hands. If anything, he seemed back to
his old self: wound up like a spring, anxious and
impatient at the same time.

I tried to raise myself. He reached out and
gently lifted me up and sat me up with my back
to the cold and clammy, but comforting solidity of
the stone wall.

'Are you okay with the pain and all? Can you
listen to me?'

I looked down at my arm. He had removed
the old filthy bandage and retied strips of banian
cloth over the wound. My trousers had gone,
shredded to the four winds, leaving me in my
striped underwear.

He waited for me to focus. Then he said, 'I
work for Indian intelligence.'

19

For the second time in the span of a week, Meenakshi sat in an anonymous hotel room, facing strangers. This time there were only two of them. One sat steno-like in the background taking notes on a small pad. The man directly opposite her was in some ways just as professorial as the earlier one with the horn-rimmed glasses, but in every other respect he was altogether different. She could tell. This one was small, his eyes large and owlish through the thick lenses of his spectacles. But it was his old-world, courtly air that gradually set Meenakshi at ease. It would have been fanciful to call his manner warm, but she sensed a friendliness in him, a certain sympathy that had nothing in common with Shukla's boss.

'Kuch chai ya coffee, Ms Pirzada? And would you like anything to eat?'

'Just water, please.'

The steno got up and poured a cup for her. She

took it and drained it in one long pull. He refilled it, set the carafe on her table and went back to his chair. The bespectacled man looked up for a while at the ceiling as if trying to compose his thoughts, then began to speak. His tone was conversational yet precise, as if it was ordered in a clear sequence in his head.

'Ms Pirzada, let me start my assuring you once again that I mean you no harm. I realize that my words will seem empty to you and will possibly do very little to ease your suspicions, yet I feel I must do what I can to set you at ease as to our intentions.'

She said nothing to that. She was on her guard. She trusted no one: not after the last two weeks. Her fingers sought reassurance, unobtrusively checking the ChilliGuard stuck into the waistband of her jeans. If the man saw the move, he showed no sign. Instead he smiled his polite, warm smile and said:

'My name is Pant – Nalini Ranjan Pant. I am acting director of the Joint Intelligence Committee of the Cabinet Secretariat. What I am about to tell you involves a matter of national security at the highest level. It is also directly linked to the fates of Inspector Syed Ali Hassan and your friend Chandrasekhar.'

He saw her face tighten and held up a hand to stall her. 'Don't get me wrong. The threat to them does not come from me; it shames me to say that it comes from certain others – some of them my own colleagues – within the government. Two have been in contact with you already, but they are just the tip of the iceberg.'

She was only half-listening and said fearfully, 'Is Chandra okay? Have you heard from him?'

Pant said carefully, 'No, we haven't heard from him. And we may not – at least not directly. But I believe he is heading into what we call the "kill zone", the area of maximum danger.'

She felt herself blanch inside but waited, outwardly composed.

'But you can help him. And your country. So I'm going to do what I've never done before with any civilian outside the government: open up. You, on the other hand, will never trust me entirely and I don't ask that. What I do ask is that you reserve judgement till you have listened to what I have to say. If afterwards you wish to leave you may do so without any conditions, other than you keep confidential what you hear in this room. Is that a fair request?'

She said, 'Who was it who tried to kill me just now?'

Pant returned her gaze levelly. 'We believe it was someone sent by Shukla.'

'But why? That man was calling me almost everyday … wanting to know if …'

She broke off, rubbing her forehead. Her palm came away wet. She started to shiver. Another reaction was beginning to set in.

Pant leaned forward and touched her shoulder in a curiously comforting gesture.

'Ms Pirzada … Meenakshi, we know what you've been through. If I may be permitted to say so, I think you're a very brave woman. But we're running out of time. Is my condition acceptable?'

She nodded wordlessly.

'Good. Then let me tell you straightway: Hassan is not a traitor as you have been led to believe. On the contrary he is a covert operative for military intelligence – the Defence Intelligence Agency, to be precise – on secondment to the JIC.'

Meenakshi rocked back in her chair. 'Hassan …?'

'Hassan is one of our top field agents. Has been for years. We now use him only on very special assignments – like this one. He's ranked a full colonel in the armed forces, by the way.'

Meenakshi was struck dumb. *Hassan … an Indian intelligence agent.* Pant paused, giving her time to absorb it, then continued.

'Approximately a year ago, a source embedded deep within the Research & Analysis Wing – which handles India's external security – came to me with a highly disturbing report. It appeared that a section within the clandestine community had gone rogue.

'The world of intelligence, Ms Pirzada, is, as you may expect, a complex one – and sometimes very treacherous. Indian intelligence is handled by no less than a dozen clandestine agencies, each fiercely protective of its turf. Each tends to operate within its silo, pooling information within its counterparts as required strictly on a need-to-know basis. If my informant was correct, this group had managed to spread its influence across multiple secret agencies, and to recruit adherents to its cause.

'I had to proceed with extreme caution, testing my findings and biding my time so as not to excite suspicion. To cut a long story short, I discovered the existence of a small, extremely influential clique: people at very high levels of policy and operations. Even more worrisome was that they had built a wide network of sympathizers throughout the civilian and military machines. You saw it yourself: they got the Delhi police commissioner to speak to you.

'The group's ultimate intent was kept completely closed off to all but a very few at the apex. Sympathizers below knew nothing of their actual plans. I dug deeper into the personnel files, looking for the common thread behind it all. It was then that I discovered that every one of the names that came up on my radar shared one common trait. Without exception they were all hard liners when it came to our two main security threats – Pakistan and China.

'That's when the pieces began to fall into place. We've fought four wars with the one and were humiliated in another with China. Geopolitically, China-Pak is a nexus that is essentially viewed by this country as anti-India. It obsesses the security establishment. Many of us see it in professional terms but to many others it has become an article of faith, driven not by cool reason but by an abiding, corrosive hatred of China and Pakistan – especially Pakistan.

'You can see it now. Only something like this could provide an ideological glue strong enough to hold all of them together. It took me even longer to discover what they were up to; what I found was so extreme and horrific that I, with all my experience, could scarcely credit it. It appeared that their plan was to assemble nuclear-armed missiles inside Afghanistan and fire them from Pakistani soil – *at India.*'

Pant paused to take a sip of water himself. Meenakshi's knuckles whitened on her armrests. She heard Chandra clearly: *some sort of nuclear strike is planned on Indian soil.* As happened to her in moments of stress, she noticed incongruous details about this musty hotel room: the grey, stained carpeting, the off-kilter lampshade in the corner and the cheap plastic film over the windows. The sun was lighting up the east; dawn was breaking after a long, hellish night.

Pant cleared his throat and continued, 'You're a historian, well up on Indian affairs, and you're probably thinking this is some crazy concoction from a cheap novel. I just wish it was, but it is not. The group has already put the plan into motion. Understand this, Ms Pirzada. *These missiles are already in Afghanistan, being armed as we speak.*

'The evidence leaves no room for doubt. The simmering resentment in this country against Pakistan has many manifestations, but this is by far the most dangerous I have ever come across. And their timing is perfect. The political leadership is supine and scandal-ridden. Our secret service has always operated with minimal scrutiny, but even those checks and balances have loosened. And our neighbour is in deep internal crisis ever since the bin Laden operation.

'Think of it: an unchecked rabid faction within the Indian establishment facing a Pakistan with its back to the wall. These people are convinced their moment to strike has come.'

Meenakshi burst out, 'That's still impossible! When we got the nuclear waiver, our fissile materials control regime was ...'

Pant interrupted. 'Fully certified. Yes. What's

not so well known is that the Bush administration was so keen to certify us that no one took a really hard look. Have you heard of the NTI?'

Meenakshi shook her head.

'It stands for Nuclear Threat Initiative. It's an independent think-tank out of the US that ranks countries by the safety of their nuclear materials. Do you know India's ranking last year?'

The question was rhetorical and she said nothing.

Pant ticked off his fingers. 'On transparency of fissile material control we got thirty-two on hundred, on material production and elimination we got eighteen on hundred and on safety in physical transportation we got a ten on hundred. *Ten on hundred.*'

She murmured, 'I had no idea …'

'It's published information. You can get it off the Internet. Now, about Hassan …'

Pant's phone went off with a soft beep. He put it to his ear. She saw him sit up and listen carefully. Once or twice, he glanced at her in an appraising way. Then he said, 'Thanks. Keep me posted.'

He put the phone away and said, 'That was my man who was watching your house. Your attacker was apparently removed in semi-conscious condition a few minutes ago by some of his colleagues. What did you do to him?'

'ChilliGuard. It's a desi Mace.'

Pant chuckled. 'Whatever it was, I can tell you it's probably illegal. It's knocked him out for close to six hours.'

He became serious. 'We have to move you to a safe house. You cannot go back till this is over.'

She felt a wash of relief laced with regret. Her little apartment, her warm and cosy refuge, had been crudely violated in the worst imaginable way. But now was not the time; she thrust her emotions aside.

'You were saying … about Hassan …?'

'Yes. When I became certain of what was going on, I brought in Hassan. For one, Hassan's DIA, not RAW. He's been our ace-in-the-hole for a long time now.'

'So the police inspector thing is just a cover?'

'Yes and no. It's a bit complicated. In India there's a big overlap between external counter-intelligence and internal security. It's part of our problem. We've worked with the IB to keep him on as a lower-order policeman when he's on internal security assignments. That way he is low enough in the pecking order that he does not attract attention, but has enough of an official position to be effective. Which is what he was doing when this thing exploded.'

Meenakshi's thoughts went back to that fateful evening when Hassan had walked into Chandra's living room. She could see him even now, etched in every detail: the rumpled, sweat-stained shirt … that haunted expression. All designed to make the right impression. No question, the man was a consummate actor. Pitch perfect. Had to be to take in someone like Chandra.

'But why pull in Chandra? What does he have to do with any of this?'

Pant took several small sips of water. She had the subliminal impression that he was carefully considering his reply. Then he said, 'In March this year, I began to sense that my activities were being monitored; despite my precautions, it appeared the opposition had become suspicious. I had to assume that Hassan would also automatically come under the scanner as my links with him were well known within the higher echelons of RAW and the IB. We retreated for a while but kept our eyes and ears open. When some key scientists from our missile programme went missing we knew something very big was going down. Then the Qutub murder forced my hand.'

Meenakshi listened, mesmerized, as Pant sketched out the happenings of the following days. His manner was precise, understated but this was the point where she too had been drawn into the net of terror and intrigue and she felt an intense connect to the chain of events that he was describing.

Hassan had no jurisdiction at the Qutub, but

Pant was convinced of a vital connection with Afghanistan and had sent him in. Instantly, the struggle had become overt, both sides marshalling their resources in a lethal game of hide-and-seek. It was an unequal game in which the dice was loaded against Pant. All the conspirators had to do was remain undetected; Pant and Hassan, on the other hand, had to actively seek out the missile site and expose the clique behind the plot. Time was of the absolute essence and it was now that Pant decided to turn to two unlikely – and unwitting – allies: the press and the Pakistani ISI.

'Chandra was our immediate choice. For one, Hassan knows him. For another, his reputation within the press corps is without question. A breaking story of this magnitude from someone like Chandra can and will stop the opposition in its tracks. But he had to be reeled in quickly and we used ISI as bait.'

Pant smiled, a wintry, dry smile. Meenakshi had a sudden fleeting glimpse of another man beneath that quiet, mild exterior: hard and ruthless.

'Hassan's cousin is a highly respected, ranked officer of ISI. We floated the missile story to the Pakistanis and let them do the work for us. As I expected, ISI contacted Hassan. ISI believes Hassan is a cop. They also believe Hassan did not know who his cousin works for. There were wrong on both counts. They thought they were reaching out to Hassan of their own volition; in fact it was we who made it seem so.'

Pant glanced at his watch. His manner was unchanged but she became aware that this meeting was coming to an end.

'ISI knows that the rogue group in RAW is an existential threat to Pakistan. My own hands were tied; it was going to be exceedingly difficult to get Chandra and Hassan into Afghanistan without my counterparts getting to know about it. So I used ISI; only they didn't know it. They were also very useful in convincing Chandra.'

There was a long silence. Meenakshi exhaled slowly, aware only now that she had been holding her breath. She to wrap her thoughts around what she had just heard, the stunning enormity of it all. She tried to match it with this man Pant with his dry matter-of-fact manner, as he quickly sketched out plot and tortuous counter-plot, the subtle misinformation, the manoeuvrings – as if it were just another routine day at work.

Pant sat slightly slouched, his owlish eyes blinking behind the soda-bottle lenses. If he passed her on the street she wouldn't have given him a glance, this man who looked exactly like a minor accountant in some dusty office. But she saw him for what he was now: a master puppeteer wielding his strings in the dark, getting each of them to do his bidding on a deadly stage.

The phone beeped once more. Pant listened briefly, turned and made a sign to his assistant, who got up and left the room. He said, 'By the way, your cracking the Kushan connection was an exceptional piece of work. When Hassan reported back to me, I knew we were on the right track. One day, I'll tell you more about the Sword of the Saviour. But not now. Shukla and his minions are starting to close in. Before I lost communication with Hassan, he had just enough time to tell me that he was following Chandra out of Ghazni. The hotel switchboard registered an Internet call to Chandra's room the previous night. I need to know what that was about.'

Meenakshi said, 'They were a set of numbers.'

The intelligence man held out a notebook. 'Write them down for me.'

She took the book and said, 'What about Hassan and Chandra? Can you get to them?'

Pant shook his head. 'Not in the time left, with no radio com. The next forty-eight hours are crucial. Whether they succeed or not, their fate is now out of our hands.'

20

Dawn was a pale wash of grey light peppered by a drizzle that fell across the cave mouth in a steady procession of punctuation marks. It was a light that gave no cheer, rather it filled me with dread. For Hassan had left me in no doubt of what we must do.

The night had been a long, sodden test of will. We had dragged ourselves into a small hollow cut into the cave wall so as to be out of sight. I forced myself to stay awake, to hear out Hassan's whispered explanations through my stupor of pain and exhaustion. He kept at it, as if it was important to him that I understood how he had miraculously appeared beneath me on the scaffolding. Listening to him, even fitfully, I felt like a child listening to a fantastic fable, desperately wanting to believe, but not quite sure that what he hears is the truth. He must have seen some of it in my face, for he said again:

'You've got to believe me, Chandra. I swear to you on my mother's soul it's the truth.'

I said nothing, trying to digest this … this almost surreal play within a play. It was Chanakya and Machiavelli rolled into one. Hassan was an operative of Indian intelligence: one of our guys after all. The Gul Mohammed thing had been a set-up – on me and ISI. He and his boss – some guy called Pant – had played us both. My role in his game was to tag along and break the news to the world when we got close enough to the evidence.

I lay there on cold stone, trying to come to terms with it all. I'd been set up, but so had the vaunted ISI. The real professionals had been taken in; what chance did I have? And given the stakes, I didn't even feel used. The real question was: was I being conned again? Was there some other subplot to this snakes-and-ladders game?

Hassan said, 'Look, I know it's too much to swallow at one go. I used you, but this thing's so big I couldn't risk your knowing too early in the game in case the enemy got to us. You've got to give me the benefit of doubt.'

I cut him short wearily.

'You saved my life, for God's sake, Hassan. You don't have to justify anything.'

Then another thought struck me.

'Where did I slip up? I thought I'd kept my call to Meenu pretty well hidden.'

Hassan grinned. 'You're one lousy actor, man. You made that first call to her when I was in the room, remember? You turned white as a sheet. Even switched the phone to your injured arm. I knew straightaway that that bastard Shukla had got to Meenakshi and she was tipping you off. After that it was a simple matter of keeping you in my sight. I saw you leave the hotel from my balcony.

'But I've got to say this, Chandra. Without the two of you, we'd never have got this far. Your Meenakshi, she's quite something. What did she find in the tower?'

'A sheet in code. From some ancient Buddhist text. It gave the co-ordinates to this place.'

'And that's it? Just the numbers? Nothing else that can help us?'

'Nothing else, or I'm sure Meenu would have mentioned it.'

'But how come you were climbing this thing?'

I told him about what the security guy had said. Hassan was quiet for a beat, thinking. 'It's got to be the place. The caves must lead into the mountain.'

He got to his feet and walked to the lip of the cave. Keeping out of sight, he looked carefully down and then up.

'I can't see any egress here. It'll be the level just above us. The poles go up another twenty feet and stop there.'

He made his way back and squatted on his haunches in front of me. His deep-set eyes regarded me seriously.

'You could have easily struck me down, you know. God knows, you had every reason to. But you didn't. I won't forget it. But right now I need to push you, to get you back on your feet.'

His idea was for us to climb to the cavern on top, where he was certain we'd find a passage into the mountain. My chest was tight, fear erupting like a lava bloom. We were entering the lion's den at last.

'Hassan, we can call in for help. You must have your cell.'

He shook his head. 'No dice. All the signals in the valley have been jammed. We're cut off; I'm sure everyone down there is too. That tells me another thing: they must be very close to launch. They can't sustain a signal blackout for very long.'

He asked me to stand up on my own and, to both our surprise, I managed it. My arm ached fiercely, and the buzz in my head was louder than ever, but I could walk.

'You go up first. I'll follow. That way I can arrest you if you slip. Don't show yourself at the top. There just could be someone there.'

I started up the poles. It's extraordinary how our senses – and our fear – define our limits. Last night I couldn't see for the dark, the rain

and storm. And I was alone. Now, with my sight
restored by light of day, and Hassan below me,
I went up the scaffolding quite easily using my
good arm. Just below where the lattice ended I
stopped. Hassan came up alongside. With infinite
caution, he peered over the lip.

'No one. Let's get up.'

We were in an altogether smaller cave, actually
no more than a recessed ledge, perhaps twelve …
fifteen feet deep. The roof was very low and we
had to stoop. It was completely empty save for a
tripod set in one corner. It carried a board with a
skull and crossbones and bold lettering in Arabic
and English:

CAUTION: EXTREME DANGER
Unstable wall
KEEP OFF

The tripod stood like a sentry guarding an
irregular crack in the wall just behind it. It looked
like the wall had split, leaving a gap less than
a foot wide. A flat iron bar straddled the gap,
hooked to nails at either end.

We looked at each other. Hassan's nostrils were
flared in that sign of tension that I was coming to
know well. We walked up to it. Moving the tripod
aside, Hassan unhooked the bar and peered into
the gap. He started to push himself in deeper,

trying to get a better view. Immediately, I heard his startled exclamation.

'What the …?'

He turned sideways and pushed hard against the stone. To my amazement, the rock was falling back against his weight. *He was actually deflecting the rock inwards.* I reached out to touch the stone and felt … rubber. It was a polymer, a sort of plastic material made to look exactly like the surrounding rock. So perfectly was it made and set in place that even this close, I could see no difference between it and the adjacent stone.

'This is it, Chandra. We've found the damn place,' Hassan grunted, pushing harder, simultaneously wedging himself into the gap. More pushes and heaves, then the rubber sprang back and he was in.

His whisper flowed out of the crack with a dull echo. 'Wait here.'

I waited in silence, then his voice sounded again, 'Okay. Get in. Hook the rod behind you.'

I was bulkier but squeezed through with an effort. The silence was immediate, closing in on us like a dark tomb. A sliver of light flowed in from the outside, showing up another semi-circular chamber, this one slightly larger than the one outside. On the far side, spaced in exact intervals of forty degrees, were four entrances.

Hassan said in a low voice, 'More caves.'

I felt the adrenaline pump as the recognition hit me. I said, 'Be back in just a minute.'

I went up to the cave in the middle, ducked through the low entrance and walked a few cautious steps in. A single shaft leading straight in. I backed out and went into the passage on the extreme left of the chamber. It too arrowed straight on but here I kept going till I hit another shaft, this one branching off to my left. Exactly as I had expected. I turned into it and came up short against two shafts – one on each side. The one to my right seemed to be travelling upwards. I retraced my steps to the cavern.

I held up a hand to Hassan, motioning him to hang on, and repeated the exercise for the other two. Both were variants of the second tunnel, except the spacing of the branch-offs varied, as did the tunnel inclinations. In two of them the passages went down instead of up, burrowing into the heart of the mountain. I had seen enough.

Hassan was waiting, clearly intrigued.

I wiped my damp palms on my trouser leg. 'It's a maze. A simply connected cross section in 3D, most likely. More than 100,000 combinations if tried at random.'

'What?'

'It's a maze, Hassan. I'll need to see a bit more of it to understand the general structure.'

'You mean that's a labyrinth there?' 'Not

a labyrinth. A maze. The two are technically different.'

It was the first time I saw Hassan flummoxed. He stared at me like I had sprouted another head – an oracular one spouting arcane gibberish.

'How do you know?'

'I know. I majored in math at college, and for a while solving complex maze puzzles was all I did. It's a branch of mathematics called topology.'

Hassan was shaken up, no question. I felt a perverse satisfaction at having him on the back foot for a change.

He said, 'Can you get through?'

I heard the mix of hope and excitement in his voice. I had to make some assumptions. From the look of the tunnel walls, this thing was clearly old. No sign of having been blasted out recently. Mazes of the ancient world tended to vary but they were usually of a 'simply connected' type, a technical term for a pattern where all the walls would be connected to each other or to the maze's outer boundary. The spacing of the four entrances strongly suggested the centre two were dummies. The devil of it was that this maze had a third, vertical dimension. 3D mazes could be notoriously complex.

I said, 'I'll need a piece of paper, and a compass.'

Hassan had the pencil and paper ready, but no

compass. But he had a good idea of the cardinal directions from where we stood. I took the paper from him and noted the direction of the first swing I had just seen.

'We'll enter through the left. Stay close to me, and let me have your best directional reading of the first turn on either side that we come across. Got it?'

He nodded and we started to move.

Light exploded in the chamber, bright as the sun. My pupils, dilated by the darkness, responded instantly by forcing my eyes shut, but even so the dazzle pierced my eyelids and filled my vision with an orange glow. I cowered back, blocking my face with my hands, then forced my eyes open, squinting through spread fingers. Four men in combat fatigues stood in front of the passage. Holding automatic weapons. Something stirred behind them, and they parted to allow it through. A saffron-clad figure filled the mouth of the tunnel. It stood stock-still, taking us in, then half-turned and jerked its flattened head at the armed guards. My blood was ice, the recognition instantaneous. It was a Kushan.

There are those who explore the nether regions of the earth for fun. But they tend to be well equipped, organized in groups and do it of their own free will. But even they will tell you that of the peculiar phantom that sits in the geoglogical recesses of our planet. It is a wraith that feeds on our most primordial fears: fear of blackness, of restricted spaces, of being entombed forever in a coffin of stone.

A subterranean maze magnifies these fears a hundredfold. For it is deliberately designed to hold and keep those that enter it, to confuse and sow the seeds of alarm that soon lead to full-blown panic as the victim rushes heedlessly hither and thither, unwittingly pulled with every step ever further into its maw – till all is lost and the conscious self spirals down into a hell of madness, starvation and death.

I too had traversed mazes for fun, a topological puzzle to be solved – nothing more. As a student, my friends and I had done the run of a maze beneath an old ruined tomb in Delhi, a ball of string running reassuringly behind us, a lifeline attached to the entrance. Even so, the claustrophobia had been severe and I had used a mental trick to keep it in check.

Hardly did I hear Hassan's whispered 'Stay with the maze, Chandra. Don't take your mind off it' the instant we entered the maze, I knew what I had to do. It would call for every ounce of will I possessed. I breathed deeply, then brought my fear up into active consciousness. I kept it in the centre of my vision, a living, boiling ball of emotion. I gave it a special colour – a sort of grey-green. Then I savagely began to pound on it; I beat it again and again, hammering it to the size of a pellet and then rammed it into a small corner of my brain. I tamped it down with brain matter, solid as cement. Then I began to focus on the maze.

The Kushan led the way, Hassan and I were just behind and the guards took the rear. It no longer mattered that my hands were manacled behind my back, that we were moving deeper into the Earth's bowels, that there was no guiding string, no laughter or murmur of small talk. And no light. The creature that led us didn't seem to need it. We marched along in absolute silence through a blackness so thick it was almost tactile; an ether through which we ploughed in a continuum of byzantine twists and turns with abrupt lateral runs. I moved through it all like an automaton, utterly intent on the play of the tunnel. The reading of the first turn had been taken, and I was a digital compass, processing each subsequent shift of direction and automatically logging it into a mental computer.

It soon became apparent that my hunch was accurate: the maze *was* of a simply connected type and the Kushan was 'following the left-handed wall': a classic tactic of negotiating such patterns. As long as one had the direction of the first turn

fixed in mind and kept one's sense of direction
from that exact relative point, it was possible to
literally feel the way out. However, the tunnels
also went up and down; wall-following meant I
had to flatten the 3D of the maze into a 2D plane
in my imagination and assign directions to each
relative to that of the first turn.

I walked on, 80 W Level, 81 NW Up, 82 NE Down
... 103 SSE Level ... the list of coded numbers grew;
my mental map swelled, curling and corrugating
within itself like a giant intestine. 116 NNW Level
... 117N Down ... 118 NNE Up ....

We were plunging ever deeper into the bowels
of the mountain. 66 S Down ... 45 SE Level ...
The list was becoming too long for my mind to
hold and I switched mental images to give my
memory fresh impetus. The numbers were now
phosphorescent flags attached to a physical string
that unravelled behind me, a lifeline to which I
held on with increasing desperation.

I was dimly aware that the pellet that I had
mashed into a corner was growing by the minute,
fuelled by the growing weight of a terrible
certainty: I would not be coming back out. This
was a monster of a maze: too long, too convoluted.
It was a malevolent demon of the deep and it was
swallowing us for keeps. It was only the clink of
metal on metal, metal on stone, the muffled steps
and the strained breath that told me I was not

alone in my fate, that the creature who led us would yet be our salvation.

A remote part of me sensed the freshness in the air before my conscious mind registered it. The tunnel was also noticeably brighter. A curve right and we could see it dead fifty yards ahead: a halo of light, the end of the tunnel.

My pupils had barely begun to adjust before we were out. The guards brutally pushed us to our knees. This time it was even more painful, a searing glare that was a hot brand over the eyelids. But I barely felt it. I knelt there, sucking in the fresh air, letting the light wash over me. I had no thought to my surroundings; all I knew was I was out of the abyss. I revelled in the blessedness of my release, bathing in the glow of an artificial sun. Then, slowly, I squinched my eyes open.

My first impression was that we were on a running track. A track the colour of burnt cinder that ran around an area the size of a football field. Banks of arc lamps on the vaulted dome way above threw a brilliant glare over the whole arena, heightening the similarity to a sports stadium. But there the similarity ended. Instead of the empty space of a playing field, here was a densely packed engineering factory. Row upon row of machines intermixed with assembly lines were laid with geometric precision across the centre space, demarcated by yellow lines. Lines of other colours marked inspection bays, cable trenches and pathways for electric pallet trucks carrying supplies from one end of the plant to the other. Immense cranes ran along overhead gantries, steel cables lashed around large crates and heavy pieces of equipment. Forklifts ran silently along the track to the far side. Glass cabins packed with computers and other electronic gear dotted the floor at random intervals. Figures in white, blue and khakhi dungarees moved purposefully about the whole place like ants in a colony. It was a scene that could have been lifted directly from a sci-fi movie: an advanced high-tech facility – buried deep in the heart of an ancient mountain. This was the assembly station for a weapon I hadn't really believed existed. There wasn't anything on the floor that resembled a missile but it didn't matter; beyond all doubt we had found what we were seeking.

The Kushan was nowhere to be seen. The guards seemed to be waiting for instructions: now and then a wireless crackled to life and there would be a muttered conversation. I glanced at Hassan. His face was bloodless, bathed in a wash of neon. He showed no surprise, instead he had a cool, calculating expression of one already thinking of the next move. He turned to me, jerked his head backwards and raised an eyebrow slightly. His meaning was clear: *Do you have the route in your head?* I nodded shortly, hoping I wasn't too far off the truth. My heart was still thumping from the stress of the maze, and stress is deadly to the memory. He relaxed slightly, then gave me a quick thumbs up.

The handset squawked to life. The guards hauled us to our feet and marched us clockwise along the the track till we came to a steel door. One of the guards opened it to reveal a long tube-lit corridor. We walked through till we came to a solid vault-like door. A video camera watched us from the wall bracket. The guard pressed a button on the wall. Silence, then a whirring as the door clicked open.

They hustled us in, padlocked our handcuffs to rings driven into the wall and left us. Bluish, low-intensity light from recesses in the roof barely dispelled the gloom and once more my pupils had to adjust to the abrupt lumen shift. Gradually I made out that we were in a polygonal chamber about twenty feet across. The walls, roof, even the floor were uneven: chisel-cut planes, left rough and unfinished. A vile odour of putrid flesh permeated the place, as if an animal carcass had been thrown there and left to rot.

Before I had a chance to take in any more of the place, Hassan half-bent his knees and said in a low, urgent voice, 'Chandra, move over and cover me. There's a camera above the door.'

I turned around and kept my back to the door, blocking Hassan off. He looked up into my face.

'Listen. We're close to zero hour here. I can't explain right now, but things are going to get ugly. They have to break me fast. These guys obviously have a collaborator in Missile Defence to get the missiles undetected through Indian airspace. They'll be desperate to know if I managed to get through to someone in the military before I reached Bamiyan. Someone high enough to get after them and expose the plot. Follow me to this place. Force them to abort the launch.

'But you're just a reporter: here for a scoop. I brought you here to break the story of the missiles. That's your cover; it's close enough to the truth, so stick to it. But I want you to switch sides.'

I stared at him, uncomprehending. 'What do you mean?'

'Tell them all you care about is the story. That if they'll let you, you can give this thing a whole new spin. Put it out in the best possible light to the world outside. With your reputation behind it.'

'You can't be serious. What about …'

'Dammit, Chandra, listen to me. This thing is going down to the wire. The warheads are close to launch. The one thing they want now – and want badly – is to know who else I may have spoken to in the forces.

'I want you to finger me; pretend I got through

to someone, but you don't know who. They'll expect that.'

'But … what will they do with you?'

'They're going to give me the third degree.' He shrugged. 'Look, I am trained for this stuff. I can hold out, long enough to give you a chance. They're never going to let me go. But you're in with a real chance: the *only* chance we have.'

'They'll never believe me.'

'They will. If you do it right. And you've got to. They'll have worked the media element into the plan post the strike. It's going to be the first offensive use of a nuclear weapon since Hiroshima and Nagasaki, the biggest breaking story of our times. It's absolutely critical for them to manage the media: to point all fingers at Pakistan. Your endorsement will be as big a boost as any they can expect.'

'And then … what?'

'I don't know. But you have to get out of this room. It's our only hope of getting to the missiles. You're not going to be able to disarm them, but you'll be able to get the target co-ordinates from the command vehicle that'll be right next to the TEL trailers and …' He broke off, listening. I was still immersed in the conversation, didn't hear the buzzer sound. Hassan's breath hissed out sharply. I turned round – and got the shock of my life.

21

Three men sat around the conference table in a basement room at the Intelligence Bureau building on Akbar Road, close to Connaught Circus – New Delhi's commercial heart. The meeting had started with seven people in the room; it been called ostensibly to prepare an inter-departmental internal security brief to the cabinet the following day. At least, that was what four of the seven in the room believed. In reality, its purpose was entirely different.

At innocuous intervals, each of the four received urgent summons from their superiors and had to excuse themselves. Within half an hour of the meeting being convened, only three were left at the table. In all direct and indirect communication between themselves they referred to each other only as A, B and C. Collectively, these three were the masterminds of the project called Shadow Throne – a series of carefully controlled developments designed to change the geopolitics of Asia – and the world – forever.

Up until now, the group controlling Shadow Throne had never met collectively in one location. It was an enterprise buried deep in the heart of an unsuspecting government and it was vital it remain that way, especially now that the mission would go critical in a matter of days. So far, Shadow Throne had moved with the speed and precision of a highly tuned machine, a signal monument to the group's mastery of the political and operational skills needed to pull off a clandestine operation of this complexity and magnitude. Two HATF Class V Intermediate Range Ballistic Missiles, each armed with a four-kiloton nuclear payload, were ready to move to the Af-Pak border in a matter of hours.

It was then that several developments converged – all in the space of the last twenty-four hours -- each important in themselves and collectively capable of representing a clear and present danger to Project Shadow Throne. So when the three received an urgent, unprecedented request from their point men – Shukla and Venkat Rao – for a PP or person-to-person meeting, they had reluctantly acquiesced.

The man called 'A' pressed a buzzer. The door opened to admit Rao and Shukla. They carefully locked the door. A red bulb lit up on the outside;

no one would be admitted into the room as long as it was on.

There were no greetings or acknowledgements. The three simply waited. Venkat Rao began without preamble.

'At 11 pm yesterday we sent someone to the target's place to terminate her. He failed. She took him out with a chemical spray. Before we could retrieve the situation, she vanished. We've issued an APB, but I don't think we'll find her.'

'A' said, 'Why not? She's a history professor, for God's sake.'

Rao waited a beat, then said reluctantly, 'We think Pant's got her.'

There was no overt reaction from the three men but the atmosphere in the room was suddenly sharp with tension. Then 'C' said tightly, 'What in bloody hell was he …?'

'A' held up his hand. 'Wait. Let him finish.'

Rao said, 'We've reason to believe lines of communication exist … existed … between the woman and that journalist Chandrasekhar. She's cracked the code on the slip of paper she gave us and fed him the information. At 0600 today Xiphos Soter intercepted Hassan and Chandrasekhar in the cave above Brihad II. Their interrogation will start any time now.'

All three looked at each other. 'A' said almost wonderingly, 'Those fucking amateurs. They almost got to us.' He allowed himself to relax slightly. 'Good work, Venkat. What's the residual threat?'

'There's two, actually. We don't know who else Hassan or the journo have been in touch with. We've jammed the communication networks in the valley but it's always possible they got through to someone. And then there's Pant. We've got to assume he knows the location.'

The room went quiet.

Shukla spoke up for the first time. 'We can neutralize …'

'A' cut him off before he could finish. 'No. *Don't even think it.* Pant's nobody's fool. He'll have taken precautions. The last thing we need right now is a murder investigation.'

He looked over to 'B'. 'Is it out yet?'

'B' nodded and tossed the newspaper over the table. 'It's out today.'

'Tell them.'

'B' said, 'We began to take counter-measures against Pant more than six months ago – when we started to suspect that he was onto us. We started a series of misinformation campaigns and dislocatory tactics aimed at the civilian and military establishments. We needed to stir up as much bad blood and suspicion as possible all around to keep them off balance, in continuous crisis mode. *We didn't have to attack Pant frontally: it was enough to deny him an audience by simply overwhelming the cabinet and the services in scandal.'*

Venkat Rao said, 'You mean all the scams … the …'

'A' said, 'The worms were all there. All we did was stir them up. The bugging of the finance and defence ministers' offices has the civilians foaming at the mouth, fingers pointed in every direction. And now we've got the army and the MI at each other's throats.' He tossed the newspaper to Rao. The headlines screamed from the front page:

Army blames MI team for rift: rejects charging of spying as fabricated fiction.

'A's voice was hard. 'Pant's acting director; he's a stopgap, still too junior in the system and doesn't have reach to the top. We've cut off his balls without touching him. But we can't take chances with Hassan. He's got real clout within the military. When are the mobile launchers due to roll out for the border?'

'Midnight the day after tomorrow. These TEL trucks move at a maximum speed for thirty kilometres per hour, so we've averaged it out to twenty-five kmph to allow for road conditions. The convoy will cross the Durand line and reach launch location in just over twenty hours. Launch is set for 4 am, 24 June. We can't advance the schedule. The ISAF is conducting ground operations against Talib remnants in the Gardez-Khost sector. We can't chance an interception so close to the border.'

'No matter as long as they hold to schedule. I'm more concerned about those two bastards. Rao, we've not told you this as it's been on a need-to-know so far, but we have a key man in Missile Defence. He's introduced a worm into the satellite control system to generate a transmission malfunction during the missile flight window. Both Prithvi and Advanced Air Defence will be blind. If Hassan's gone to someone over his head then we're finished. We need to break him: to find out who he might have spoken to. Hassan's been around a long while in MI; he knows people there, people who can't be bought, high enough in the set-up to cause some real damage.'

'We'll break him,' Shukla said.

'Who's working on him?'

Shukla's lips pulled back over the buck teeth in a devil's grin. 'The big man himself.'

Before us was a statue. An enormous Kushan statue. The flat head was the size of a boulder, with a topknot that stopped just short of the eight-foot ceiling. The face was that of a Greek-Asian goliath, and it fixed us with a remote, unseeing stare of the ages. Then the statue took a step forward.

Its titanic presence filled the room: an emanation of primordial power that had me cowering back, the shock now battling for dominance with fearful awe as it dawned on me that this was no statue: it was a living thing. I could not call it a man; it was altogether too monstrous for that. The form itself was a perfectly proportioned work of sculpture, only its sheer scale robbed it of any human quality. But it was the face that sent an icy barb up my spine. Eyes of pale blue swivelled in their sockets, each independent of the other, like those of some electronic robot. One orb fixed on me and the other on Hassan, examining us like we were interesting specimens.

'Welcome, my friends, to the Bamiyan Valley. Xiphos Soter has been expecting you for some time.'

I was conscious of a fleeting amazement. The voice was a deep accented rumble, but in every other respect it was completely at odds with the raw physicality of the giant figure; the English was flawless, the words perfectly enunciated.

'I regret the circumstances of your visit are somewhat … difficult. Soon, the world as you know it is about to change. The time of the Saviour has come – and the time for you to choose. Choose wisely and live.'

'Cut the shit, you big ape. I'm giving you nothing.'

Hassan's voice sliced through the chamber like a knife. I spun around, shocked. He was still crouched back against the wall, but there was a contemptuous nonchalance about him as he faced the giant.

The chill in the room deepened; both eyes slid together and locked on Hassan. A hand the size of a meat cleaver reached down and held him by the top of the shoulder. The fingers splayed out over his back, the hammer-like thumb fixing itself on the joint. Instantly Hassan was writhing; drops of perspiration erupted like boils over his face. I saw him trying to twist to one side, to ride out the grip but the hand held him completely imprisoned, like a child its toy. The veins bulged on his forehead and the neck corded as he stretched his head back, his face contorted in a terrible rictus. But he made no sound. There was a loud crack; Hassan jerked like he'd been shot and the hand released him. Hassan fell back against the wall, head hanging lifelessly on his chest.

The Kushan said conversationally, as if nothing untoward had happened, 'You do not give, Mr Hassan, it is we who take.' The orbs flicked to me. 'And we will take it bit by bit from your body. Despite what some may say, Mr Chandrasekhar, let me assure you that we are – in very large measure

– our bodies. Have you ever thought of what it means to live without your eyes, your limbs, your tongue, your sense of …'

I found it took very little for me to put as much fear as I could into my voice, 'Look, sir, whoever you are. I'm just a reporter. Please tell us what you want. *Don't hurt us, please.*'

The giant looked at me speculatively; despite the cold, I felt my shirt clinging to my back. He turned and glanced up, seemingly making a sign. The door opened and a man walked in: human, normal height, ordinary clothes. The knowledge that he was the enemy still didn't prevent the huge relief that expanded inside me. Anything than being alone with this nightmarish creature. Then I heard Hassan speak and spun around.

He was still slumped against the wall, his face ashen. He croaked, 'Shukla, you fucking traitor. You shit-faced bastard. You're going straight to hell, you …'

I noticed the newcomer had red hair and protuberant teeth. His smile was unpleasant. 'Well, well. Mister-too-clever-by-half Hassan. Not so clever this time. Looks like you still have your face left. You're not going to have it much longer if you don't do some serious talking.'

'Go to hell, you bastard.'

I said desperately, 'Hassan, don't be a fool. For God's sake … Look, Shukla, that's your name right, Shukla … just tell us what you want from us.'

Shukla's attention was on Hassan but he said to me, 'We need to know who the two of you talked to before coming here. Every name, every call. We need it. Now. Did you call or speak to anyone, tell them you were headed to Bamiyan?'

I said swiftly, 'No, I didn't. I wanted to call my contact in the home ministry but there was no time in Ghazni and when I got here, my phone went dead.' Then I hesitated, started to say something, stopped.

Shukla waited, then said, 'But …?'

I looked at Hassan. He started to swear at me, softly, viciously. I said, 'Hassan, I'm doing this for the both of us. You've got to tell them about that call or they'll …'

'What call? Who did he call?'

'That's it, I don't know. He used a call booth near the parking lot. I was outside when he made the call.' I put all the pleading I was capable of into my voice, 'Hassan, *come on, man. Tell them*.'

His face was pinched with pain; he said nothing, just turned his back to me.

Shukla said quietly, 'Excellency, how much time to break him?'

'By the evening. We will rest him in between.'

The giant's accent was noticeably thicker, with a throaty undercurrent. The eyes had filmed over, as if reflecting on something pleasurable. I realized the giant was actually looking forward to working on Hassan.

I shuddered, overcome by horror and remorse. I could not play Hassan's game, could not send him to this ghastly fate. He must have been watching me, expecting this weakening of resolve. Before I could speak, blurt out that it was all a charade, he said:

'Don't you dare write their stories for them. Don't you dare betray your country.'

I pulled back from the brink and said in a trembling voice, 'It's you who betrayed *me*, Hassan. You never told me a damn thing. What we were getting into. I almost lost my life twice in the last few days. I can't take this shit any more, man. I'm not going down with you.' I looked at Shukla, pathetically eager. 'Mr Shukla, listen. I'm a journalist. Hassan promised me a scoop and I came along. I can still do it. This story's big ... huge. Let me handle it for you. It's my chance of a lifetime. I have contacts in the media. Just tell me how you want it written.'

Shukla's horsey face had the smug look of a cat with a mouse beneath its paw. He shook his head in mock regret. 'We've got our own stooges lined up in the press and it's too risky to ...'

I said quickly, 'But I know about Xiphos Soter. I can do a real build-up on them. The lost race of the Bamiyan Valley. *A race of supermen.* With a leader to match – a world leader. It'll be the story of the decade.'

It sounded incredibly weak to me but I was aware the Kushan was listening intently.

Shukla smirked and said, 'The first thing the media is to scream about is the goddamn nuclear fallout. Millions of deaths. With all the shit hitting the fan, no one's going to worry about Xiphos Sot ...'

The giant's voice hissed out like a serpent's. 'The deaths are nothing. The world will see the Kingdom of Kanishka rise from the ashes of history. And they will see the Sword of the Saviour.'

He said, as if issuing an edict, 'This man will write about us. The glories that have been and the glories to come. Xiphos Soter has waited a thousand years. Let the world see us now – and wonder.'

Shukla shot a poisonous look at me. But I knew he couldn't go against the Kushan. It had been a last-ditch gamble that had worked – only just. He said deferentially, 'As you wish, Excellency. My only request is that you put your people around him at all times. He must not be let out of sight. The weapons leave the bay in less than forty-eight hours. This man is a potential hostile; he should be brought back and secured here by nightfall.'

'It will be done.' The Kushan turned to me,

'The guard will come for you.' The hand reached out and took Hassan by the crushed shoulder. 'And for you.'

They filed out. The door had barely shut, when Hassan said in a strained whisper, 'Move over.'

I placed myself as best I could between him and the CCTV camera. He had moved as close as he could to me and flattened himself against the wall. His face was pale and sweaty; he was slumped over and the crushed shoulder stuck out at an odd angle, making him look like a hunchback. His words came out choppy, pushed out through clenched teeth.

'Chandra. You played that well, really well. The TEL mobile launchers top priority. Don't know how … but get to them. The missiles will be a Pak design … likely set for a fixed trajectory point to point with pre-loaded target co-ordinates. Stay away from the missiles, you won't be able to disable them. Watch out instead for the command vehicle. Used for missile targeting and system check at launch point. It'll be right next to the TELs. Windowless van with antennae sprouting from the roof. It'll be the one with the target co-ordinates. You have to get in and secure them.'

'But how'll I recognize them?'

'Maps with the GPS co-ordinates. They'll be displayed inside with the ballistic flight trajectory.

Then get to a phone and call them out to Pant. Clear?'

I acknowledged with my eyes. Even as he spoke, I was miming for the camera's benefit, my body rigid, shaking my head as if I was arguing vehemently with Hassan. There was no point telling him the chances of my getting anywhere close to the missiles was negligible. He knew that already. All I could do was to pray for a break and trust to my wits if it came my way.

'What's his number?'

Hassan gave it to me, a long satphone number. 'The line will be open 24x7 and will reach him instantly. One more thing. It's a long shot but worth trying. The Qutub murder. One of the Xiphos guys turned against his own. I'm now sure he was coming to give us the tip-off when he was killed. If there was one, there could be others. Keep it in mind if you get to meet any of the other weirdos.'

Hassan smiled, a pain-filled grimace. 'That's it. Good luck. I'm sorry it had to turn out this way. I don't know how to say it without sounding cheesy, but it's been a privilege knowing you, Chandra.'

I looked at this man who faced a horrible, lingering death but who could still smile. In that moment, my respect for him soared to the ultimate plane. My hands were manacled behind me, otherwise I would have embraced him, held him to me – as brother to brother. But I could not. My eyes were filling and I couldn't trust myself to speak. I just nodded. Hassan looked at me a long time, then turned his face away and closed his eyes.

It was now T minus fifty-six hours and counting.

22

Nalini Ranjan Pant kept away from the office that day. The enemy knew he had Meenakshi and it had become too dangerous for him to even show himself in the open. Instead he had set up his transit HQ in a house near Palam, an old mansion leased out from the PWD which had acquired it just after independence. Hassan had helped set it up with military intelligence, and there was a good chance that RAW knew nothing of it. It sat by itself in a sprawling compound behind the airport staff colony with a single access road.

Pant was now bending his every resource to the task at hand, and he straightaway recognized that in Meenakshi he had another one – a smart, intuitively gifted one at that. At noon, he had her woken up from an exhausted slumber downstairs and brought up to his office.

Entering the room, Meenakshi saw Pant talking with a military man. A Sikh.

With no word yet from Hassan and the rapidly closing window of manoeuvre, Pant had decided to gamble on his instincts and take Air Commodore Jasjit Singh into confidence. He had sketched out only the bare bones of the plot, eliminating the more bizarre aspects of the affair such as the Kushan angle. As expected the officer had been frankly incredulous, ascribing the whole thing to some fantastic figment of Pant's imagination. He sat now, stiff and uncomfortable in his chair; it was clear he wished to leave. It had taken all of Pant's persuasive powers to get him to stay a while longer.

'Jasjit, this is Meenakshi Pirzada. She's a civilian seconded to my team. Meenakshi, please meet Air Commodore Jasjit Singh.'

Jasjit nodded shortly to her. Pant's aide walked in with a tray. Pant waited till the tea was poured, then said:

'I've called you both here to seek your advice and views. Jasjit, I've given you a bare-bones briefing on what I suspect. I realize you're sceptical. Let me tell you that Meenakshi here has been directly targeted by the opposition: they sent someone last night to her house to kill her. That's an absolute fact. Now, I'd like to summarize the whole thing once more, put it all in perspective to both of you and see if there's anything we can do in the very limited time – literally hours – that we likely have left.'

Pant rapidly sketched out the backdrop to the conspiracy; he laid bare the facts, hid nothing. He dealt with the essentials of the plan: the smuggling of missile parts with the Afghan aid convoys, using Xiphos Soter to foment the rise of the Hazara people and the ultimate dismemberment of Pakistan.

He explained how it went to the very highest levels of the intelligence bureaucracy, effectively outgunning him so that he had very little traction to take them on. His belief that some of the unending scandals were being deliberately blown up to sow the seeds of further paralysis in the country's decision-making apparatus.

But it was all nebulous: a connection that existed in the mind of a single intelligence officer of middle rank. Pant did not have a shred of hard evidence. The decision to send out Hassan and Chandra, to inveigle ISI into spiriting them into Afghanistan was an effort by Pant to get precisely that: clear evidence of the existence of a rogue missile site under Indian control.

Thanks to Meenakshi, the mission had succeeded in establishing the likely site as the Bamiyan Valley. But then the trail had petered out. Completely. Chandra had left for Bamiyan, Hassan in tow. Pant had no doubt Hassan intended to establish contact from there, but that had not happened. Instead there was absolute silence since almost two days. Sending in another agent was impossible: RAW would be watching. And now time had run out.

He had, Pant said, three options. One – go to the press now. Allege a conspiracy and hope that would create enough of a stink to put a crimp in the enemy's plans. Pant's career would be finished and he would probably face a prison term, but that was a price that had to be paid. Two – do their damnedest to get through to someone high enough in the government. Somehow persuade him or her to take them seriously and initiate counter-measures. Three – wait and hope that Hassan and Chandra could still pull it off.

Pant was cracking his knuckles as he spoke, a measure of the wound-up tension in a man normally always still and composed.

'I need ideas. Do we just wait here, or can we do something?'

The air force man said, 'I'm still trying to take it in, Nalini. Are you sure about this? Couldn't it be some gigantic mistake? I mean, I'm having serious difficulty believing the whole thing.'

'Jasjit, bullets don't lie. They tried to kill Hassan and Chandra. Then Meenakshi here. That murder at the Qutub. They are stopping at nothing. Why? What are they protecting?

'And then I made discreet enquiries at the AEC and the DRDL in Hyderabad a few days ago. Guess what? Four of our senior scientists are on leave. *Four.* One of them's K. V. K. Sastry, their leading guy on gyros and triggers. And they're not saying more without higher clearance. Even if I'm wrong about this stuff, can we afford to take a chance?'

Jasjit Singh rubbed his forehead. He had the air of a man who had been dropped into *The Twilight Zone*. He said reluctantly, 'No, that's the one thing I agree with. We can't take the smallest chance. So here's my take. I don't think Two is an option. Let's say you get to someone at the top: say the cabinet secretary or the principal secretary to the PM. Then what? Even if they decide to act immediately, they'll send for the national security advisor. The NSA's very likely above board, but what's he going to do on his own? He has to refer down the chain of command. Then they'll be on you like a ton of bricks. You're dead before you've even begun.'

'Yes. But I would have brought it to the attention of the powers that be. They'll have to initiate some sort of an investigation. And I could go to the media: pull the wraps off this thing.'

'Sorry, Nalini, but I don't see it. The launch happens, the evidence pours in and it all points to Pakistan. The investigation will be a non-starter. The whole country will be up in arms. The press, the politicians baying for blood. *You'll* be seen as the traitor for pointing fingers at us instead of the real bad guys across the border. And think of the immediate aftermath. The government will have to respond. The pressure to launch our own nukes at them will be enormous. Think of it – an all-out nuclear exchange. The airwaves will be jammed solid for days – everywhere around the globe. Your voice won't even make it through the mayhem. You'll be blown just away. That is why your first option looks damn weak.'

Meenakshi said hesitantly, 'Mr Pant, you said the missiles could be launched in a matter of hours. What is the basis for the time frame?'

'When Rao and Shukla came to see me, they agreed to a meeting that could potentially expose their hand. In a week's time. That was four days ago. It's an indicator at best, I agree. But my instinct tells me it is the correct one. They'll launch from just over the Pak border so the location can later be traced back to satellite images to tie up the evidence. That means the launchers will have to exit the Bamiyan area under cover of darkness sometime the day after tomorrow.'

'Can't we mount a surveillance over the area and stop them when the vehicles are coming out?'

Pant said simply, 'I don't have the bandwidth or resources to do it. It'll mean going up the chain of command. Back to Option Two.'

Jasjit Singh said, 'And back to the question of

time. No way to roust the PM and get him to take any effective action in the time we have left.'

Pant nodded, 'Exactly.'

Meenakshi said, 'That poor man at the Qutub … the Kushan. He was killed trying to reach us. If there was one, there could be others like him. I'm positive Hassan and Chandra would know that. So maybe they're not alone there.'

Pant blinked slowly. 'Absolutely. It's a small hope that I've kept alive. Jasjit, these guys have a mole in Missile Defence. *They have to*. It's the only way they can be a hundred percent sure the thing will get through. Anything we can do on that? Check and see if our satellites scans are pucca? Are we fully covering our airspace for intrusions of any kind?'

'We do – for aircraft interception. Missiles are tricky; speeds and altitudes are quite different. The last anti-missile exercise we had was encouraging. But the AAD grid is still in the test tube. The plan is to cover Delhi around one year from now and gradually the rest of the country. Right now it's 50:50. And no way we can handle multiple targets unless we have their flight path co-ordinates.

'And, as for the mole …' Jasjit shrugged. 'I don't know, Nalini. In this scenario anything is possible. But can we get to the guy in time or even do a complete systems check? I don't think so. Not without solid evidence and clearance at the highest level.'

Meenakshi said, 'How will they take the missiles to the Pakistan border?'

It was the air force man who said, 'TELs. Transporter Erector Launchers. They're massive, but they're squat and flat, easy to disguise as specially made up cargo trucks. But I think they'll cover them with tarpaulin, not a hard top like a container.'

'Can't we somehow intercept them en route?'

Pant went quiet for a bit, thinking. Then he said, 'The container traffic in those parts is huge. It'll be like finding a needle in a haystack. I just don't have the resources.'

Meenakshi said, 'There is a fourth option.'

'What?'

'We reach out to Gul Mohammed.'

One character on whom I had lavished a fair share of my pre-teen fantasies was Phantom. I still saw him, etched clearly through the unchanging prism of my youthful imagination, the masked superhuman sitting on his stone seat within the skull cave, deep in the heart of the jungle.

This was that seat: a carved block of gargantuan proportions. It appeared to be from an archaeological site: the dimples, cracks and yellow blemishes on the stone glimmered in the russet glow of the fire lamps, its edges limned with a pulsating radiance, giving it an eerie – almost living – aspect.

I was in the great hall of Xiphos Soter, and upon the seat, filling it completely, sat Autokrator. I had been standing before him for almost an hour: an hour in which I had fought desperately against the primordial presence on the throne. The more I fought it, the more it seemed to hold me in its thrall, claim me for its own, a willing instrument to its will.

The vision that Autokrator – for that was what he called himself – laid out before me was that of a new world order: a grand design worthy of an Alexander. The new Bactrian kingdom – to be called Theophila (I knew now what 'Tofulu' meant) – would be just the beginning of a New Age, a fusion of the religions of Central Asia. In its perfection, Theophila would conquer all before it, not so much through war but through the minds of men. Kanishka the Saviour had foreseen it, chosen Autokrator himself as the instrument of its accomplishment.

I listened, my face eager, my manner craven. But inside I was rocked. I thought of Shukla and his masters back in India and wondered whether this was also their doing. For this Theophila was as unreal as Shangri-La. It was a jagged piece that would be force-fitted into the ethnic and religious jigsaw of Central Asia, an island of Hazaras –

fervent followers of Shia Islam – sitting bang in the middle of a sea of Sunni Afghanistan-Pakistan. Ruled by a group of fanatics from another age. The whole thing was a disaster waiting to happen.

Autokrator's eyes of washed blue were on me, as if he had caught a dissonance in my manner. I caught at myself.

'Excellency, your vision takes my breath away. Not for one moment did I dream that such a thing was possible. Only you, Autokrator, could have made it possible. Only you. Sire. It is a story that will astonish the world.'

A pinprick of light flared in those dead eyes. 'Yes. The world will look on in ...' He stopped, as if listening to something, then he said, 'I wonder about you, scribe. You're too eager, too cowardly. Your outside: it does not sit well with what I see inside you. Inside you do not believe.'

I said nothing, felt my skin prickle, the sweat bead my forehead. Autokrator stirred. 'You do not believe the vision. Even though it has been foretold by the Saviour himself. No matter. In yourself you are an insect. Of no importance. But you will write and you *will* tell the world of him who whose rule is to come. You are wondering how Theophila will hold, are you not?'

Before I could respond, he said softly, 'Pars–Iran will help us.'

Iran. I'd completely forgotten. Directly to the

west – sharing an entire border with Theophila – was the enormous landmass of Shia Iran. Iran – with its rallying cry to Shias the world over.

That was when I knew. This first-century monster understood enough of twenty-first century politics. Autokrator's pillar-like arm rose and swept all before it.

'Behold now the Sword of the Saviour. Hundreds more of the brethren have gone out into Bactria, preparing the people for the moment that is upon us.'

Lined to one side were perhaps three dozen Initiates. Tall, with that massive build I had come to expect, the plagiocephalic skulls, the Greek profile. In some the almond eyes were more pronounced, showing up the ethnic mix of the centuries. All wore saffron robes in the manner of Buddhist monks, the cloth crossed over half the chest leaving the other half bare. Acolytes were filing in, many more of them, massing behind the Initiates, a sea of white robes and shaven heads. These were ethnic Hazaras, and there was no mistaking the look of profound reverence on their faces.

A thrill of awe rose in me as I took in the scene. The dimly lit vaulted hall soaring to the heavens, the massed audience like ancient statues, the raw power of this gigantic figure on the throne. For a moment I felt dislocated, transported back centuries to another age. I felt insignificant, immaterial: a mere speck in the grand sweep of history.

Then the image of Hassan flashed before me. Hassan, speaking in short staccato gasps, laying his charge on me, a charge made sacred by the totality of his self-sacrifice. The missiles. They were all that mattered. I would get to them or die in the attempt. But this could be no kamikaze death, no leap to glorious martyrdom. I had to use my brain coolly at the very moment when he was being subjected to unspeakable torment. Something bared its teeth deep inside me, breaking me out of my thrall.

Autokrator switched to Dari and said in a loud voice, 'My children, this is a scribe from Hind. He is here to record our moment in history, when the will of Kanishka shall be …'

One of the guards with the SMGs moved near the hallway entrance. There was a murmur of voices and then an Initiate came hurriedly in. The bile rose in my throat. His robe was spattered with blood. He spoke in Autokrator's ear. The giant rose up and pointed to the guard and then to me.

'Wait here.'

Then he was gone and I was alone with the Initiates, with just the guards in attendance. It had all happened so quickly it caught me unprepared. But here it was: my chance in a million, the chance I was waiting for. My thoughts raced. I had to get through to the ones in the hall who might know and make a clear connection to the dead man at the Qutub, yet keep it innocuous. I raised my voice and said in English, 'Is there one among you who will translate my English to Dari?'

My heart was thudding. I faced them squarely, didn't look at the guard.

There was a shifting in the ranks, then a Kushan strode forward. 'I know. Little. Enough if you simple.'

'Thank you. I will keep it simple.' I raised my hand with my notebook in it. 'Brothers, I am here to write of the glorious rebirth of Theophila.'

I waited for the Initiate to translate, which he did in a halting voice. The serried rows stood straighter, drinking in my every word.

'I am no student of history, but I am from Hind, and who in Hind does not know of King Milinda – he of the Milindapanha? Who does not know of his great successor, Kanishka?

'He who brought Milinda's questions to Al Hind has passed on. May he rest in peace. But the Word lives, and we in Al Hind – in the world – have desperate need of its true meaning. I am here to receive it from Xiphos Soter.'

There was a ripple of puzzlement in the ranks; some of the monks turned to look at each other. Before I could continue, the guard's wireless crackled. He lifted it to his mouth and answered briefly, then gestured to me with his weapon. I folded my hands in a namaste and bowed. Then I walked out of the hall.

My being put back with Hassan was doubtless deliberate, an attempt to crack his will with the comfort of my presence. He lay on the floor, naked, breathing heavily. Now and then he jerked up, spasming before falling back on the floor. Even a novice like me could see they had worked him carefully. There were some horrific overt signs of damage: his fingernails had been yanked out and the top phalange of his right thumb was a crushed pulp, but I was sure the real torture had been of a different kind. There were raw burn marks on his torso and near his testicles. He had bitten through his lower lip and the blood covered the lower half of his face and neck.

I strained desperately against my handcuffs, yanked at them savagely to reach for him, to let him know I was there. He spasmed again and cried out. I felt a burn of hot, incandescent rage at our captors. In common with much of the press community, I was a cynic. I had seen too much taint in people to be convinced that one could act in a spirt of true virtue, that all altruism was ultimately not thinly veiled self-interest. But nor did I admit to the existence of pure evil. The world was neither white nor black, just shades of grey. I saw now how utterly wrong I had been in my self-satisfied belief. This was as black as it came – pure, unalloyed evil.

I squatted down as far as my manacles would allow and whispered, 'Hassan, it's Chandra. I got through to Xiphos. I managed to convey the message. If there's another of them, he will know. I am going after the missiles soon. Hang in there, Hassan. *Hang in there.*'

There was no reply. I didn't know if he had heard me or not. I turned and looked once more at the door. It was smooth inside, no handle. I could almost sense its heavy steel. The video camera watch me with an unblinking eye.

Hassan said in a hoarse whisper, 'Chandra.'

I was bent over in a flash, straining towards him. The words came slowly, laboured and distorted through his severed lip. 'Electric shock. Some new ga...gadget. Next time ...very bad. Will try ... hold back. Give you time ... get to command van ...' His voice trailed away and he fell back into his private blackness.

I sat there, trying to get a grip on myself, to tamp down on the incendiary mix of rage and despair before it overwhelmed me. My whispered assurances to Hassan were to comfort him in his pain, nothing more. The odds of finding an ally in Xiphos Soter were next to zero.

The missiles. I had to get to the missiles and the command vehicle would be parked next to them. But how? My mind scrabbled uselessly at the problem before I forced myself to focus on what I already had. Slowly, deliberately, I began to construct a visual layout of the place in my mind. I'd been taken three times along the track that lined the factory arena, and each time I had done an automatic visual sweep of the place. I could see it now: the main floor like a hub with tunnels radiating out like spokes in different directions. I placed the exits precisely as I remembered them. I labelled those I had already navigated. Some of the passages clearly were dead ends, lined with rooms like the one we were in. Others linked the hub to various parts of the subterranean complex. One of them had led to the great hall of Xiphos Soter. There had to be another leading into the missile chamber.

I had no idea of the size of these things, but an ICBM or whatever it was would be at least a metre in diameter and possibly eight ... ten metres tall. And filled with fuel. *So: tall and heavy.* Probably carried out on a trolley of some kind. So the exit opening from the assembly area would have to be big enough to allow the missile to pass through and it would have to be within direct access of the gantry crane. I reviewed my mental map. There were two that matched in size, both covered by retractable shutters of clear plastic, at either end of the west wall. *Which one?* I closed my eyes, letting my thoughts flow intuitively, did a slow scan of the map displayed in 3D before me … And then I had it.

A discontinuity in the assembly area. The entire shop floor was densely packed with equipment and workbenches. Every square foot had been used up – except in the southwest corner. A section there looked empty, recently vacated. I could see it now: littered wiring, empty cardboard cartons, a long rest-rail, all lying loosely around. The missile assembly area. Had to be. One of the shuttered exits was directly adjacent to it.

There was an electric buzz and the door clicked open. I jerked up, startled; the chain of my thoughts broke and I stared uncomprehendingly at the guard. He gestured with his SMG. I went up to the door. He swung me around and unlocked my cuffs. I picked up my notebook and pencil.

We marched counter-clockwise along the track. Presumably I was being taken back to the big hall. To the left, the factory floor was mostly empty except for a few technicians inside the glass cabins: an ominous sign that told me a great deal.

No one was looking at us. At a subliminal level, I think I had made up my mind to act. To seize a chance: any chance, however slender, however foolish and impossible. I *had* to.

We walked past the exit of the maze, the point where we had first entered this place. *Now.* I spun right and sprinted into the tunnel. I heard the guard's startled shout, half-smothered as I raced straight through and then darted into the first passageway to my left. As I had expected, the guard did not raise an instant alarm. I had watched these security guys from the time we had been brought here. They were all scared witless of this place, of the Kushans. My escort was no exception. He probably understood that a slip-up like this would be dealt with mercilessly.

He came in after me. I crept back another ten yards, came to another right channel, moved in and waited. My heart thudded in the dark. I could hear him clearly, the stillness and my heightened senses magnifying the scrape of his feet. Closer … closer. I heard him stop in front of my shaft. His breath was shallow, uncertain. I made a small rustling sound and he froze. A metallic click punctured the dark, then silence. I knew he had snicked off the safety catch. It lasted for a full minute then I heard him again, entering the tunnel after me. I stood completely still, my senses reaching out, probing. He was now just a few yards out. I could hear the rasp of his gun strap, the clink of metal, feel his hair-trigger tension. He shuffled forward another step, then another.

I judged the distance and threw my notebook

with a hard underarm swing that sent it flying over him. It landed with the sound of a pistol shot in the muffled gloom. I launched myself after it. The guard had spun about in the direction of the sound, for I rammed into his back full tilt. He buckled and fell with my bulk on top of him. He grunted in pain as the weapon dug into his torso and tried to roll from beneath me, but my clenched fist was already scything down, smashing into his temple with all the force I could muster. He slumped and went still.

My chest was heaving. I rolled him over and with shaking fingers began to undo his uniform. Fumbling in the dark, I stripped him down, pulled off my own shirt and ripped the sleeves out. Twisting them into ropes, I tied his hands and feet and then stuffed a wad of cloth into his mouth. There was no way of knowing how long the trusses would resist his struggles, but I repeated every knot twice and pulled the ends tight with as much strength as I could muster.

Less than five minutes later I walked out of the tunnel in uniform, the cap pulled low over my face, the SMG slung over my shoulder. The guard was smaller than I was and the uniform was way too tight. His shoes crushed my toes. But I hoped it would pass a casual inspection. Anything more than a casual look and I would anyhow be dead. I paused, looking around. Nothing untoward.

All the action had happened inside the tunnel and no one had noticed. I started off counter-clockwise along the track at a brisk pace, towards the southwest side of the floor. I took a look at the guard's wristwatch. 1800 – 6 pm. Exactly twelve hours since we had been taken prisoner; over seven hours since Hassan's interrogation had started. I felt the perspiration run down my face and back. Any moment now I expect the bell to sound, boots to pound on the track behind me, soldiers to burst out the doors. Even if the guard didn't get free himself and raise the alarm someone would be coming soon to investigate, to see why I hadn't been produced.

I quickened my pace, circling the arena. The plastic shutter came up on my right. It was one of those jobs that could be mechanically retracted. I pressed the green button on the wall console to rack it up a few feet and ducked through.

The scene before me could have been right out of the James Bond film *Moonraker*. I was in a hangar of sorts. The missiles were right there, directly in my line of vision. Two tall olive-green cylinders, shining dully under the arc of the fluorescent lamps. The half-moon crescent of Pakistan was prominently visible just below the nose cone as were the letters GHAURI. Each missile was mounted on a ladder-like frame. Twin hydraulic shafts on either side propped up the frame at a forty-five-degree angle. The whole system was mounted on enormous trucks, the largest land vehicles I had ever seen, massive as battle tanks, but much longer and low slung with a serried train of tires along the entire length. Festoons of wire ran from the missiles to a computer bank set inside an open van with satellite dishes and antennae on its roof. The rear doors were open and I could see several men in white coats clustered around the screens. Two others were bent over an open panel on one of the missiles, calling out from checklists in their hands. Security men were everywhere, SMGs at the ready.

The snapshot appraisal had taken me just seconds. A few heads were already turning in my direction. I raised my hand in greeting, stepped back through the shutter and thumbed the close button. I forced myself to walk away slowly, back the way I had come. I had found the missiles, but there was no feeling of satisfaction that my surmise had proved accurate. Instead, my mouth was dry, I was having difficulty breathing. My stupidity had almost done me in. It was blindingly obvious that security around the missiles would be tight. Had I really thought I could just stroll up and take the readings? My jaw was clenched, and my fingers dug painfully into my palms. Feverishly, I tried to think of something: anything that would get me back there with a chance.

Maybe I should just brazen my way through. Pick up a conversation with a guard, wait for them to break for dinner and ... I thrust the thought away. It was a pipe dream. They were never going to leave the missiles alone, not till the trucks left the place. The trucks ... I paused, the thread of an idea forming. I crossed the exit that led to the great hall and kept going, stepping up my pace. The maze presented the best option for what I wanted to do next.

I heard someone call out behind me. I ignored it, kept walking. The call was repeated, louder this time. I turned around, keeping my head down. A half-naked figure stood at the mouth of the tunnel I had passed with two armed men in tow. It was the man I had disarmed. He started to gesticulate, to ask me something, when his eyes widened. He opened his mouth to shout, but I was already bringing up my gun. I pressed the trigger. The gun rode up, the recoil huge in my untrained hands and the burst of automatic fire shattered the stillness of the dome. And then I was running, ducking and weaving. The staccato chatter of answering fire was almost immediate. The air about me filled with a high whine as bullets whizzed past. I tore around the corner, making for the maze. Glass blew out of the cubicles, dissolving under the hail of bullets. I was distantly aware of more shouts, commotion in the arena. White coats were scattering away from me, getting out of the line of fire, but one outsized orange figure detached itself from the rest and moved to cut me off. It was a Kushan.

He was at the far end opposite. I raised my gun, sighting from the hip and let loose a burst, more as a deterrent than with any hope of hitting him at this range. The Kushan ignored it, accelerating instead. I pressed the trigger again. Nothing. He was on the track now, coming straight at me. Even through the intensity of the moment, I noticed the man's loping stride, the perfect balance and fluid power of a big cat running down its prey. The tunnel mouth came up. I squeezed the trigger one more time with the same result: just a click. I unslung it from my shoulder and let it drop. Then I sped into the maze.

I was drowning once more, flailing about in waters oily and black, sinking like a stone into the darkness closing above me. Never since that morning – so long ago it seemed lost in the mists of time – when the Fates had taken me to the Qutub and then sent me hurtling down a corkscrewing slide of treachery and evil, had I ever known the utter helplessness that now claimed me for its own. Not even when I hung face down in the void, or when I first came face to face with the demon that called itself Autokrator.

The footfalls behind me were sure. I was being hunted in the dark by a remorseless enemy who knew the maze better than I did. I had run out of time. I had failed Hassan. My plan of making it through the tunnel, shooting my way out the other side and getting to the ASI camp in the valley was always a wild fancy born of a desperate impulse to act – to do something – at any cost. I had no idea how I would reach Hassan's controller and, if I did, what he could do stop the warheads, but either way the chances seemed at the time infinitely better than being trapped by the rapidly closing options before me. But even that slender hope was now gone, shredded and scattered in these tunnels.

My pursuer made no effort to disguise his presence; he knew he had me unarmed, trapped inside the winding warren. The exits would be blocked on either side and it was only a matter of minutes before he caught up with me. I reversed the 3D map in my mind as I ran, re-ordering it back to front, staying now with the right-hand wall. But the time had come for an all-or-nothing move. Even as the thought came to me I broke the iron law of the maze, moved away from the wall and cut left. I kept my fingers splayed, letting them brush against the sides to guide me along. The passage went straight for a bit, then bent itself into a U and almost immediately started to climb. The traverse became steeper. Soon I was panting with the effort of traversing the incline. My fingers told me the chute was narrowing, the walls closing in with each step. Soon I was bent double and then forced onto my knees. The tunnel narrowed some more; I had the sense of being slowly crushed inside a tube. I grit my teeth, fighting against the surging panic that threatened to swamp me, the scream starting to build up inside.

My hands touched a sharp ridge. I ran my fingers over it, felt the divider. The tunnel pipe had broken into a Y junction, each branch around three feet in diameter the size of a sewer water pipe. I lay there in the murk, my chest heaving, trying to decide. It was getting difficult to breathe. Crawling back was impossible now; retreat was not an option. *Left or right?* I tried to place my position on the maze map. I had traversed well to the left of the main channel, so the right-hand path was seemingly the way to go. But there was something about this diversion; it had a malignant feel to it, as if left there to trap those foolish enough to venture into its reaches. I wriggled into the left pipe.

It was a never-ending crawl that tested the limits of my sanity. I scrabbled savagely at the dirt, burrowing like an animal. Now and then a moan escaped me as the terror of that hole, the complete, total mind-destroying horror of it consumed me. I ground my teeth, gnashing them together. I pushed and pushed and *pushed.*

I dug into the dirt with my fingers, thrust forward with my toes; inched forward like a centipede. I was sloping down now, correcting for the earlier climb. I scrabbled faster, thrusting with my hips. The tunnel widened and then it debouched into a level passage. I felt the onrush of an enormous blessed relief; my instinct hadn't played me false.

I eased myself out violently, careless now of noise. I fell out of the tunnel and lay there in the passage, trembling violently all over, like a man with ague. There was a whisper of a sound, a gust of movement behind and then I was gripped by arms like steel hooks.

23

The adrenalin that hits the bloodstream in moments of crisis is the pure physical reaction of a biological organism preparing for its supreme purpose: survival. The textbooks call it 'flight or fight'. But overlaid on it is a kind of a sixth sense, an instantaneous awareness of the nature of the threat. And when it knows that neither fight or flight is possible, it trips the body into a default mode: paralysis. That was what happened to me. In the flash of a nanosecond, I knew I was utterly outmatched; nothing I did against that kind of strength would make the slightest difference to the outcome.

I stood passive and unresisting, allowing the Kushan to turn me by the shoulder. I had expected to be clubbed down, beaten to my knees. Instead, though the grip on my shoulders did not slacken, I had the curious impression of being studied, as though the creature was somehow taking my measure in the pitch-dark. Then a giant hand locked my wrists together in a crushing grip and the other fastened itself around my throat.

My captor lifted me off the ground and took off. He flew like the wind, with long even strides, holding me up in front like a bizarre standard. I had no idea why he was holding me in this awkward way. I supposed it was the position that best immobilized me. His orders must be to deliver me back alive. It was no longer fear of certain death that haunted me. It was the realization that I had failed. All chances of getting through to the missiles were gone. In my pathetic efforts, I had failed Hassan. Failed the country. Millions would die. I closed my eyes as the anguish of it washed through me. The dice was loaded against us from the very start, the enemy possessed unlimited resources and power and they were expecting us and ready. But none of it took away the pain.

The darkness rushed by, thick as flowing water. My captor must have had the eyes and the perfect co-ordination of a cat, for not once in all the twists and turns of the maze did I feel even the smallest brush of stone on my body. We went on like this went on for what must have been a quarter of an hour. The Kushan never let up pace; only once did he stop, as if listening. His breathing was even, showing no sign of stress from the punishing run. I smelt sandalwood incense mixed with sweat.

Then we were off again. I had lost my sense of direction, knowing just enough to realize we were following another route; a diagonal seemed to arrow across the maze, accessible only to those who knew it intimately. And then it struck me that we had been on the move for much longer than necessary to get back to the main holding area. My arm – miraculously dormant the last few hours – was again throbbing in fierce protest against being forced back and pinned. My throat was seriously hurting with the pressure on the windpipe. But through all of it, a sliver of doubt was beginning to creep up inside me, small, hesitant, but edged with uncertain, unbelievable hope.

A wink of light showed up ahead, then faded, then came on again, flowing through a gap in the stone some fifteen feet to our right. My captor slowed down. He negotiated a dogleg, then set me down. I could see his backlit outline, pointing now to an orifice in the wall. It was less than three feet high, so I got down on my hands and knees and crawled in. It was still dark, but a glimmer of luminescence from the light source outside bounced off the rock and showed up a boulder on the floor, a shapeless boulder. I reached out and felt cloth – and flesh. And a shock of recognition. It took all my self-control not to cry out. I crawled closer, put my head close, ran my trembling fingers over the body to check if it was not some mistake. Even in the murk, there was no mistaking the angular profile, the faint odour of Benson & Hedges. It was Hassan.

He didn't react to my touch, clearly unconscious. But he was breathing. I caught him to me, cradling him to my chest. Hassan. In the flesh. Solid. In my arms. I felt the emotion well up in a tidal wave, my face crumpled and … The Kushan tapped me roughly from behind. I turned around to see him gesturing urgently. I backed out slowly, holding onto Hassan. The Kushan was on his feet, his outline limned with the radiance from the passage. He held up his hand in warning and pointed unmistakably. *We must go. Now.* I stood up, then bent down to pick up Hassan, but the Kushan thrust me aside. He lifted Hassan carefully and slid him over his shoulder. The body looked lifeless, hanging there like sackcloth. I felt a stab of anxiety but there was no time for speculation. The Kushan was moving off. I could see the orange glow getting brighter. He jerked his head at me: *Keep close to the wall.*

The tunnel had a disused look. Cobwebs straddled the corners in thick cottony festoons and the smell of bat dung was heavy in the air. Light came through in pinpoints between piled stones that covered a two-foot hole at the base of the wall. After the long dark, even the little holes of light stung like needles. I peered ahead through half-shut eyelids. From the mud and dirt caked about the joints, it appeared to be a long abandoned shaft.

The Kushan put Hassan down gently and stepped forward with infinite caution. I felt a familiar chill at the sight of the flat skull now silhouetted like a puppet's in some monstrous shadow play. He squatted by the pile, listening intently, then he pulled out a single rock, exposing a hole. He put his face close to it and listened again. Then beckoned me forward.

In a few minutes, we had cleared the pile and crawled through. We stood on a black-topped tarmac. Bracketed industrial lamp fixtures mounted all along the wall threw a bright light over what seemed to be a highway tunnel. By their illumination I saw my rescuer clearly for the first time. It was the Initiate who had offered to translate my English to Dari in the great hall. He bent and put his mouth close to my ear and breathed in a guttural whisper, 'I Dinna. Man died in Al-Hind … name Sena. My brother.'

The Kushan stepped back and regarded me gravely. I looked at him, stunned. Sena … the brother at the Qutub. I leaned weakly back against the wall, my legs all rubbery. I breathed deeply, struggling to absorb it. The wafer of a hope that had risen in the tunnel was now the truth. Thanks to Hassan, a one-in-a-million chance had paid off. In the darkest moment of my whole life, I had been sent a deliverer. I was back with a chance. And so was Hassan.

As it all started to seep in, the joy and elation started to rise inside me like a sweet nectar. My blood sang and I was filled with a new, heady resolve. If at that moment Autokrator himself had shown up I believe I would have faced him coolly.

Dinna. I looked wonderingly at my saviour. It was astonishing to know he actually had a name; I had never associated names with these strange men of Xiphos Soter who seemed ancient as time itself. Yet here he was: Dinna. The hunter who had miraculously turned out to be an ally. I held out my hand to him impulsively.

'Thank you, Dinna. Thank you for helping us. I am sorry about your brother.'

He took my hand shyly, in the manner of one not used to it. Till then, the Initiates had been one identical, sinister mass. But as I looked into Dinna's face with newly awakened eyes, I saw how wrong I had been. Other than the shape of his head, there was an almost perfect symmetry to his features. His brow was wide, the eyes fine drawn, almond shaped, the irises a warm brown, flecked with gold – like a fawn's. His expression was sombre, weighed down, but even so the immediate impression was of a sharp intelligence.

Then he dropped my hand and shook his head grimly, pointing ahead as if to say *I don't know how we're going to do it.*

It came home to me then with a thump; we still had the mission ahead of us. I recognized that I had been in thrall to the drug high of this incredible reprieve. He was right: we still had an impossible task ahead. Four impossible tasks actually. Even with Dinna's help, I could see no way to the command vehicle, to get the readings and transmit them to Pant. And come away alive.

The Kushan tapped me on the shoulder and started his sign talk. He mimed the missile cylinder, held his palms parallel and moved them forward. Then pointed at the lit tunnel. The trucks. This was the way they would exit the mountain. The wall-mounted lights, the width of the thing: it matched. He had taken me directly through the maze to the truck exit roadway. My excitement mounted; I nodded to show I was with him.

Soon we were hastening along the road corridor, with the Kushan in the lead. It looked like Hassan was coming awake on Dinna's shoulder; he twitched and I thought I saw him mouth something in his sleep. We'd been on the move some 500 yards when the illumination ended and it got progressively darker, but a wash of residual light still reached us. Dinna slowed a little, seemingly looking for something. Then he grunted.

It was a steel cabinet, the type that houses an electrical panel. It stood to our right, against a recess in the wall, but still projecting around two feet into the tunnelway. Dinna put Hassan down and with an effort squeezed himself into the gap between the wall and the cabinet and entered the alcove behind it. I helped him transfer Hassan inside and then joined him.

As we crouched there in silence, I could see the outlines of our new-found ally's plan. We were waiting for the missile convoy. I tried to imagine it: the two huge flatbeds I had seen in the missile bay. The things were trailers, where the driver cabin was distinct from the goods section coming up at the rear. I guessed they would probably be sandwiched between escort vehicles for protection. The roof of the tunnel looked low and clearance would be tight. That meant a slow, steady progression through the tunnel. We would be making the jump when they crossed.

Dinna was looking at me intently, as if following the train of my thoughts. His English was passable as I knew from the hall, but clearly he wasn't taking the slightest risk in case there was somebody about. He jerked his hand emphatically, the right hand slicing down and moving, separating. He was drawing the shape of the articulated missile transporter. We would make the jump in the gap between the driver's cabin and the loaded rear section. He mimed once more, shutting his eyes with his palms and jabbing his thumbs in the direction that we had come. The vehicles to the rear would be on the blind side: the rear of the first truck and the narrow gap between the vehicle's sides and the panel would give us a moment – no more – of concealment. The timing would have to be split-second accurate.

We waited. The minutes ticked by in silence. My nerves were beginning to crawl. By now a massive manhunt would have well and truly been launched at the heart of the complex. I wondered by what magic Dinna had spirited Hassan out of the torture chamber. *That* would have set the cat among the pigeons. I had been seen running into the maze, Dinna in pursuit. What would they make of it? Did they know of this exit? If Dinna did then surely other Initiates would know of it too. My thoughts swirled through a myriad possibilities. Only one thing was certain: the search was going to spill here soon. I could only pray that our escape had scared them enough to evacuate the missiles fast. The trucks were our only ticket out of the mountain.

Hassan stirred, called out aloud. I quickly placed my hand over his chest to calm him. His body went still, then abruptly he awoke. My vision had adjusted to the ambient light by now and I could see clearly. His gaze fell first on Dinna. His face contorted into a rictus of agony and he shrank back visibly. I thought it was from fear, but I saw he was actually drawing tightly into himself, as if he was shutting himself down. He had probably done the same thing every time they had hit him with the electric prod and that was his first reaction on seeing the Kushan. Gently, I turned his face towards me. He looked at me, uncomprehending, as if his brain was not registering what his eyes were telling him.

I smiled at him and whispered, 'It's okay, Hassan. He's the one you asked me to watch out for. He's one of us. He got you out of there.'

Still that blank look, then very slowly I saw a spark awaken. A growing awareness … then an unasked question in his eyes. I nodded, put my head close to his and spoke in a soft undertone, pausing with each word.

'We escaped; now we're in the exit tunnel. Waiting for the missile carriers. Have to get on when they pass us. How are are you feeling?'

He didn't answer. His eyes flicked back and forth between me and Dinna, looked around him, as if he didn't quite believe me. His lips opened, trying to form words.

After many tries he said huskily, 'And the big … big …'

'The big guy will be looking for us. Our escape must have caused a huge stink. They'll be coming soon. The trucks should be coming any ...'

Dinna gestured, cutting me off. He pointed to his ear and then up the tunnel. I froze, all my senses at a high pitch. The noise was faint but distinct, funnelled to us by the passage walls: the throbbing sound of idling engines. Instinctively we moved deeper into the nook.

Hassan was trying to get up on his own but could not. Other than the horrific damage to his fingers and the broken shoulder, his body seemed whole. But it clearly wasn't responding to him. I tried not to think what the torture might have done to his nervous system. Dinna and I held him on each side, supporting him, then the Kushan effortlessly hoisted him on his shoulder.

A high whine of hydraulics came floating down the tunnel followed by the throaty growl of exhausts. I wiped my palms on the uniform tunic. I was starting to sweat, very little of it was from the heat.

The engine sounds magnified; the vehicles were starting to move. Dinna beckoned me forward, against the right side of the panel, and positioned himself just behind me.

And then we heard the dogs.

24

Gul Mohammed's staff car swung into the Chakala Air Base compound at Rawalpindi. The summons had been as sudden as they had been mysterious; a caller on the India-Pakistan strategic forces hot line had got through to his counterpart in Pakistan's air defence HQ in Rawalpindi with a terse message: *Bring in Gul Mohammed from ISI. Now.* A single phrase had been added to the transmission: Xiphos Soter. That message had reached the ISI HQ in Islamabad at 1200, minutes after the call. Gul had been in a high-level review meeting but had rushed out immediately and choppered out to the Chakala suburb where the AD HQ was located.

He waited now, just him and the phone, alone in the communications room. The phone buzzed at 1400, exactly as indicated, and he put it to his ear.

'Gul Mohammed, JD SIGINT ISI,' he said clearly into the receiver. For the next fifteen minutes he sat hunched over the phone. Now and then he asked a brief question but for the most part he simply listened. When he had replaced the phone in its cradle, he made three calls to the ISI, army and air force headquarters in rapid succession. Within ten minutes of the calls, the commander of ADF Rawalpindi received explicit instructions from Air Force Command HQ In Islamabad: the entire base was to be placed at Gul Mohammed's total disposal; he was to be given a carte blanche on men and materiel and his instructions were to be followed without question. The ISI JD went into a telephonic huddle with his ADC and other members of his staff via video satellite. After a quick confabulation rapid-fire instructions were issued.

Within the hour – at 1450 PST – a helicopter lifted off the base airstrip with Gul Mohammed on board heading directly west towards Jalalabad just across the Durand Line. On the ground below, forty kilometres northeast of Chakala, two eight-tonne troop carriers with forty Pak special forces commandos roared out of the Eighty-first Ranger Division Barracks at an undisclosed location heading in the same direction.

From the chopper cockpit 4400 feet in the sky, Gul reviewed the astonishing call in his mind once more. The caller had been one Nalini Ranjan Pant, Acting Director for South Asia, Joint Intel Committee. Gul had asked his staff to pull up the

file on the man immediately and send it across to
the server in Rawalpindi. It appeared that Pant was
a middle-ranker, filling in for his superior who had
been taken ill. There wasn't much about Pant in the
ISI dossier, but Gul now suspected that the slimness
of the dossier was of Pant's doing. During the
conversation, Gul had formed his own judgement
of the man on the other side of the phone. Pant
came across as an exceptionally able professional.
He conveyed only that which had to be yielded to
Gul to allow him to act, not an iota more. He had
kept the conversation couched in general terms,
yet to someone like Gul – a seasoned pro himself
– it was as complete a briefing as anything he had
listened to. No mention of any complicity within
the Indian security apparatus. Listening to Pant,
it might be some unknown nuclear terrorist group
that was plotting this thing.

Gul wasn't sure if Pant was acting solo but if he
was, it put the man in a totally different league.
He could taste the bitter ash in his mouth. Syed Ali
Hassan and Chandrasekhar – one or both – were
intelligence operatives for India. Pant had played
him like an angler, used him to bait Hassan. And
he had fallen for it. He smiled grimly to himself.
Two could play that game. But not now. No time
for pointless recriminations of any kind. For
the moment, the supreme task was to stop the
plotters.

Pant had stressed that he believed the
launchers would leave the Bamiyan Valley
any hour now – if indeed they had not already
done so. The target vehicles would be TELs
most likely disguised as long-bodied flatbeds,
probably escorted. So, a convoy. Probable border
destination unknown. Kabul lay directly east of
Bamiyan and then Jalalabad further east, close to
the Durand Line. It was possible the launch point
would be south or north of the Jalalabad sector,
but this was pure guesswork – based on the need
to get to the launch point quickly. Very much
north or south meant greater distances and, more
importantly, danger of a Taliban ambush or an
ISAF interception.

Gul had agreed with Pant's logic and had
set course for Jalalabad. As soon as the three
carriers with the ranger company joined him
at the border post at Torkham on the Pakistan
side, they would illegally penetrate the border
and take up positions. One would monitor the
highway traversing the Gardez-Khost sector south
of Jalalabad and the second ranger group would
sit athwart the Charikar-Mehtar Lam sector sixty
kilometres north of the city. A third would be the
mobile carrier, parked equidistant between these
two companies and ready to rush to the support
of either at quick notice. It was like throwing pin-
sized darts on a board the size of a building but,

with the options rapidly dwindling, there was nothing for it but to gamble.

Hassan and Chandrasekhar still remained fading but potentially key factors in the equation. If either of them managed to reach Pant with the convoy location, he would in turn alert Gul who would move to intercept.

Gul's wireless crackled to life. 'Ranger group leader reporting in. ETA Torkham 1900, sir.' Gul acknowledged. The helicopter banked steeply and headed for the frontier.

In their search for us, the enemy had made one unwitting mistake. They could not possibly guess at our position and so whoever was directing the operation had likely placed top priority on getting the convoy away. That meant the underground road was as yet uncombed, and we had emerged and then remained undetected for a half hour or more. The trucks had started up and were now advancing down the tunnel. The stink of benzene was heavy and clogging, filling up the air in the closed space. And it must have confused the dogs behind. We heard the deep-throated baying of the hounds mixed with excited whines, but could see nothing of them.

The wash of headlights threw the corridor into harsh relief, the halogen turning the rough stone to pure silver. I braced myself, every muscle rigid with anticipation. The roar of engines filled the air and then the first escort jeep rumbled past. Dinna's hand sought mine, gripping it tight. The steering cabin of the flatbed followed. We were in plain sight, completely exposed. But the driver was elevated a good four feet above us and the high door prevented a direct line of sight.

The linking platform hove into view. *Now*. I moved in smooth unison with the Kushan. One step forward and a leap. We hit the flat steel girder that linked the two sections of the freighter. I put both hands on the bar and vaulted clumsily up. From the corner of my eye I could see that Dinna had caught the rails and drawn himself into the gap, one hand looped firmly around Hassan. The Kushan caught at the side rails, then extended his hand to stabilize me. We made sure of our footing then ducked down quickly and sat hunched over the pivot joint, suspended two feet above the floor. The light from the posterior vehicle lit up the ground beneath us and we watched the gravel flash past, sparkling like gems. Suddenly I felt the unreality of it came home to me. Not two hours ago I had given myself up to a bitter end. Now here I was, huddled like a stowaway in a hold, trundling out of an invulnerable fortress. And I was no longer alone. Dinna was with me and his outsized hand held me balanced upon the frame. I could hardly grasp at this turn of fate. I knew without a shadow of a doubt that I would meet my end soon. Even if Dinna was by my side, it was too much to hope that we would get out of this alive. We were stowaways surrounded on every side by hostiles. Getting to the co-ordinates and then to a phone through to Pant was going to be next to impossible. But if together we could somehow pull it off, do what Hassan had set for us, that would be enough. But I had long before come to the conclusion that my own death mattered little in a calculus where millions of lives were at stake. I looked at the still waxy face of the man who had taught me that before he had been taken away to be tormented.

The echoes of the tunnel suddenly receded. Up ahead the mechanical grating of a shutter came through clearly above the engine sounds. The air became suddenly cool. The truck picked up speed and we sped out into the open night.

At precisely the same time in New Delhi, the controllers of Shadow Throne were gathered together for an unprecedented second time. The venue was a five-star hotel on Man Singh Road. 'B' and 'C' checked in under an alias and went straight up to 'A's room.

He was waiting for them. A large sat map

was spread over the table. He began without preamble.

'We've had an incident. Hassan has escaped and so has Chandrasekhar. We have every reason to believe they are still in the complex. The only routes in or out are the maze and the truck tunnel. We sealed off both; there's no way they could have got out by either.'

They stared at him in open shock. 'B' said, 'When did this happen?'

'Shukla called in at 1830. I ordered an immediate advancing of the schedule. Systems checks on the missile were speeded up and they have been despatched from the mountain as of midnight. Our advance patrol has also reported that the ISAF have exited Gardez, so we'll have a free run.'

'C' said worriedly, 'No chance then they could have been anywhere close to the missiles?'

'None. Hassan was worked on quite a bit by the big man. They used one of those new pain prods. Apparently shreds the nervous system. He was unconscious when they left him last.'

'Then how …?'

'He had inside help. One of the Sword turned. Seems like the Qutub guy had an accomplice still in the mountain.'

'Fuck. That fucking Shukla. What in hell was he doing?' 'B' exploded.

'He's as good as dead, or will be when we get to him. So are those two. But let's stay focused here. The convoy is on its way. It was searched thoroughly just prior to departure, so no chance of any sabotage. ETA Anwat Tal 0100 day after. Site techs confirm they'll be ready to launch sixty minutes post arrival.'

'Co-ordinates?'

'Pre-programmed in and locked at the base itself. We'll effect final systems check and lock them in from the command van on arrival. Once they hit the trigger, the missiles can't be stopped.'

'So we're safe?' 'C' said.

'So far. I made discreet enquiries at Air Headquarters and SNC. All seems normal. I don't think anyone's got through to them. Looks like Hassan was bluffing during the interrogation.'

'And Pant?'

'He's taken off. Can't be found. It's the one thing that worries me. He's a tricky bastard. I've told the escort vehicles to keep their eyes peeled.' He ran a trace on the map with his forefinger. 'We've also switched the route from Parikar. They'll swing north from there and take a kuccha road instead of the highway.'

He said to 'B', 'Are we in control on the media releases?'

'It's going to be mayhem out there. Print, audio and visual from every country in the globe will be on us like a pack of wolves. The evidence is tied up pucca and we'll release it in stages. Rumour first, then doctored conversations within their command and control and then satellite photos. We'll overwhelm them with the damn stuff. Sitting on top of the carnage in Mumbai, it's going to explode like a volcano.'

'Good.' 'A' looked solemnly at his two colleagues. 'Comrades, we severed the East from Pakistan in 1971. That was a price the enemy could pay. In less than twenty-four hours from now, we will sever the West as well and leave him limbless and bleeding. No China will come to his aid. A new kingdom shall be born, ruled by the Shadow Throne. We are about to achieve what four wars have not done. We have only read our history, now we will make it.'

There was a burning fervour about him, the fiery light of a true believer.

'Let us get to our homes now. All is to be normal. We will all meet together only when we are summoned to headquarters and faced with the news that the world as we know it has changed forever.'

As they rose, the clock on the room console said 12.30 am. T minus four hours and counting.

25

The convoy did not stop. We had been crouching in our positions for over twenty hours and exhaustion had set in. My limbs felt leaden and my lungs asphyxiated with fumes. The day went by in a blur; all I could see was that the convoy was on a minor road, a rutted mix of sand and broken boulders, and the launchers were having a hard time of it. By evening, we had swung back on to a black-topped two-lane highway and the engines kept to their steady grinding beat that ate up the miles through the vast Afghan night. It was empty at this hour, with just the odd goods carrier roaring past us from the opposite side.

I crouched awkwardly in the articulated space. The steel members that connected the two parts of the vehicle swayed to and fro with the swing of the truck and made for a precarious seat. Much of my earlier euphoria had evaporated into the wind that soughed past in the wake of our passing. We were practically next to the command van, but might as well have been light years away. It didn't take a genius to see that I had to do four things. First, I – or we – had to get into the command vehicle. Second, take the readings. Third, somehow convey them to Pant. Fourth, we had to get away ourselves. Four was the icing on the cake; I had no illusions about our chances on that one. There was practically no way we were going to survive the next halt. Ergo, we had to accomplish one to three before the convoy stopped. *But how?* Most of a day had passed and we were clueless, were no closer to seeing any way forward.

Hassan seemed to have slid back to unconsciousness. I looked over at Dinna hopefully. He'd done the near-impossible by getting Hassan and me onto the missile convoy. Perhaps he was already working on another miracle. The Kushan was squatting on the girder, looking about him curiously, taking it all in the manner of a peasant who has hitched his first ride.

Then it struck me: how much did Dinna know of what had to be done? My contact with the Sword had been altogether too brief for me to form anything other than the most fleeting impression of the Initiates. If Dinna was anything to go by, their physical prowess was clearly extraordinary. If they were ancients, relics of a long-forgotten empire, they were also savvy enough to navigate the contraptions of the twentieth century. Two of them had gotten as far as Delhi – one to kill and the other to be killed. Dinna had spirited Hassan out and got us on the convoy. So they were possibly extremely resourceful. But for all that, I had the feeling that the Kushan was irredeemably of another age, the product of a peculiar time warp created by the unnatural solitude of their abode within the mountain.

I tapped the tarpaulin that covered the flatbed, and indicated I had to get in.

Dinna's eyes widened. 'You want … inside?' He kept his voice just above the beat of the engine.

'Yes,' I nodded. 'The missiles … inside.' I mimed the missile in flight, closed my fist and exploded it open. He stared at me, turned and looked at the tarp. I nodded slowly and jabbed my forefinger at it.

'Yes. It's there … what Sena … your brother died for.'

He thought about that for a minute. He raised his eyes upward and said something softly in a voice full of melancholy.

'What was that, Dinna? Were you saying something to me?'

He pointed up. 'I speak to Sena. I do for him.'

Without further ado, he hitched his robe higher and, keeping a firm grip on Hassan with his right arm, started to probe the canvas awning.

We soon realized that the side that faced us was entirely fabric attached to a steel frame. Together, we examined the fastenings. The tarp had holes crimped into it. Steel cables threaded their way through the holes like laces, lashing the canvas to the frame. The cables were inch-thick hawsers and rigid as rods. Impossible to shift even slightly. We could not see where the lashings ended from where we were. The cloth itself was some sort of reinforced composite; it looked very strong and would probably be extremely tough to slice through even if we had a knife, which we didn't. Dinna strained some more at the cables, then gave up. A dead end.

Then Hassan said, 'It's hollow from the bottom.'

It was the last voice I expected to hear. The hair rose on the back of my neck.

'What?'

'It's a Korean TEL design. The missile sits on a ladder frame which is directly supported by the chassis. That cuts the tare weight so the TEL's weight to distance can be optimized.'

Hassan might have been delivering a technical lecture. His voice was weak but clear. Dinna was also taken aback, his fawn eyes filled with surprise.

'Hassan …!'

Hassan pre-empted me. 'I'm feeling better now, Chandra. That cattle prod fucked up my nervous system; I don't think I can move yet. But Dinna snatched me before the third degree really started. Now, get under the canvas, walk along the missile and look out through the rear awning carefully. I have a feeling the command van is sandwiched between the two TELs. If it's there, come back and we'll decide what to do.'

There was a tremoring thread of pain behind his words. I remembered how Autokrator had mashed his shoulder; the crushed thumb, the torn nails and the electric shocks would have all extracted a terrible toll.

I said nothing; I think he knew how I felt. I saw his teeth flash white in a grin. 'Let's get to it, man. I hope your arm is in better shape than mine.'

That's when I remembered my injured hand. By some incredible mind-body calculus, the sheer stress of the last hours had severed all physical signals from my hand to my brain. I had literally forgotten about my arm. Now, I could feel Hassan's banian bandage beneath my uniform sleeve, covering a dull but bearable ache.

I twisted over and lay with my back to the pivoting girder. Dinna held me by the thighs and started paying me out like rope as I slowly wriggled backwards below the lashed cables. The headlights from the rear vehicle seeped through the bottom of the truck and provided the illumination I needed. I saw at once that Hassan was right:

a ladder frame. The one I had seen raised at an angle on the truck. I reached in, caught hold of a strut with both hands and started to haul myself in. Dinna had me in a firm grip, moving in unison. My fingers caught at other holds inside; the space was full of fabricated metal and I had no shortage of holds as I pulled myself up into the black space. I hit my head against something hard and almost let go. I smothered an obscenity in my fright. The place was a forest of metal; carefully I inched up, probing the space with my right hand and weaving my torso through the network. I was through to my thighs; I wiggled my feet to get Dinna to let go and pulled my legs up. I was in.

The air was full of the smell of oiled metal, an engineering workshop smell. Motes of headlight bounced up from the tarmac and played like little phosphorescent beetles on the immense cylinder by my side. I ran my hands over it, feeling the matte-painted smoothness of its curvature, dimpled in places by rounded rivet heads, a cold, lifeless feel to the metal. A WMD. I was actually touching, feeling beneath my palms a weapon of mass destruction. I could see the dull sheen of the black nose cone in front of the thing and, just below, just two feet away – the warhead.

I tried to absorb the enormity of it. In a matter of hours this long, shiny tube would lift off in a roar of flame and flash at incredible speed hundreds of kilometres through the ether to an exact pre-chosen spot over a densely populated area of India – of home. There it would jettison a small part of itself: *this* part. I saw the small cross section that was the warhead fall away in a gentle curve towards the earth below. I saw the city wake up, the shops open, the commuters wait at the stops for buses or honk impatiently in cars. I saw mothers bathe their babies at muncipical taps, old men read newspapers over tea, boys congregate in the maidans, playing cricket with sticks and stones. I saw the instant of explosion, a giant soundless blast, then an immense fireball radiating from the epicentre in an all-consuming tsunami of fire and death. Then I saw no more. Millions dead or dying: my mind could not grasp its horror. Instead a procession of faces spooled out before my mind's eye like a film: my own friends and Yamini's; people I knew once and then no longer cared to know; I saw my parents, and Meenakshi.

My head swam and I tottered. I would have fallen had not the canvas been buffeted violently on the other side.

Dinna hissed, 'You well? Inside?'

With a huge effort I took a hold of myself. I said, 'Yes,' as loudly as I dared. 'I am taking a look now.'

I walked unsteadily along the length of the trailer till I reached the rear. I parted it carefully at the centre lashing and peered with one eye through the slit. I saw it at once: the boxy mini-truck I had seen earlier beside the TELs inside the mountain. It was holding carefully at a distance of two metres from the rear of my trailer. I spun around and walked back as fast as I could.

Hassan was waiting tensely. I told him what I had seen. He closed his eyes, lying there, body swaying with the truck. I thought he'd fainted and was reaching out for him, when he opened his eyes and said, 'Great job, Chandra. When you get into the command van, don't remove anything. If these guys realize you've grabbed the co-ordinates, they may be tempted to launch from right here. Just write down or memorize the numbers and get out of there quick.'

'But how am I going to get into the van, for God's sake?'

'Dinna and I have been talking. He's going to create a diversion.'

'A what?'

'He's going to jump off the truck.'

The plan was quintessentially Hassan in its total co-option of anyone, including himself, to accomplish the task at hand irrespective of the consequences. If we all had to die, so be it. Given the stakes this time, I had to admit to the logic of Hassan's methods. Still, it made me extremely queasy, more for Dinna's sake than my own. The

man had risked his life for both of us and had
made a bad bargain in the process.

But it turned out the Kushan did not need
to be persuaded. He had adopted his brother's
mission as his own; he was completely clear in
his mind. Just seeing that immense figure there,
calm and determined, filled me with a fresh sense
of purpose.

Hassan's plan gambled on his belief that our
convoy would reach its destination when it was
still dark. It would be far too risky to cross the
border by daylight. My watch said 11.30 pm. We
were travelling at around thirty kilometres per
hour – the best that apparently could be managed
by these mobile launchers – and he thought we
would reach the border in another hour. Now and
then the vehicles came onto a bad patch of road
and tended to slow down. At the very next such
occurrence, the Kushan would leap off the carrier
and sprint away at a right angle to the convoy
in full view of the escort vehicles at either end. I
would wait inside the first truck, at the rear, but
just behind the awning. The sighting of the Kushan
sprouting as if by magic from the running truck
would trigger a panic reaction: the two escorts
would get after him, leaving the two launchers
parked head to tail. That would be my cue. I
would drop down from inside the launcher, hit
the road and crawl beneath the command vehicle,

get to the rear, open the doors and get in. I would then take the readings, jump out and get beneath the rear trailer. 'When you hear my signal, you get as far away from the road as you can. Run like hell in the opposite direction to one Dinna's taken. Then you hide behind the best cover you can find,' Hassan said.

'But won't the guys in the rear TEL see me? ' I said.

He smiled lopsidedly. 'Someone's got to draw the attention of the cabin crew of the second TEL and the command van away from you. I'll drop off and start crawling away. That'll grab them for sure. You'll hear me shout something, as if I'm in pain. That's your cue to take off.'

'They'll suspect a rat.'

'I doubt it. These are limited mission guys. Techs for the final launch set-up and guards. They won't have the whole picture. Sure, they'll call HQ, ask for instructions. I can guess what HQ is going to tell them. They've thought of nothing else but this launch for two years, even a lifetime. As long as Rao and Shukla and their bosses believe the mission is not compromised, they'll still give it top priority.'

'That's my whole point, Hassan. They can't know that. All they'll know is that you were found on the missile convoy, right next to the damn things when by their every expectation you should have been screaming your guts out in the torture chamber. How can they be sure of anything anymore?'

'Because Pant will reassure them.'

'Pant …?'

'Yes, Pant.'

———

Gul Mohammed glanced at his watch, the second time in as many minutes. 0245 hours, 2.45 am. The Pakistani ranger division had crossed the Durand Line at Torkham into Afghanistan at 2000 hours. The crossing was conducted at a wild scrub valley north of the settlement. Ranger Group One broke off immediately and headed cross country towards highway A1 south to Khost and Ranger Group Three towards Jalalabad and then on the road north. Both would set up surveillance blocks close to the highway. Gul Mohammed remained with Ranger Group Two close to Torkham, almost directly on A1 east. Both Pant and he had agreed that it was a very likely route for the missile convoy. Mohammed maintained direct operational control over the other two over a satellite GPS line, and maintained a separate scrambled satlink with Nalini Ranjan Pant. The two exchanged communication every ten minutes. The Pakistani had been in many hot situations before, but he was on the edge of his seat with a tension he had never experienced to this degree in his working life. Despite the distorting echo of the satlink, he thought he detected the same undercurrent in Pant's voice. They had both handled dangerous assignments, but none where failure meant nuclear catastrophe. And if his Indian counterpart was right, they were almost out of time.

Pant was red-eyed due to lack of sleep. He had been awake for over fifty hours at a stretch. Reports from his office poured in in a continuous flow, routine intel from everywhere. He had parked it all, ruthlessly put everything aside to focus on this thing. He knew he could not keep this up. As an acting director in the JIC, he had meetings, Cabinet Committee of Security briefings and a huge basketload of matters to attend to. The JIC was the spider at the centre of the intelligence web, and for him to be incommunicado was unsustainable beyond a short span of time.

He had done everything that seemed humanly possible for someone in his position. Through Jasjit he had gotten through to the CO Strategic Missile Forces. In answer to his enquiries, he had been assured that both Prithvi and Advanced Air Defence Commands – together designed to intercept an incoming missile upto an altitude of seventy-five kilometres above the earth – were on routine alert. He had dared not go further, not knowing how much of his hand to play. An obscure instinct also told him that it was vital to keep up an appearance of normalcy, so he had word put out through his office that he would be attending the next day's cabinet briefing in North Block.

He looked at the wall clock. The LED winked 0245. His lookout in the office had reported earlier that evening to say that there was no sign of the RAW duo. Several others both in the IB and the RAW had not come in for the last couple of days. There was a strange silence in the air, and unhealthy quiet, a sense of expectation. Or maybe he was just being paranoid. He rubbed his eyes tiredly. For the hundredth time that night – the longest he had ever experienced – he found himself thinking about Hassan and Chandra. *Where the hell were they?*

He waited some more, leafing through some reports, his mind elsewhere, sluggish now, barely able to process information. There was a brief message in from Gul at 0300, just a routine call in. The two ranger groups were in position but had nothing to report. He decided he could not keep up this vigil any further, he was burning the candle at both ends. He would put an assistant on watch and take at least an hour of rest. He was reaching for his set to call Gul when his emergency satphone line shrilled to life.

I crouched by the tail fins of the missile. The exhaust growl filled the interior. The TELs' engines were big and the decibel levels high. I had no line of sight and hoped to God I would know when Dinna had made the jump when the escorts veered away.

As it turned out, I needn't have worried. The blaring of the horn and the screeching of tires executing a rapid turn happened simultaneously. I heard shouting then more honking. I guessed the rear escort was trying to get the attention of his counterpart up front. The vehicles sped off the highway to my right in Dinna's wake. The trailers were already slowing; soon they ground to a halt in a squeal of brakes. I was already dropping to the tarmac. It was hot as a furnace from the radiant heat of the engine. I started to crawl forward. There was burst of fresh air as I hit the gap between the vehicles, then I was below the command van. I wormed my way as fast as I could over the tar of the highway, getting deeper under the truck. Then I waited. I became dimly aware of more shouts outside. Doors opened and then banged shut. The cabin crew was spilling out. They had spotted Hassan.

I waited a bit, then crawled forward and threw a quick look around. The second TEL's front doors were open and the cabin was empty. I got to my feet and yanked the van's doors open. I scrambled in and pulled the shutters close behind me. The van was crammed full of electronics. Against the far side was a huge screen and, pasted right next to it, a large ordinance survey map and then – two square sheets with geometric squiggles. With long arcing lines. Longitude and latitude numbers and a string of other alpha-numerics at either end. I pulled out my scrap of paper and pencil. With shaking fingers, I wrote them down. I blinked away the pouring sweat blinding my eyes, and re-checked them. I turned back, cautiously opened the van doors and glanced front and then sideways. No one. I dropped to the ground and dived beneath the second TEL and started to crawl furiously to its centre. I lay prone on the hot tarmac, my heart bursting. I heard Hassan shout loudly, a yell of pain.

'Oh my God, my hand … my hand …!'

I rolled to the left, got between two gigantic sets of tyres and was out the far side. I got to my feet and hobbled away as fast as my legs could carry me. I ran into the night as if I was possessed by a demon; I was out of shape, overweight, but the adrenaline once again lent me unnatural strength. I hit the shoulder of the road and kept going. I plunged up and down gullies and sandy ravines; several times I tripped over a bush or stone and fell heavily. But I did not stop. After some ten minutes of this, I dropped half-dead into a hollow. I retched, dry vomiting sounds that produced nothing. I had forgotten when I had last eaten. My lungs heaved and I felt dizzy with the nausea.

At length I dragged myself up the small slope and poked my head over the top. The trailer's halogens were on, lighting up the convoy. The escort SUVs were back. I could see nothing of Dinna but presumably they had got him – dead or alive. Hassan was being held up by two men and dragged to one of the SUVs. I breathed in short gasps through my mouth, watched them take their positions in the front and rear. The TELs gunned their engines and the vehicle train moved off. I kept my eyes on them till the tail lights faded away into the darkness. I was alone in the desert.

I rolled back down into the shallow of the ditch and lay there like one dead. I could barely move. The whole operation must have lasted less than ten minutes but it had felt like an age during which every cell in my body was in turbocharged overdrive, and now I was utterly drained. I could have lain there forever, given myself up to the grey lassitude that was upon me like a thick cloud. Except for the numbers. Fifty-six of them – sitting within me. Trapped inside those digits were millions of lives reaching out to me, crying aloud for deliverance. And I – I alone – carried within me the seeds of their salvation – or destruction. Even through my torpor I felt the terrible weight of it, the weight of the whole earth pressing down on me.

My brain started to scream. *The numbers. Pant. Phone. Get the hell going, you bastard.* I groaned out aloud and pushed myself up on my elbows, then got shakily to my feet. I started to weave drunkenly in the general direction of the highway. I made it with more falls and bruises, till I stood by the roadside. No trucks, no cars. Nothing. Just a strip of grey snaking away into the blackness. I started to walk away from the convoy's direction.

Ten ... fifteen ... twenty minutes. No cars, trucks ... nothing. My stomach burned as if it was filled with hot coals. I kept jerking my head about in all directions, looking frantically for any sign of life, anything. I whispered to myself with terrible intensity. *Come on ... come on. Someone come, please ...*

Then I saw the pinprick of lights ahead. My heart leapt into my mouth. I jogged forward, walked, then jogged again, willing it towards me. I had to get the thing to stop. *Had to.* My last chance. Better not to give him warning. I kept to the side of the road, judging speed and distance. The headlights neared. I couldn't see its outline but the spacing and height indicated it was a car. I felt quick relief. Easier to stop a car than a goods carrier. It was now about fifty yards out and closing at average speed. I thrust out my arm waving, watching his reaction. As I half-expected he kept coming, wasn't slowing down. I waited some more then sprinted towards the car, cutting diagonally across the highway and directly on its path. The car swerved onto the shoulder, engines gunning, trying to get past me, but I flung myself forward in a frenzy. My outstretched hands caught at the door sill by the driver, then I was scrabbling inside, catching at his steering wheel. He shouted something I couldn't hear, then floored the accelerator. The car bucked like a rearing horse, almost tearing my arms off their sockets, and then stalled.

The driver yelled out aloud: a curse filled with fright and furiously twisted the starter key. Once, twice. The engine neighed but would not start. I yanked the door open and pulled him out. His face crumpled, he folded and fell to the ground at my feet. He caught at my ankles and began a loud wail I could barely catch, some sort of an entreaty. That was when I saw the woman and child in the rear.

They were huddled in the far corner against the door, the woman in a black abaya, the child on her lap no more than six or seven. They were both terrified, their eyes shining with acute fear in the dispersed light of the car's beam. The woman screamed as I tore open the rear door; the man – I took him for the husband – started his wails again, clutching at my feet.

I stooped, caught him by the shoulders and yanked him to his feet. He was middle-aged with a seamed, windblown face. His head was covered with a white woven kulla and he wore a typical Afghan jubba. His eyes rolled as he saw my uniform. I struck me then: he thought I was military. I shook him roughly and said:

'Hindi … Hindi … ya Urdu?'

He nodded eagerly, held up his thumb and forefinger separated by a small gap. 'Urdu. Thoda thoda.'

'Cellphone chahiye. Cellphone.' I put my cupped hands to my ear.

To my spiking joy he nodded and pointed to his wife. I held him firmly by the collar and marched him to her. Held out my hand. She shrank back with her child. I felt shame even as I snarled at her in English.

'Give me that goddamn phone!'

She tossed it onto the seat, her arms around her trembling child. I snatched it up and held it to the headlight. Two bars in the tower signal, one of them coming on and off intermittently. Faint but serviceable. I felt the relief pour over me in a wave. I waved the phone at the man curtly and motioned. *Go. Get the hell out of here.*

He didn't even argue. He was back in the car in a flash, teased the engine to life and roared away. I didn't hear him. Instead I was trying to get my trembling, sluggish fingers to punch in Pant's satphone number. Twice I pressed the wrong button and had to clear it. I hit the green call button and pressed the phone to my ear. A single beep and a voice came on.

'Pant.'

'This is Chandrasekhar.'

There was a pause for perhaps a nanosecond, but it filled the ether with its supercharged potency. Then he said in a clipped tone:

'What do you have for me?'

'The flight co-ordinates.'

Again, silence for a beat. Then: 'How many are there?'

'Two sets.'

'Noted. Read out slowly, please.'

I had the paper but no light. I should have commandeered a light, a box of matches or whatever from the guy in the car. But the possibility hadn't even occurred to me. Then it struck me: I had the phone.

I put it on speaker, held the lit screen over the paper and read it out to him. Fifty-six letters and digits together. I enunciated each numeric carefully, I followed the letters with words as in 'B' for 'bravo'; and on his instructions I repeated everything once more and finally heard him repeat it once more for me to confirm.

When Pant finished his voice was hurried, but it shook a little. 'Chandra … I … Chandra, I have to go. Where is Hassan?'

'I don't know. He's been taken by the enemy. They're heading somewhere for the border.'

The tremor in his voice was stronger now. 'Chandra … keep your phone line open. We'll triangulate you. Help will reach you soon. Bye for now.'

The connection went dead. I kept the phone on, dropped it into my shirt pocket. I walked off the road into the sandy scrub. Stumbled, walked, stumbled again. Then I dropped into a hollow. Leaned back against the slope and stared out into the night. I had no idea how long I was there. All time ceased to exist as I sat there unmoving. Perhaps I imagined it but suddenly, far away in the distant east I thought I saw a flash lighting up the sky, then another one: sputters of flame that flared and died as suddenly as they appeared. I saw too a faint lightening in the east, the coming of dawn: old as the centuries, newborn each day. And then the tears began to flow.

26
Aftermath

***Times of India*, 26 June 20—**

The Defence Research & Development Organization of the Ministry of Defence announced today that a successful missile interception test had been carried out somewhere over the western sector as part of its Prithvi Missile Air Defence System capability check. 'This is a new landmark achievement in terms of our strategic anti-ballistic missile interception capabilities,' the Director of the Indian missile defence programme, Dr VS Khanolkar, told a gathering of media persons today. 'In this technology demonstrator, we simulated a low-level missile launch from the western border into Indian airspace and intercepted it at an altitude of 15 kilometres. The test has conclusively established the country's capabilities in this exclusive technology domain and the robustness of our anti-missile capabilities. We will now be working to build a missile defence grid that will cover the entire country in stages.'

China News Monitor, Beijing, 30 June 20—
It is of great satisfaction that good neighbourly relations between India and China have been steadily going forward. To the continuing economic and political exchanges have now been added another link: military-to-military exchanges. A new high was reached recently when India's military and that of China collaborated in a simulation missile defence exercise where both countries jointly tracked a hostile missile from a third country and deployed missiles from their respective air defence systems to neutralize the threat. People's Air Force General Hue Bao, Commander of the Chinese Strategic Missile Division and his counterpart Air Marshal M.K. Palit, Commander of Indian Strategic Forces Command, issued a joint statement in which they said, 'This exercise is a unique example of how mutually assured defence collaboration works to the advantage of both countries. We are already planning for more such exercises.'

The Chinese Premier today called the Indian Prime Minister on the hot line and congratulated him on the successful outcome of the test and reiterated China's willingness to strengthen mutual co-operation with India in all areas, including defence.

The New York Times, 10 July 20—

Pakistan has recently been convulsed by a rumour that its nuclear missiles have been secretly suborned by NATO and US forces. Street demonstrations in Islamabad, Karachi and other major cities in Pakistan have forced both the civilian government and the military to issue repeated statements denying that there is any truth to these rumours. 'There is no country on earth that can deprive us of our divine right to protect the motherland,' Pakistani President Alim Khazdari said at a public meeting in Islamabad yesterday. 'Pakistan's missiles are in – and always will be – in our hands and our hands alone. Let no one misunderstand this.'

Reacting to developments, the US State Department issued what seemed a non-response in which it merely said, 'We have no comments whatsoever on the matter. The United States does not response to rumour and unconfirmed reports as a matter of policy.'

The Hindu, 18 July 20—

The government today announced sweeping changes in its military and intelligence establishments. Taken together they appear to represent the most significant and far-reaching reform of India's national security structure since Independence.

Reading from a prepared statement in the Lok Sabha today, Prime Minister Charanjit Singh Mann said, 'Let me say once more that these changes have been in the making for a long period of time. The twentieth century has been a challenging one for India from an external security standpoint and the twenty-first will likely prove even more so. No country can hope to cope with these challenges without significantly modernizing not just its arsenal, but also the structures and systems by which such arsenals are deployed. For India, that time has come: we can no longer live in the twenty-first century while working with legacy systems of the nineteenth.

'No less than twenty-five expert committees have examined the various issues that have hobbled our control and command structures and have made clear and perceptive recommendations. My government intends to lose no time in implementing these and ensure an India proud and strong in her self-defence. We owe it our citizens, to the brave jawans and countless others who work day and night for the safety and security of the nation.'

Commodore Karthik Narayan of the Institute of Defence Studies & Analysis said, 'It is a hugely welcome move. We have not yet been able to study all the changes proposed as many of them are still classified, but the main thrust is timely. The government seems at last to have woken up to the manner in which this over-bureaucratization of the military and intelligence wings is crippling our national security.'

When asked by The Hindu *as to what could have prompted these changes so suddenly, that too in the middle on the current session of parliament, he said, 'It's puzzling. Though the PM presented it as if it is some new thinking, these reports have been gathering dust for years. I can only put it down to the coming elections. Maybe the government wants to send a message that it is taking national security seriously at long last. After the drift that we've seen, any change, however incremental, is welcome. We have really hit the trough.'*

The meeting with the prime minister was set for 3 pm but with my paranoia about Delhi traffic, I had got in half an hour early. I walked through the scanner at the entrance to South Block. As a journalist, I had always found it a nightmare to get into South Block: even the security guard at the gate seemed to be able to smell the media from several feet away, and then it was all shutters down. This was a government that lived from scandal to scandal and reacted accordingly – especially with the press.

Not today, though. The guy at the front desk took one look at my ID and practically stood to attention. He punched in a number on the intercom and whispered urgently into the mouthpiece. He replaced the phone and came round the desk.

'Sir, please take a seat. Kunwar sahib is on his way down.'

'No, thanks. I'll stand.'

He stood beside me awkwardly. *He's not used to this*, I thought amusedly. The VIPs or VVIPs got whisked straight through. And they never came half an hour early. The day was saved when a clerk type hurried down the passage towards me. 'Mr Chandrasekhar? Namaste, sir. Sorry, we did not expect you so early.'

'No problem. Do you want me to wait here?'

His horrified expression said it all. 'No … no. Please come with me. You can wait in the visitors room, sir. Till the others come.'

So I was seated in a plush waiting room. The arched cupola of the period window opened directly above the inner gardens of the complex; I could see the beds of roses, petunias and dahlias lining the central water concourse. All laid out in Mughal style. At one end of the lawn a single jacaranda tree spread its gorgeous purple bloom, filling the sky with colour. The summer sun shone brightly but in here it was cool and quiet, the air conditioning deadening heat and sound.

I sipped at the black tea with a twist of lemon, served in a bone-china cup and thought again about the mysteries of the human mind. All the events of the past month seemed to be overlaid now with a patina of unreality, as if everything that had happened had been to someone else, not me, a dream in which I participated only as an observer. That first night I woke up bathed in sweat from a dream filled with a mosaic of terrible images: the demonic face of Autokrator, Hassan crying out in death agony, of me trying to reach him through a maze filled with serpents. And in the background, the numbers. Always the numbers: red flashing digits winking their baleful message at me through the night, beating like a metronome beneath my closed lids, till I felt like tearing my eyes out with my bare hands.

The next day, the military psychologist at the command hospital examined me and pronounced that I had a mild form of DID: Dissociative Identity Disorder. A split personality condition, he explained, induced by extreme, pathological levels of stress. There was no reason why it would not fade, given time and rest. He had given me some pills, but as soon as I got home, I threw them into the waste basket – and immediately felt better.

Home. I smiled, remembering. Pant had been as good as his word. The chopper had landed right on the highway close to where I lay. Within fifteen minutes we were airborne, heading north for the Tajik border, then south towards Delhi. It was only when the city showed itself to me through the late afternoon haze that I knew that Delhi at least still lived. The helicopter set down at Palam Air Force

Base, close to where much of my journey had started. I had indeed come a full circle. A small man with owlish eyes and thick glasses waited for me at the airstrip and at last I put a body and face to the name: Nalini Ranjan Pant.

There were no greetings. He seemed to know exactly what I would ask for he said simply, 'We got both the warheads in mid-air.' He grasped my arm firmly and steered me to his staff car parked on the airstrip. He sat silent beside me as we sped away into the city, opening his mouth only to say that we were headed to the command hospital.

I had the feeling that he was in the grip of some powerful emotion and did not trust himself enough to speak. I too was content to look out of the window: the autos, the commuting crowds, the cows and the shopfronts spooling like a film across the window frame. I sucked them all in, feeling them deep into my soul, suffused by a deep wonder that I was here at all, in this heartbeat of dense humanity, the heartbeat I called home.

The car swung into the huge driveway of the command hospital. Pant looked at me and smiled, this time a sly smile full of humour and mischief.

'Your co-conspirators are waiting for you.'

That was when I knew. We got out of the car and he led me upstairs. We hurried along a long spotless corridor with rooms on either side. Till the last room to the left. A large airy room.

On the bed, wearing a white hospital gown, his hands swathed in bandage and his arm in a sling, was Syed Ali Hassan. Two figures were seated by the cot. A giant frame that dwarfed the chair and beside it, another form, looking altogether dimunitive in comparison. I stood at the door and stared. Hassan. Face lit up with a huge smile. Dinna getting up, overturning the chair with a crash. And Meenakshi, also on her feet. Our eyes met in a long look till she dropped her gaze. My heart lifted; I felt an unfamiliar lightness, and a sense of something coalescing within. I turned to Hassan, who was still grinning at me. I went up, took his hands carefully in my own and raised my eyebrows.

He answered my unspoken question in a normal voice.

'Hello, Chandra. Welcome back. I'm much better now. Should be back on my feet any time now.'

He indicated towards Dinna. 'This guy. I wish I'd found him sooner. His phyiso sessions feel like the third degree, but it's working. The docs say I can chuck my crutches in a month.'

I looked at Dinna and inclined my head, put out one hand to him. 'Thanks, Dinna. For everything.'

He ignored it, put his arms around my chest and squeezed till my ribs creaked.

Meenakshi had moved away and stood

unobtrusively in the background, watching us. I disengaged from Dinna and walked up to her. For a long moment, neither of us said anything. I stood there, taking her in once more: the fair face with its cleft chin, eyes welling with tears, the petiteness of her.

She extended both her hands to me. I took them in my own and said, 'Hello, Meenu. That was one hell of a break you gave us.' I stopped, tried to continue, but no words would come.

Pant coughed to draw my attention and said, 'Not just you, Chandra. It was the resourceful Ms Pirzada who had the idea of using ISI to get Hassan and Dinna out.'

He faced us, hands behind his back, looking every inch like a professor about to deliver a lecture.

'Friends, I am charged by the PM and entire union cabinet to thank each and every one of you for the extraordinary service you have rendered to this country and the people of India.' He paused. 'And China.'

I thought I hadn't heard him right. He said grimly, 'That's right, China. The second missile was aimed at Urumqi, in Xinjiang. They'd caught a gap in the Chinese missile defence network. The idea was to sever the China-Pak nexus forever.'

I clutched Meenu's hand tight, feeling the chill blow over me. China. You had to hand it to the plotters: whatever else, they didn't lack for sheer imagination – and coldly brilliant execution.

Pant continued, 'Thanks to you, Project Shadow Throne has failed. We have most of the ringleaders in custody. Shukla's vanished into Afghanistan, but we caught Rao and got everything out of him.'

I had to know right away. 'How did you get to Hassan and Dinna so fast? I thought they were as good as dead.' Pant's faced cracked into a smile. 'Ah, that was my good friend Gul Mohammed to the rescue. Thanks to Meenakshi's idea, we got the Pakistanis into position on the main highways to try and intercept the missile convoys. When the co-ordinates came in from Chandra, they showed the launch point just four kilometres north of Torkham, pretty close where Gul himself was parked. I tipped them off and a Pak ranger group got there minutes after the launch. There was a firefight in which the launch crew was outgunned by Gul Mohammed's men. Zero survivors.' Pant shook his head mournfully. 'Those rangers are nothing if not killers.'

'And Xiphos Soter? The Initiates … Autokrator?'

Pant's face was drawn, suddenly grim. 'Gone. As if they never existed. I think when Dinna vanished, they knew it was over. The Hazara monks too: just dispersed into the population. But it's not the end. The Sword has waited forever; they're not going to give up a dream that's been with them for centuries. We're just going to have to keep our guard up as far as they are concerned.'

I thought about that. The giant. Surely he would find it impossible to hide for long. But the Sword had survived for thousands of years in the most hostile and unforgiving of environments. I looked at Dinna with a new-found awareness: the rock-like strength of that body, that preternatural awareness of an animal that took no account of night and dark. Survival was built into their genetic code.

Pant was still speaking, tying up those last loose ends for us. 'Thanks to Dinna here, we penetrated the Bamiyan Complex through the road tunnel a little after midday. Our techs and scientific teams are still scoping out what we found. It appears that four key scientists were working against their will on the missile programming and the triggers. Their families were being held hostage.'

I said, 'My God. The poor people.'

A cold nimbus played about Pant. He was suddenly different, hard and sharp as a steel blade. 'There is nothing poor about them. They are traitors who will be dealt with as such.'

Then, as if by an effort of will, he relaxed. 'Look, I'll have to leave you to it now. Chandra, you need to see the doctor tomorrow. It's standard protocol for all my agents returning from the field. And, by the way, the PM wants to meet with all of you at the end of the week. To thank you personally.' He waved at us airily and walked out of the room.

I said to Hassan, 'Did I hear him call me his agent?'

Hassan grinned. 'Now that I've been singing your praises, I think he's determined to recruit you.' Then he said seriously, 'He's not been entirely candid with some other stuff as well. Do you know what that son-of-a-gun did? Just after alerting Missile Defence with the co-ordinates, he tipped off the CIA. US satellites caught the launchers just as they fired and, what's more, they got high-res images of Gul Mohammed on the scene with his rangers.'

'My God,' I said, awed.

'Yes,' Hassan nodded. 'He's some bastard. I wouldn't want him against me.'

'Nor I,' I said with fervour. 'Nor I.'

Meenakshi got out of the car and smoothed her sari down. Pant was helping Hassan out and handing him his crutches. Dinna had resolutely refused to come. From his sign language they made out he wanted to visit the Qutub. Some sort of a pilgrimage, he said.

The three of them walked up towards the entrance to South Block where the protocol officer was waiting for them. They went up the stairs into the waiting room. Chandra was sitting there, sipping from a cup. Meenakshi felt her heart lurch. She had been shocked when she had laid eyes on him in the hospital. In the twelve days since he had seen her off at his door, he had aged as many years. His stoop was more pronounced, as if he carried the world on his shoulders, and his face was sallow and shrunken. There were bags beneath his eyes. His clothes hung loosely over his frame. To her relief, he looked much better now. He had made an attempt to dress for the meeting: his shirt was ironed and his hair combed.

They greeted each other wordlessly, touching hands. The PO came into the room and said, 'The PM and the cabinet will see you now. This way, please.'

So this is where it's done. The historian in Meenakshi looked around with wonder. This was the room where the all the cabinet committees chaired by the prime minister met, where the destiny of the country, the fate of millions was decided.

Five persons sat at the far side of the table: the core of the union cabinet, ministers who handled the vital portfolios of the government. The PM sat in the centre, with Finance and Defence flanking him on either side. Then Home, Foreign Affairs.

They took their seats opposite. A turbaned

bearer entered with a tray. There was silence as tea was served, a silence during which the ministers gazed at them with undisguised curiosity. Meenakshi dabbed her face with her kerchief and shifted in her seat.

Then the PM said formally, 'Mr Pant, Colonel Hassan, Mr Chandrasekhar, Ms Pirzada. Thank you for coming to this meeting. I know this past month has been ... difficult, even traumatic for all of you – especially for you, Colonel Hassan and you, Mr Chandrasekhar. What you have done for the nation can never be repaid. Never. On behalf of my colleagues – and on my own behalf – I wish to place on record our deepest gratitude to each one of you for your supreme sacrifice in saving this nation from disaster.'

The prime minister paused, looking round the table at his colleagues. They all nodded, murmuring in agreement.

'It is a matter of the greatest regret that we can never acknowledge what you have done publicly; indeed, it can never even leave this room. But I give you my word: if ever any of you need the services of this government, if there is something we can do for you, you only have to say. Mr Pant here will see to it.'

Pant said, 'Yes sir, of course. It's the least we can do.'

Meenakshi and Hassan also said their thank

yous. The prime minister was about to rise from his chair to greet and shake hands with each of them when Chandra said quietly but clearly, 'If I may have a minute of yours and the cabinet's, Prime Minister.'

There was a stir at the table. The PM said, surprised. 'Yes, Mr Chandrasekhar?'

'You know that I am journalist. It's my job to report on what goes on in this country. There is much that is good and also much that is wrong – terribly wrong.'

Pin-drop silence. The PM paused as if he hadn't heard it right. 'I beg your pardon?'

Chandra said, 'For too long now, sir, the country has been on a slippery slope. I look around and I see it everywhere: a bureaucracy that is increasingly distanced from the people it is supposed to serve. A government that has abdicated its duty to govern and is instead mired in scandal. Let me say this: there will be more missile plots, more conspiracies. The nation almost paid a terrible price. Millions of lives were almost lost; they were saved only because you still have men like Mr Pant and Colonel Hassan. The next time we may not be so lucky.'

Meenakshi did not dare breathe. The ministers were staring as if they could not believe someone was actually speaking to them like this. Chandra pointed at Hassan.

'Colonel Hassan had his thumbs crushed, his

nails pulled out, electric shocks applied to his body. In the name of God, ministers, do not let his sacrifice go in vain.'

He rose heavily, pushed his chair back. Meenakshi took a quick look at the PM. The face beneath the turban was white, shaken, all response stricken from it. The ministers' heads were down with embarrassment or some other emotion, it was hard to tell. Pant nodded to her and they rose together, Meenakshi helping Hassan with his crutches. Then they followed Chandra out of the room.

———

We got into Pant's Ambassador. An escort Gypsy with a revolving red light and filled with armed commandos led us through the traffic. Hassan sat in the front passenger seat by the driver, Meenakshi, Pant and I in the back. Dusk was falling. The car swung the car around the gol chakkar around India Gate where the evening crowds milled about the Eternal Flame.

Pant said, 'We're dropping you off first. Where to?'

I said, 'My place, please. Chandni Chowk. If that's okay.'

'No problem.'

I said to Meenu, 'Will you come with me? Have a bite together?'

She nodded, 'Yes.'

'What about you, Hassan? Care to join us?'

'No thanks, Chandra. I've got to drop in on my mother. She's used to my absences but she's laid out one rule: report in as as soon as you're back.'

Meenakshi said, direct woman fashion, 'No wife?'

Hassan said, 'Nope. Any suggestions?'

'For James Bond? Are you kidding me?'

We all laughed. I could see the spires of the Jama Masjid coming up on the left. I quickly said, 'We'll get off here, if you don't mind.'

'Are you sure? I can drop you off at your place. It's only five minutes away.'

'No, I'd rather walk.'

The driver pulled over and Meenu and I got out. I leaned in and said, 'Thanks for the drop. And congratulations.'

'For what?'

'Hassan told me that you've been made director of the JIC.'

'Oh, that. Thanks. Chandra, you really were something in there, you know that? I've attended more cabinet meetings than I care to remember, but this is something for the record. They didn't like it but they couldn't say a thing. You really had them in knots.'

His owlish eyes blinked at us. 'Well, one lives and learns about you press types. You know what my promotion means, don't you?'

'What *does* it mean, Pant?'

'I have the right to call on your services at any time in the service of the country. You too, Meenakshi.'

I said, 'Dream on, Pant. Dream on.' He laughed loudly at that. Hassan and I waved to each other. See you soon, I said.

We watched the car's tail lights fade into the distance and then turned and started strolling down Chandni Chowk.

'What's for dinner?' Meenu asked.

'My mother called yesterday. She's made some sambhar and rice and left it in the kitchen. How's that sound?'

'Mm … yummy. Did your parents know … about all this, I mean?'

'Pant's been in touch with them, pretending to be from my news agency. He told them that I had to go to Afghanistan in a hurry on an assignment for him and they should not worry: I would be back in a fortnight.'

'Sometimes I think that man has more heads than a Ravana.'

'Yeah, he's scary.'

Meenu stopped in the middle of the sidewalk. 'Did you see that look of his?'

'What look?'

'When he just left us. When he said he could

ask you to work for him any time.'

'Meenu, he was just joking.'

'I just don't trust him and Hassan ... at least where you're concerned. I'm not letting you out of my sight. For a while anyway.'

She threw a glance at me, a look at once vulnerable and apprehensive, as if the words had slipped out and she wasn't quite sure how I would react.

I smiled, took her hand and drew her arm through mine. Chandni Chowk danced to its own cadence; no one paid us the least attention as we wound our way down the crowded thoroughfare that was once a fabled street of the East, a canalled way designed by Shah Jahan's daughter Jahanara to reflect the light of the moon.

Author's Note

It is my intent to place *The Shadow Throne* against a backdrop that mirrors current underlying reality – especially as it applies to India's current political predicament and its inevitable impact on our geopolitical security. That we are passing through challenging times on the internal and external security front seems widely accepted, and political and bureaucratic stasis in times like these can have far-reaching consequences. That said, this is a work of fiction and the standard disclaimers that apply to any such work hold for *The Shadow Throne* as well.

Acknowledgements

The Shadow Throne was essentially written over a period of six months. To keep it reasonably grounded in fact I have relied heavily on that crutch that now forms such an integral part of our lives: the Internet. But, alas, the Net doesn't (yet) read the book and tell you how to improve on it. So there is much in the novel that has benefited from incisive comments from a number of people. I would like, in particular, to thank the following people who have at various stages contributed to the making of *The Shadow Throne*:

My wife, Afried Raman, for bringing out her editorial scalpel and sharpening most parts of the novel. Priya Doraswamy of Jacaranda who piloted me to Pan Macmillan and has been a pillar of support throughout its journey. Niranjan Natarajan and Aparna Ponnappa who put together a powerful marketing plan for the work and helped me execute it flawlessly. The following people read and offered valuable comments on either the whole or part of the book: Vishal Ponnappa, Maya Ratnam, Manu Raman, Christoph Emmerich, Megha Lohia and Naresh Bala. For setting me right on certain facts and also providing me with relevant contacts and information sources, I owe thanks to Group Captain A. K. Sachdev (Retd), Air Marshal T. J. Master (Retd) and Dr Nabeel Mancheri. C. K. Devarajan and his team at Fomax Technologies worked closely with me to create a visually arresting author website that so well captures the essence of *The Shadow Throne*. Finally, a big 'thank you' to Saugata Mukherjee and Pallavi Narayan at Pan Macmillan for their solid editorial and marketing support to the book and to me as a debut author. Needless to say, all errors seen and unseen that remain are solely my responsibility.